BLURB

KEEPING MY G.

The girl I fell in love with was ripped from my arms, never to be heard from again.
She was sold to the cruelest man on the planet, Constantine Carbone — my family's number one enemy.
Over the years, I haven't stopped looking for Selina.
And then one fateful night, I finally find her.
In a move that will undoubtedly bring war upon my family, I save Selina, killing Constantine's son in the process.
I soon come to realize that Selina is nothing like the girl I once fell in love with, but none of that matters.
She's mine.
She's always been mine.
And when her past comes back to haunt her, threatening to steal her away from me again, I vow to do whatever it takes to keep her safe.
This time I'm not letting her go.

AUTHOR'S NOTE

Keeping My Girl is Nico Vitale's story. He is the son of Luca and Verona Vitale, the couple from the first book in this series, Keeping My Bride.

******

Due to the sensitive subject matter contained in this book, it may cause triggers to some readers.

Reader discretion is strongly advised.

DEDICATION

To my brother.

There isn't a day that goes by when I don't think of you. I miss you more than words can describe.

I wish you were here.

PLAYLIST

Smashing Pumpkins – *Mayonaise*
Kate Bush – *Running Up That Hill*
Lorde – *Buzzcut Season*
Whales – *Souvenir*
MISSIO – *Bottom of the Deep Blue Sea*
Serhat Durmus – *Hislerim (ft. Zerrin)*
Rita Ora – *Poison (Zdot Remix)*
Sia – *Elastic Heart*
K.Flay – *High Enough*
Em Beihold – *Numb Little Bug*

PROLOGUE

Nicholas Vitale

Ten Years Ago

I STAND IN the doorway of Selina's room, watching her pack. My heart aches at the thought of her leaving today, and I absently rub my palm against my chest in an attempt to alleviate some of the pain. She's become such a huge part of my life that it will be as if she's taking a piece of me when she goes. Selina has been living with my family for the past six months. I would like to say it took that long to fall in love with her, but I'd be lying. It only took the first day. Maybe even the first hour.

I'll never forget the first time I saw her. The tall, thin girl with two different colored irises, one green and one blue — a condition known as complete heterochromia, as she later explained to me. I barely even thought about girls before that point; but the moment I laid eyes on her long blonde hair, heart-shaped face, and her strange, ocean-colored eyes, I was a goner.

Selina had been rescued from a human trafficking ring that my parents, Luca and Verona Vitale, dismantled. They are constantly on missions to help women and children from being sold and trafficked. And when no one came to claim Selina, my parents offered to take her in temporarily until her family could be found. Little did we know what a life-changing decision that would be for both her and me. She's been here every day since. And she would continue to be here, maybe forever, if her mother hadn't suddenly appeared out of nowhere, demanding her daughter be returned to her.

Sighing, I walk into Selina's room and sit on the edge of the bed as she folds up a white t-shirt and a pair of sweatpants, her long locks swaying with every movement. Even though we knew this day would be coming eventually, it's still hard to believe she's actually leaving here.

Her bottom lip trembles as she zips up the suitcase, finalizing the reality of the situation. "I don't want to go," Selina confesses with a sigh before she sits down next to me. I don't know much about her past, given that she hasn't told me much. But from what she has told me, her mother is a real piece of work, unstable and wildly unpredictable.

"I don't want you to go either," I say, my voice heavy with emotion. But the unmistakable truth of the matter is she's thirteen and I'm fourteen. We're both minors, and there's not a damn thing we can do to fix this situation. Her mother is, by law, her legal guardian whether we like it or not, and she's currently waiting downstairs for Selina to pack her things.

"I wish I could stay here," she says, her eyes filling up with tears and nearly gutting me in the process.

"I know. I want the same thing," I agree. I put my arm around her shoulders, squeezing her tightly to me in a hug. God, she smells like strawberries and wildflowers, and I breathe in her scent, stamping it into my brain.

"Selina, hurry up!" her mother yells from downstairs. Her voice is husky and coarse like sandpaper and is followed up by some loud hacking, which sounds like she's coughing up a lung.

Selina grimaces at the sound of her mother's voice before slowly pulling away from me. She stands and grabs her tiny suitcase, which is filled with clothes that my parents bought for her while she was living here. Her eyes are wide and sad as she looks around the bedroom one last time before we retreat out into the hallway. Every single step feels like a thousand as we walk down the hall. I don't want her to leave, but it's not up to me. God, I wish it was.

We reach the top of the staircase when Selina suddenly turns and flies into my arms. "Don't let her take me," she begs in a shaky whisper against my ear.

I hold her and smooth my hand up and down her back soothingly. I remember how skinny she was when she first arrived, but now she's filled out. She's healthy. She's *happy*. "I'll find a way to get you away from her, Lina," I promise, calling her by the affectionate nickname that I gave to her on the first day we met. Maybe my parents can pull some strings. Maybe they can buy her mother off. She sure as shit didn't care about Selina for six months before showing up out of the blue to put claim on her daughter.

She's practically shaking in my arms, and I curse under my breath. I wish we were older. I wish it didn't have to be this way. Pulling back, I stare into her eyes and tell her, "Everything is going to be okay. We'll be together again soon. I won't just let you disappear."

Before I can utter any other words, Selina leans in and places her lips against mine.

Our first kiss.

My first kiss ever.

I've been imagining for months what it would feel like. We're both inexperienced and young, having done nothing more than hold hands.

Her lips feel soft and undemanding against mine. I deepen the kiss, pulling her closer, and stroking my thumb over the small heart-shaped birthmark on her neck. She hates that damn mark, but I think it's cute as hell.

"Promise me, Nico," she pleads when she pulls back, staring into my eyes. "Promise me you'll come to see me."

"I promise. Your mom will just have to get used to the fact that I'm going to be around. I don't care where you go or where she takes you, I'll still come to visit." I know, without a doubt in my heart, that I would follow Selina to the edge of the earth if I had to. "We can text, email, write letters. Whatever you want."

"I want all of that and more," she says before wrapping her arms around me in a hug.

I hold her tightly, inhaling her strawberry-scented shampoo and memorizing the way she feels in my arms. I want to be with Lina forever, but I don't tell her that. I don't want to scare her, but I think she knows how I feel. And I'm pretty sure she feels the same way.

"I feel safe with you," she whispers against my chest.

She guts me again with her words, but I know right now I have to be strong for the both of us. Nothing is going to change the current situation. Pulling back, I stare into her blue and green eyes. I hate when I see so much sadness reflected in them. "Tell you what. How about tomorrow I'll come pick you up, and we'll go for a picnic on the beach," I offer in an attempt to cheer her up.

"A picnic," she says as if the idea is so foreign to her.

"Yeah," I muse. "I'll pack us those juice boxes that you love, a bag of Doritos, and some of those chocolate and marshmallow cookies that you keep sneaking out of the jar in the kitchen." That earns me a smile, and I can see some of her tension melting away. "And, hey, I'll even make you PB and J with the crusts cut off." She hates the crust, and it makes me laugh every time I see her cutting off the extra bread.

"So it's a...date?"

"It's a date," I promise. "I'll see you tomorrow. I know my mom will drive me over to visit you." According to Selina's mother, they are going to be staying at a motel for a couple of weeks before she finds an apartment to rent for them. My mother offered to help with the rent, and her mother immediately took her up on the offer, demanding money up front to help with the costs. My mom, of course, handed over the cash, because in the time that Selina's been here, my mom has come to love her just as much as I have and would do anything to ensure her happiness and wellbeing. And I know that, as long as Selina's mother promises to get an apartment nearby, my mom and dad will keep footing the bill. Lina's become part of the family. There's no doubt about that.

"Selina, come on!" her mother crows from downstairs.

Selina reluctantly pulls away from me, takes a tentative step towards the stairs, but then suddenly stops and turns to look at me over her shoulder. "My mom is not who they think she is," she says cryptically. But before I can ask what she means by that, I hear her mother's screeching voice calling for her again.

"Hurry up!"

We round the corner and slowly descend the staircase. My parents and my little sister Aria are waiting patiently in the foyer. My dad has a frown on his face, my mom looks worried, and Aria has tears in her eyes streaming down her red cheeks. She's just as upset as I am about Selina leaving.

And when I finally lay eyes on Selina's mother standing by the front door, I almost begin to plead right then and there with my parents to tell her to leave. She's skinny, way too skinny, with ratty blonde hair and blue eyes. She has wrinkles on her face even though she can't be that old since Selina told me her mother was a teenager when she gave birth, and her fake nails scratch down her arms nervously as she watches her daughter with bloodshot eyes and a thin-lipped smile.

"It's about damn time," Miss McCall mutters angrily to her daughter. But when she notices everyone is staring at her and her cold demeanor, she suddenly changes her tune, plastering on a fake smile that stretches out the cracked red lipstick on her mouth. "Did you get everything, sweetie?" she asks, laying it on thick but not fooling a single soul in this room.

No affection or warmth comes from either one of them during their little reunion, and the red flags just seem to keep popping up. Lina turns and runs into my arms one last time, and I hold her tightly to me, not wanting to ever let her go. I can feel the apprehension and nervousness coming off of her in waves, and all I can do is whisper in her ear that I'm coming for her. Soon.

Her haunting words come rushing back to me just then — *My mom is not who they think she is.*

If it's the last thing I ever do, I will find out a way to get her out from under her mother's control. I'll run away with Lina if that's what it takes. We're both young, but we'll figure it out. I don't care about the consequences. I just want Lina in my life. Forever.

"We have to go, Selina," her mother says, roughly grabbing her daughter and ripping her from my arms.

"Wait!" I call out, but her mother is dragging her out the door and onto the sidewalk before I can even say goodbye.

Aria stands silently next to me, holding my hand tightly as my father puts a hand on my shoulder in support while we watch the only girl I've ever loved being taken out of my life by force.

"Call me!" I yell to Selina as she reaches the old, white, beat-up sedan sitting in the driveway.

She longingly stares back at me and gives me a nod and a little wave before ducking her head into the car and slamming the door shut.

I know she'll call. I made sure she packed a piece of paper with my number on it into her suitcase. That was the very first thing she put in there. *The most important thing*, she had told me.

I watch as the car speeds away, and my stomach sinks. I feel like this will be the last time I'll ever see her again, but I know that's silly. I'm going to see her tomorrow. My mom already promised to drive me to the motel, so that we could check on them.

"When we go to see them, I'll make sure Selina has everything she needs," my mom assures me. "And if she doesn't, well, then social services is getting a call from me."

Forcing a smile, I nod. See, everything is going to be okay. None of the Vitales are going to let Selina McCall fall through the cracks. She'll be taken care of no matter what.

I stand at the doorway watching the car pull out of the driveway, refusing to move or even breathe until it completely disappears out of sight. I end up staying there for over an hour, just hoping that Lina forgot something she has to come back for or that her mother changed her mind. But they don't come back, and it makes my stomach sour at the thought of Lina being with that horrible woman.

The sick feeling stays with me for the rest of the day and evening, and that night I have trouble sleeping. I expected Selina to have at least called me or something when they got to the motel, but I don't hear from her. And by the next morning, I know something is terribly wrong.

When my mother and I stop by the motel that Selina and her mother were supposed to be staying in, we learn that they only stayed a few hours and then dipped, leaving no information behind with the desk clerk.

I knew right then and there that I would probably never see Selina McCall again. She was gone forever. And all of my heartfelt promises to get her away from her mother and keep her safe were fucking broken.

CHAPTER 1

Nicholas

Present Day

TWO HORRIBLE THINGS happened when I was fourteen years old. The first thing was losing Selina. We were never able to find her after that day. She just up and vanished without a trace. And despite our best efforts, we could never locate her or her mother.

The second thing that happened was when Constantine Carbone was released from jail on a technicality. Carbone was the man who was arrested for human trafficking charges years ago when I was just a toddler. My mother and father had been the ones to bring him down, supplying the feds with all the information they needed to arrest him.

Carbone made appeal after appeal after appeal until something finally fucking stuck. He had more money than God and used it wisely, effectively buying his way out of jail.

Prison did nothing to reform the horrible bastard. Just months after his release, word on the street was that he was right back into the flesh trade once again. He was more careful this time around, however, moving people in shipment containers and keeping them out on the ocean instead of on the land. Out in the vast water, the laws don't really apply there and it's harder to get caught. The son of a bitch was smart; I'll give him that.

My father kept tabs on him, however, and still gave information to the feds as often as he could. But Constantine evaded the police and the law at every turn.

Justice needs to be served on that bastard.

And maybe I need to be the justice.

I remember the horror stories Selina told me about being taken from her mother and locked in a warehouse for days and weeks on end. She was rescued by my family before she was sold, but that didn't mean that bad things didn't happen to her. She was emotionally, physically and mentally scarred.

After she was ripped from my arms by her awful mother, who chose to take her daughter and the money my parents gave her and run, I vowed to always help people like Selina. One way to help would be to take down Constantine Carbone once and for all. And I'm beginning to think the only way to stop him is a bullet between his eyes.

"Champagne, sir?" a waiter asks me, offering up a tray filled with several crystal flutes of bubbly liquid.

"Thank you," I mutter before grabbing a flute by the stem. I take a sip of the expensive champagne and watch him walk away. I'm not even supposed to be at this party, but Aldo, my father's best IT guy, was able to secure me an invitation under a false name.

"If your father finds out about this..." I hear Aldo's voice murmuring in my ear thanks to a micro-Bluetooth earpiece that's undetectable to the naked eye.

"He won't," I breathe out quickly right before I finish off my glass and set it down on a nearby table.

Aldo is stationed about five blocks away in a nondescript black van. He agreed, reluctantly, to this little reconnaissance mission.

Carbone has been flying under the radar ever since his prison release, but we know he's still dealing in the flesh trade. It's just harder to pinpoint his whereabouts. And when I get close to him tonight, I'm going to plant a tracker on him. Aldo will take it from there, securing his coordinates and, thus, gathering the information we've been desiring for years.

If we can just get a tail on Carbone, we can figure out where he's hiding his warehouses, ships, everything; ultimately saving hundreds, if not thousands of young lives. And even though it's dangerous getting close to the bastard, I'm willing to do the dirty work if that means bringing Carbone's empire to its knees.

Laughter breaks out to the right of me, catching my attention. I look around the crowd of people, dressed to the nines with elaborate, colorful masks complete with jewels and feathers. It's a Mardi Gras themed party, and that is exactly why I chose this one in particular to make an appearance. The simple, gold mask I'm wearing will help conceal my identity from the cameras around the property. It will be easier to move around, looking for my target all while staying hidden within the throng of people.

Alberto Berlusconi throws the most extravagant parties for New York's most elite, including the largest crime bosses. Alberto enjoys drugs more than girls, however, which is the only reason he's still breathing. But if Carbone was going to show up at any parties this year, it would be this one. Alberto and Constantine are great friends with mutual tastes and connections in the seedy underbelly of New York City.

Berlusconi's mansion is situated in the upper east side of Manhattan. I've seen him making his rounds at the party, throwing around his extra weight, boasting about his twenty-seven bedrooms and how many maids he's had to fire because he fucks so many of them and they get too attached. He's a real piece of work, but he's not my target.

My gut is telling me that Carbone will show tonight. He never misses an opportunity to attend lavish events and show off his money and power while meeting potential clients. The wealthiest people are sometimes the most perverse, buying young women and children and not even batting an eye. When you are rich and powerful, you can have anything you want, and no one in their inner circles even questions it, no matter how taboo or out of the ordinary their wants actually are.

Constantine has been out to sea for far too long. If anything was going to draw him inland, it would be this. All of the big hitters are here tonight. The only person missing is *him*. I check the Rolex on my wrist, watching the seconds tick by. I'm a patient man, but my patience is growing thin. I risked a lot to be here tonight, so he better show.

A tall blonde passes by me just then, and my breathing stops. But when she gets closer and her dark brown eyes meet mine under her green and yellow mask, I quickly look away. Closing my eyes, I shake my head subtly.

There's not a day that goes by when I don't think about Selina McCall at least once. The image of the sad look in her unique blue and green eyes as she glanced back at me one last time as her mother led her away will be forever ingrained in my memories.

It's been ten years since I last saw her, but I still remember every detail about her. My fascination with her is borderline obsession, and over the years I haven't stopped looking for her. We have tried everything to find her and get her back to no avail. She vanished out of thin air like some kind of cruel magician's trick.

The world doesn't really seem that big until you're trying to find one person in a vast sea of billions. And my fixation with her disappearance haunts me to this very day.

A waiter passes by me, and I grab another flute of champagne. I'd drink something stronger, but I want to keep myself level-headed and alert. I don't need expensive whiskey tripping me up even though that's my preferred drink.

I decide to leave the corner of the room and walk around, my eyes scanning every single face I pass. The masks make it a little harder to tell who is who, but I'm glad mine is hiding my true identity. I can't risk my face being seen. I look so much like my father that I have no doubt Constantine would be spooked. My family has been coming after him for years and will continue to do so until he's rightfully behind bars for good...or dead. Preferably the latter, but I'd be content with him spending the last years of his life rotting away in a maximum-security prison.

"*Any sign of him yet?*" Aldo's voice comes through the earpiece secured in my right ear.

I give a subtle shake of my head. Aldo has eyes everywhere in the room, having hacked the security cameras, and I know he can see my response.

"*Ten more minutes, and then I want you to get the hell out of there.*"

I can't help but smile. Aldo Allaband is head of my father's IT team. When I proposed the idea of somehow implanting a tiny tracker on Carbone, Aldo was all for it. But now that I'm here and the danger is real, he suddenly wants me to leave.

Not a fucking chance.

I'm not leaving until I do what I came here to do.

If I can get close enough to Carbone to place the tracker on his suit, Aldo can then trace wherever he goes after this party. Hopefully it's to his home base, which we haven't figured out the whereabouts of yet. This will be a huge win for our team. We've been trying for years to figure out where Carbone stays when he visits the city. His driver is very good at eluding our men, taking way too many turns and running too many lights for us to be able to follow.

I continue to walk around the room, searching for him. If my mother and father knew I was here, they would have my fucking head. But they're in Colorado on their wedding anniversary trip and none the wiser. In fact, this is the perfect time to get this done.

Finishing off the champagne, I set the glass down on an empty tray and walk towards the doorway leading out of the ballroom.

"You're leaving?" Aldo asks, and I can hear the relief in his voice.

"Gotta piss," I inform him in a whisper as I make my way towards the restrooms.

As soon as I round the corner, I barely have time to catch myself before I nearly crash into a woman. She bumps into my chest, her fingers grasping the lapels of my suit jacket in a white-knuckle grip. "S-s-sorry," she mutters, her speech slurred. She stumbles backwards in her heels, head down as her mask flutters to the floor.

"No. My apologies," I tell her, quickly reaching down to scoop up the purple and gold feathered mask that she dropped. My eyes drift to her feet, locking on to the gold sky-high stilettos that she's currently teetering on. Then, they slowly venture up her long, lean legs to a sparkling gold dress, if you can even call it a dress, that's so short and low cut it should be illegal.

When I finally stand at my full height, I hold the mask out to her, watching her delicate hand grasp it tightly as if it's some sort of lifeline. "Thank you," she says softly, and there's just something about her voice that makes me think that I have met her before. Her fingers lightly brush against mine, the brief contact causing my heart to skip a beat inside of my chest. My feet suddenly become rooted to the floor. It's as if my body doesn't want to leave this spot until I see her face.

She's about to walk away, her head still down, denying me what I want to see — no, what I *need* to see — but I reach out to stop her. Ever so gently, I put my hand under her chin and force her gaze to mine. And suddenly, all the air in my lungs escapes in a rush.

I blink a few times to clear my vision, thinking I'm imagining her, dreaming all of this up. But when she's still there, still looking longingly up at me, I know she's real. Long, blonde hair cascades over her bare shoulders, and she's so damn beautiful that it almost hurts to look at her. But her beauty is not what has my hand clenching into a fist at my side. No, it's her eyes.

One blue.

One green.

They're both bloodshot, and her pupils are nearly blown like she's riding high on whatever poison is in her system, but I can clearly tell they're different colors.

Our connection only lasts for a few seconds, even though it feels like minutes, before she mutters another apology and stumbles past me, securing the mask back onto her face. I listen as the sound of her high heels echoing on the hardwood floor fades into the distance.

Sucking in a deep, unsteady breath, I hurry to the restroom. I take care of business and then wash my hands. Staring at my reflection, I watch my chest rise and fall rapidly. I'm barely holding it together. I'm wound up like a rubber band, ready to snap at any given moment. "Holy fuck," I mutter.

"What? What happened?" Aldo asks in my earpiece.

"I think I just saw her."

"Her? Her who?"

"Lina," I hiss in a whisper.

"Holy fuck," Aldo says, repeating my exact sentiments. Aldo knows the entire story. Hell, he was there when Selina was living at the compound. He probably loved her as much as the rest of us did. She was so damn easy to love. So full of light and life even though she had been through a horrible ordeal.

And now she's here. But why? Who is she here with? I have to know.

"There are a lot of people with complete heterochromia," Aldo reminds me.

Yes, and I found that out the hard way. I've scoured the world looking for the girl with one blue eye and one green eye. It's rare, but definitely not improbable.

"There's one more thing I can check," I tell him. Selina had a heart-shaped birthmark on her neck. She always hated it, but I loved it. "I just need to get close to her again."

"*I don't like this, Nico. What if you run into Carbone while your guard is down?*"

"I'll be careful," I say, but even I can hear the lie in my voice. My previous mission is completely forgotten. I just want to find the woman and see if she bears the birthmark. I need to know if Selina is still alive. After all these years, all the searching and longing, I need to know for sure.

CHAPTER 2

Selina McCall

I STUMBLE MY way back towards the ballroom. My hands are still shaking from my encounter with the man in the hallway. He was the very definition of tall, dark and handsome, wearing an expensive, black tailored suit. But the way he looked at me, with those steel gray eyes behind his gold mask, unnerved me. It was almost as if he were trying to figure me out somehow; like a riddle he wanted to solve. And I hated the way his eyes seemed to stare through me to my very soul, like he could see all of my fears and flaws that I so desperately try to keep hidden and locked away deep within me.

I grab a flute of champagne from the nearest table as I absently rub at my chin, remembering the way he touched me, so gently, like I'm made of glass. I've never had a man touch me like that before. A violent shiver runs through me just then as I glance over my shoulder, expecting to see him following me. But he's not there.

A sense of relief surges through my veins as I down the expensive champagne in one long swallow before setting the empty glass back down. I need to avoid any other encounters with that man...and everyone else at this party, for that matter. God forbid if I would do something wrong or cause a scene. I would probably never see the light of day again. I shudder at the thought of that. The fact that I'm even here right now, in public and away from the man who has held me captive for the past decade is almost unimaginable.

I don't even want to be at this stupid party, but it's not as if I have a choice in the matter. No, Constantine Carbone does whatever he wants. And tonight, he decided to rent me out to his son like a hooker.

The thought of running has crossed my mind a time or two, but I know I wouldn't get very far. Constantine always finds me. And the last time I tried to run...let's just say it scarred me for the rest of my life. I won't ever try to get away again. I will remain his perfect *little pet* just like he wants. I won't be responsible for anyone else getting hurt because of me.

I drink three more glasses of champagne before I steel my spine and make my way towards my date for the night. I'm going to need all the liquid courage I can get. Gino Carbone is cruel and demanding, just like his father. A cookie cutter cut-out of his old man — minus the good looks and charm.

When Constantine first bought me at the tender age of thirteen, Gino was only a few years older than me. I made the mistake of thinking that he was kind, that he would help me. I learned my first lesson a few weeks later when he and his father took turns beating and raping me.

I never trusted that bastard again. And I loathe the fact that I have to be here with him tonight while he parades me around like a *real* date and not just the woman he occasionally assaults and uses as his own personal punching bag.

Once I'm at his side again, I reach for another glass of champagne from a waiter passing by, but Gino clucks his teeth in disapproval. "I want you sober," he says before pulling me close and nipping at my earlobe like we're two lovers who can't keep their hands off each other. I pull away from him in disgust, and he grabs my arm in a bruising grip. His dark eyes glare at me as he mutters angrily, "Do we need to go over your manners again?"

"No," I say with a vehement shake of my head.

"No, what?" he demands.

"No, *sir*." It takes everything in me at that moment not to roll my eyes. Constantine tried to break me over the years, and maybe he succeeded, but the drugs he supplies me with make me feel like I have superpowers, like I can conquer the world. I think deep down he likes the defiant streak in me. It makes it that much harder to break me, something he loves doing to all of his women. And I've seen him break so many that they will forever haunt my nightmares.

"I like my whores compliant. Don't make me beat your defiance out of you again," Gino warns under his breath.

I wince at his words and at the memory of him whipping me with his belt just a few days ago. I still have the bruises all over my body and the cuts from when the buckle caught my skin. He was high on blow and his girlfriend had just cheated on him. Reason enough to take his anger out on me I suppose.

I fidget in my high heels. The concoction of benzos I took hours ago are beginning to wear off. Constantine promised me that his son would give me some whenever I needed, and that was the only way I agreed to this little outing. Constantine knows I'm addicted. I can't go without my precious *medicine*. And I have done some foul, unforgivable things in order to catch the next high. The pills are the only thing that keep me going most days. Otherwise I would probably sink down into a dark void, never to be found again.

"Stop fidgeting," Gino snaps, bringing me out of my racing thoughts.

"I'm sorry. I need my pills. Your father said —."

"Fuck what my father said," he says, cutting me off.

If Constantine could hear those words, his son would be in major trouble. Nobody defies the great almighty Constantine Carbone, not even his own son.

My skin feels like it's on fire, and I have the urge to scratch until I open my flesh and begin to bleed. I start at my wrist, but Gino snags my hand and holds it sternly between us.

"What the fuck is wrong with you?" he growls angrily.

"I need my pills," I beg him.

"Let's go upstairs. You're pissing me off." He grabs my arm roughly, pulling me along with him.

I nod in agreement. Yes, let's go somewhere private where I can take my medicine. Constantine promised me Gino would give me my pills before he tried anything.

We start for the staircase when I hear someone call out, "Carbone!"

I wince, thinking that Gino will turn around and begin talking, delaying me my high. But luckily, he just waves off the person, and we continue up the stairs to the second floor.

I can barely walk in a straight line. Sweat beads on my brow, and I feel like I'm going to pass out or be sick. I've never gone this long without my medicine before. The fear of going through withdrawal has me trying to hurry along, but Gino keeps a firm grip on me, guiding me at his own pace.

My mask feels like it's suffocating me, so I rip it off my face and drop it in the hallway, not caring if I ever see the damn thing again.

We walk down hallway after hallway until he finds a suitable room. He opens the door and shoves me inside. I stumble, banging my elbow against the wall. "Ouch," I whisper before I shake off the dull ache and continue on inside.

The bedroom is opulent, decorated in deep browns and reds with a massive bed in the middle situated under a huge crystal chandelier. Antique furniture fills the rest of the room — a mirrored dresser, a large armoire, and two nightstands with lamps, which illuminate when Gino hits a switch on the wall.

Any other time I would take time to appreciate the décor, but there's one thing and only one thing on my mind right now. I turn to Gino, who sticks a fat finger in the knot of his tie, pulling it loose. Before I can even open my mouth, he tells me, "Take off your dress."

Shaking my head, I back away from him to the nearest wall, pushing my back against the cool, floral wallpaper. "Please. My pills. I need my pills first," I plead with him.

"I'm not giving you shit until you fuck me," he says, making my stomach drop.

"Your father promised! He promised that you would give them to me!" I practically scream, growing more hysterical by every passing second. I can't fuck him unless I'm high. *I can't.*

Suddenly, Gino crosses the room in a few big strides, swallowing up the space between us quickly. He grabs a fistful of my hair and slams me into the side of an antique armoire. My bones rattle upon the impact, and I catch myself on the corner, wheezing from where it poked me hard right in the stomach.

"Take off your dress and get on the fucking bed," he orders.

Straightening my spine, I give him a nod, symbolizing that I'm going to behave and do what he tells me to do. He releases my hair, and I walk towards the bed, putting a little distance between us.

I can hear his heavy footfalls as he comes closer. And then I feel him at my backside, his hands on my waist. I turn slowly in his arms and stare up at him. He's tall, just like his father, but about a hundred pounds heavier.

I take a step back from him and pretend that I'm reaching for the zipper of my dress.

"That's a good little bitch," Gino murmurs.

If I've learned anything over the years, it's that being good only gets you in more trouble. Being good only gets you hurt in the end.

Raising my leg, I kick forward as hard as I can, aiming for his balls. But my foot only comes into contact with his fat stomach. And I realize in that moment the grave mistake I have made.

Gino's face grows red with anger as he latches onto my foot and pulls my leg, making me cry out in surprise as I lose my footing. I slip and fall to the floor, hitting the back of my head on the footboard of the bed on the way down. The room spins around me as I suddenly feel him pinning me on the floor, his heavy weight on top of my chest. He's crushing me to the point that it feels like my ribs are breaking and I can't even pull in a single breath.

"You fucking bitch!" he spits out before punching me in the side of the head.

Pain blooms along my temple, jarring my skull and making my teeth chatter. I try to bring my hands up to protect my face, but my arms are dead at my side. I can't even feel my fingertips.

The lights in the room flicker, and I'm starting to think that this is the end. That I'm finally dying and escaping this hell on earth. But then that's when I hear Gino ask, "Who the hell are you?"

Out of the corner of my eye, a dark figure enters the room, a dark gold mask covering most of his face. *It's the man from the hallway*, I vaguely think to myself.

His piercing gray eyes meet mine for only a split second before he turns his attention to my attacker. I see the blade before Gino even does. Suddenly, like in a real-life horror movie, the man grabs Gino from behind and slices through his fat neck. Blood instantly sprays out, soaking through my dress and spattering my face as Gino gurgles a horrific sound.

I'm instantly taken back to that tragic day...

The blood.

The blood coating my skin.

I'm wearing their blood.

The next thing I hear is a hard *thud* as Gino slumps over, his head resting on the edge of the footboard above me, his wide, vacant stare locked on my face as his gaping mouth spills forth a river of blood that trickles down to my forehead and cheek.

I whip my head back and forth, trying to somehow stop it from touching me. I can't bear the horrible coppery smell or the fact that I'm covered in his blood. It's too much like what happened before, and my anxiety begins to crawl its way to my throat as I struggle to breathe.

My mouth opens on a scream, but no sound comes out. I'm still being crushed by the dead bastard, and my lungs are on fire, desperate for air. I start to gasp, my mouth gaping open repeatedly like a fish out of water.

The room begins to violently spin around me, and I close my eyes as I begin to fall into a black abyss. My entire body feels weightless, like I'm floating, and I revel in the feeling. I'm in a beautiful, silent void of absolute darkness. There is no fear, no anxiety, no pain here.

Sweet, merciful death is finally coming to claim me...and I welcome him with open arms.

CHAPTER 3

Nicholas

I PUSH GINO Carbone's lifeless body off of the woman. Then, I wipe the blade of my knife off on the dead man's shirt before securing it back inside my suit jacket.

"What about in and out undetected did you not understand?" Aldo hisses in my earpiece.

"Just a minor complication," I mutter.

"*A dead man is not a* minor *complication, Nico,*" he chides.

"He was hurting Lina."

"*You don't even know if the girl is Lina.*"

"Well, even if it's not her, he was still hurting an innocent woman."

Aldo has no response to that because he knows I'm right. In the end, I had to intervene. There was no other way.

I reach down and press my fingers to the girl's neck. There's a pulse, but it's very faint. "I need to get her out of here," I inform Aldo while grabbing a blanket from the bed and wrapping the poor girl in it.

"And how the fuck do you propose we do that, Nico?" he asks angrily.

Obviously, nothing is going as planned at this point, and I know Aldo hates it when things deviate from a certain path. But it's too late to turn back now.

"You're gonna have to work some magic, man," I tell him before scooping the woman's limp body into my arms. Her head falls back, and I stare down at the heart-shaped birthmark on her neck just below her ear. "Lina," I gasp, my chest aching. A million different emotions flood through me just then all at once. Fuck, I can't believe I finally found her.

"It's her?" Aldo asks, and I can hear his fingers tapping rapidly on his keyboard.

"Yes, it's her," I manage to say. Swallowing hard, I cradle Lina against my chest, holding her tightly.

"There's a service entrance," Aldo says urgently. "You need to hurry, though. The guards are going to be doing their rounds soon. All of the video is still on loop, so they won't see you on the cameras, but I can't protect you from running into the wrong guy."

"Got it."

"Coast is clear in the hallway. Go out of the room and turn right. Go to the end of the hall and down the staircase."

I follow Aldo's instructions carefully. I stop when he tells me to stop. I disappear into various rooms when he alerts me to a guard nearby. And my chest doesn't stop aching until we're finally out the back entrance of the mansion and onto the street. It takes sheer willpower and a lot of luck, but I manage to carry Lina the whole five blocks back to the van without incident.

"Were you followed?" Aldo asks when he pops open the side door. His dark hair is disheveled like he's been running his hands through it for hours. I probably took ten years off of his life tonight by pulling all the shit I did, but I don't care. It was worth it. I would do anything, and I mean *anything*, to save Lina.

"How the hell should I know?" I hiss before gently setting Lina's limp body down on the floor. The blanket falls open, revealing her bloody dress and the bruises beginning to form on her arms and temple, and I cringe at the sight.

Aldo's eyes grow wide. "Okay, okay. We need to get the hell out of here before someone discovers his body. After you left, I took off the looping video and cleared the entire security system of all the footage for the past few hours since you arrived. When we get back to the compound, I'll work on the CCTV footage in the area, but I might not be able to erase everything. Someone could have already seen you carrying her for that distance and reported it."

"We'll cross that bridge when we get to it," I growl before closing the side door. Then, I run to the driver's side and jump into the seat and slam the door shut. Ripping off my mask, I throw it to the floor. Then, revving the engine, I pull out of the parking spot and speed down the street back towards the compound.

I glance back at Lina lying on the floor, and I have to blink several times to make sure I'm not imagining her. "You're safe now, Lina," I tell her softly. "I'm taking you home."

The moment Aldo and I return back to the compound that we call home, I see a huge, dark figure standing in the driveway.

"Fuck," I mutter under my breath.

I park the van and step out. Benito walks over, tall and menacing with tattooed-covered muscles. He is my father's number one, and he's a huge, mean-looking son of a bitch, but he holds a soft spot in his heart for my family and my family alone. He's actually my godfather and has always been like an uncle to me, watching over me and protecting me over the years while I was growing up.

His huge muscles bunch under his t-shirt, threatening to rip the seams as he stares me down. Aldo climbs out of the side of the van and shuts the door. I can practically see him trembling from here.

"Tell me you two weren't just at Berlusconi's party in Manhattan," Benito starts.

I glance at him and give him a one-shoulder shrug.

"Goddamn it, Nico!" he practically roars. "I hope to fuck you didn't have anything to do with Carbone's son being dead."

Damn. Word travels fast.

I wince at his accusation, and I can't even meet his eyes. I'm not scared of anyone, but I am scared of Benito's disapproval. I always want to make him proud. And my actions tonight are going to bring a lot of repercussions; ones that I haven't even had time to think about yet.

"You better have had a damn good reason," Benito hisses.

"I did." Slowly, I walk back to the van and open the back doors before moving aside.

Benito steps closer, checking out the cargo, his eyebrow suddenly arching in surprise. "Who the fuck is that?" he questions.

"Selina McCall."

His head whips to the side and he meets my eyes. "*Your* Selina?"

"Yes." I turn to look at the blonde beauty sleeping in the back. "She was at the party. Gino was hurting her. Hell, he might even have killed her if I hadn't intervened."

"How do you know it's her?" he asks, and I can hear the unease in his voice, because I've been wrong before. I've saved what seems like a hundred Selina McCalls before, claiming they were her before finding out they weren't.

"It's her," I tell him confidently. "Not only the eyes but the same birthmark on her neck. I'm a thousand percent sure it's Lina."

"Holy shit. After all this time..." Benito's voice trails off as he shakes his head. Then with a grim voice, he tells me, "We'll deal with your father's wrath when he gets home."

"You're not going to call him?"

"And risk ruining their anniversary trip? No fucking way," he grunts. "They'll be home in a few days. We'll figure out what to tell them by then."

I nod my head in agreement, and then I glance over at Aldo, who emphatically nods. He doesn't want to piss my father off either.

"Your team is freaking out over Gino Carbone's death," Benito tells Aldo. "I suggest you guys cover Nico's tracks to lessen the fallout from tonight."

"Right away, sir," Aldo mumbles before jogging off towards the part of the property that houses the underground network of computers, servers, and IT equipment.

"Carry Selina inside," Benito starts. "I'm going to phone the on-call doc and tell her we need her ASAP."

I give him a nod before I lean down to scoop Selina into my arms. Her head lolls against my chest as I carry her into the compound. It's hard to believe that after all these years she's finally home where she belongs.

CHAPTER 4

Nicholas

I WATCH SELINA sleep. She's currently in a room down the hall from my own, and I've been sitting here for hours, waiting, while the doctor ran some tests and a nurse cleaned and bandaged her wounds. It's still hard to believe that she's really here. I'm terrified that at any given moment I'm going to wake up from this dream and she'll be gone again.

Needing to ground myself, I reach out and skim my fingertips down her forearm, her skin soft under my touch. My hand finds hers, and I hold it, squeezing gently to reassure her while she's unconscious that I'm here, that I'll protect her.

I never stopped looking for Selina ever since that horrible day when her mother took her away from me. Hell, Aldo has been on the case for the past decade. And that's exactly how long it's been since the last time I've seen her.

Ten long, agonizing years.

Despite the dark circles under her eyes and all the cuts and bruises, Selina is still breathtakingly beautiful; an older version of the girl I fell in love with long ago. But things were different back then. *We* were different. And when she finally does wake up, I'm going to have a million questions. To be honest, I don't even know where to begin. I'll stick with the most crucial inquiries first. I want to know where she's been. I want to know how she came to be under Gino Carbone's control. And most importantly, I want to know who got her addicted to drugs.

However, for right now, the questions will have to wait. I have to let her rest. Her body needs to recuperate from all the trauma it has suffered not only over the past several hours but for the past fucking decade.

Reluctantly, I pull my hand away from hers and walk out of her room. Selina is sedated for now while the illegal drugs work their way out of her system thanks to IV fluids and medicine, so I feel safe leaving her alone for a brief period.

When Selina does finally wake, I know that she is not going to be the same girl from all those years ago. I need to mentally prepare myself for the new version of her that I got a glimpse of at the party. I don't know if I can ever fully prepare myself, however. There's still a part of me hoping that she'll be the same sweet, funny, charming girl I once knew and loved.

Dr. Fay Catalano, the physician on call that's been looking after Selina, is waiting for me out in the hallway. When she sees me, she motions for me to follow her, which I do. I've been eager for an update on Selina's condition. We enter an office a few doors down the hall, and I watch as she grabs a thick manilla folder from a table, flipping through it as she studies it silently.

The doctor is an older woman with salt and pepper hair. Her short stature may fool some people, but she can stare down even the bravest of men and have them backing down in a matter of seconds. I've seen her do it firsthand. She's seen a lot in her sixty-some years of life, and it shows.

She takes a seat opposite of me, and only gives me a moment to settle into my own chair before she begins talking. "I've run numerous tests on Selina," she starts, peering up at me through her thick glasses. "She's malnourished and dehydrated. I have her on an IV, giving her the fluids she needs as well as some antibiotics." She continues with, "Selina suffered two broken ribs from the assault at the party, which resulted in a punctured lung. She's going to need a few days at least of bed rest and then six to eight weeks to recover from those injuries alone." She pushes her glasses up the bridge of her nose. "When I deem her fit enough, she can have some light physical therapy to get her back into shape, because I noticed some muscle atrophy in her arms and legs. Perhaps she was tied up for long periods of time. I mean, that would explain the scars on her wrists and ankles," she says as she reads over the reports with a grim expression on her face. "I also discovered a lot of old bruises and untreated fractures, so I would say, unfortunately, this young lady has a very long history of abuse."

My hands curl into fists at my sides, and it takes everything in me to sit there and listen as the doctor explains what's wrong with Selina. Outside, I appear calm and understanding, but inside I'm a fucking wreck. I want to destroy the world, starting with Constantine Carbone and his entire lineage. I already took out his son, but it wasn't enough. I won't stop until his whole empire is burning to the fucking ground.

The doctor scribbles some notes down in her chart. Then, she frowns and hands me a copy of the toxicology report. "Also, Selina has multiple substances in her system. She was on a number of psychotropic drugs that we're still testing to try to learn the names of them. More than likely they were some type of street benzodiazepines. She's coming down from a dangerous cocktail, I'm afraid, and I'm doing my best to keep her stabilized while she goes through withdrawal."

"How long will that take?" I ask as I look up from the laundry list of drugs on the paper.

"She should start feeling better in a week or so," the doctor concludes. "She's going to be pretty out of it for the first few days of her stay here, unfortunately, as she goes through a variety of side effects — incoherent babbling, excessive sweating, paranoia, vomiting, the whole nine yards. Sarah will keep a good eye on her while she goes through the withdrawal."

Sarah Benson is the nurse who works full time at the compound. She's here during the day and on call at night in case any emergencies arise. I've known her personally for years, and she's great at what she does. I'm more than happy to entrust Selina's care to her.

Dr. Catalano clears her throat and then tells me, "Selina also has a birth control implant in her upper arm that I discovered. I left it alone. I'm sure Selina can decide whether she wants that removed or not when she's alert and coherent."

I find some comfort knowing that Selina at least didn't have to deal with unwanted pregnancies while she was being held captive by Gino. I can't imagine the unspeakable horrors she went through, and I know she would have never wanted to have a child go through that, let alone her own child.

"If you don't need anything else, I would like to go home for the day," the doctor informs me.

"Yes, of course. Thank you for all that you've done."

"Sarah has my number on speed dial. I can be here in ten minutes if anything happens," she assures me.

"Thank you, Doc. For everything," I tell her before standing up and leaving the office. I walk down the hall, passing by Selina's door, on the way to my room when my feet suddenly stop, my shoes rooted to the hardwood floor. Groaning, I scrub a hand down my face. I know I should get some sleep; but for some reason, I feel an overwhelming need to check on Selina again.

I tell myself it will only be for a few minutes, but the minutes quickly turn to hours, and soon I'm just sitting there, watching over her...and waiting.

CHAPTER 5

Selina

I WAKE UP slowly, my vision blurry as I rapidly blink away the moisture in my eyes. Once my vision begins to clear, I study the room I'm in. It's lavish, luxuriously decorated in muted grays and purples. And the first thing that comes to mind is that I'm back in Constantine's clutches.

I try to remember the last thing that happened, and my heart begins to pound rapidly in my chest like an angry war drum when the memories come flooding back in a rush.

Gino was assaulting me.

The man with the gray eyes was suddenly in the room.

The knife.

Gino's neck being sliced open.

Me being covered in blood...and other gross stuff that I can't even think about right now.

Me struggling to breathe.

And then...nothing.

Now I am here, and I have no idea exactly where *here* is. Did the man at the party work for Constantine? No, he couldn't have. Constantine wouldn't have sent a hitman after his only son. And if I'm not with Constantine but with the murderer who ultimately kidnapped me, then I might be in even bigger trouble than I was with my original captor.

Sitting up, I stare down at my right arm, which has an IV needle sticking out of it. Wincing, I pull the needle out and quickly climb out of bed. My heart beats in a weird staccato as I grab onto things to help with my balance and make my way over to one of the large windows on the other side of the room.

It's getting dark outside, so I can't see much. My eyes dart around, fixating on the high fence surrounding the property. *Have I been here before?* I search for anything that looks familiar. Constantine has many homes scattered all over the US and in other countries, and I think I have been to all of them. Perhaps I've been here before with him.

I try to think harder, but my brain is fuzzy and I'm having trouble focusing.

My pills. I need my pills.

I stare down at my wrists. The fact that I'm not chained or handcuffed in some way and the fact that I am dressed, albeit in a hospital gown, is all new to me. I was Constantine's property, and he liked to remind me of that often.

The door to the room swings open suddenly, and I jump back from the window, alarmed. A young woman dressed in dark blue scrubs enters the room, and her eyes widen when she sees me.

"You're awake," she says, clearly surprised. Her bright blue eyes immediately shift to my arm, and I follow her gaze there. "And you pulled your IV out." She frowns when she sees the blood dripping down my arm. "Please get back in bed. I'm going to go get some bandages and disinfectant. I'll be right back."

She leaves the room, and the door is left open. When she disappears into another room down the hallway, I decide now is my chance to try to escape.

My bare feet slap against the tiled hall as I run. I don't even think. I just run. I don't even know if I can get out of here, but I don't want to feel Constantine's wrath for his son's death. Who knows, maybe he even blames me. Knowing that sick fuck, he was just trying to get me hydrated and well again so he could torture me...and kill me. I wouldn't put it past him. His sickness knows no bounds when it comes to me. I've become his outlet for his anger over the years, and I don't want to see how much worse it can get.

My legs are weak, turning to jelly, but I force them to keep going. A grand staircase is off to my left, and I jog down the steps, gripping onto the handrail for dear life as my feet slip and my knees continuously give out. I'm dripping sweat, the moisture running down my forehead and into my eyes, and I'm completely out of breath by the time I reach the ground level. I look left and I look right, having no clue where to go...or where to hide. There's a huge door in front of me that looks like it leads outside, but I doubt if Constantine would just let me walk right out, so I don't even attempt it.

I decide to go to the right, my lungs screaming for oxygen and my entire chest feeling like it's going to cave in at any given moment as my pace slows against my will. I'm struggling to breathe by the time I force my way into the next room. There's a tightness in my chest on the right side that is almost excruciating. I need to get out of here before it gets any worse.

I hear numerous voices suddenly stop as I burst through the double doors. Inside the large room are six people, and they all turn to stare at me at the same time. I look around at their blurry, unfamiliar faces until I recognize one.

The black hair and silver eyes. Even though he was wearing a mask, I'll never forget those eyes.

It's him.

The killer.

The man who killed Gino and then obviously kidnapped me,

doing Constantine's bidding like the good dog that he is. I need to know why I'm here, why he took me and what Constantine has in store for me now that his only son is dead and gone.

"*You*," I wheeze out accusingly. A sharp pain hits me in the chest like I was just run over by a Mack truck, and I collapse onto the floor. I try to draw air into my lungs, but I feel like I can't catch my breath.

Black spots fill my vision until the pain becomes too great, and I finally let the darkness take over as I pass out, not knowing if I'll ever wake again.

CHAPTER 6

Nicholas

MY PARENTS RETURNED from their anniversary trip a few hours ago. Benito confessed everything the moment they stepped foot onto the property; and now we're all gathered in the common room, facing the wrath of my father.

"How the fuck could you do this, Nico?" my father asks as he paces the floor and runs a hand through his short, dark hair. I've never seen him so upset before. Well, at least not with me. His gray eyes, the same color as mine, pin me to the spot I'm standing. "Why the fuck would you think it was a good idea to go after Carbone on your own? What the hell was going through your goddamn mind?" he yells, anger seeping out of his every pore.

I glance around the room at my mother, Benito, my sister Aria and my best friend and Aria's bodyguard, Renato Bianchi. Everyone is quiet with a solemn look on their face. No one is coming to my defense, nor do I expect them to. I know I fucked up. I fucked up majorly, and now I have to face the consequences of my actions.

"I know we all want Constantine put behind bars...or dead, but you can't do it alone!" my father exclaims.

I stand with my hands in my pockets, staring down at the floor while my father scolds me. He's totally right. I went behind his back and could have gotten myself hurt or worse. We've discussed in the past about tracking Constantine, but he probably never wanted *me* to the be one to actually do it.

I wasn't even going to raise any suspicions with Constantine at the party; just get close enough to him to plant a tracker on him. But all those plans went right out the fucking window when I saw his son beating on a woman, who ultimately turned out to be Selina. *My Lina.*

"And then you ended up murdering Constantine's only son. Do you know what kind of hell he will bring down upon this family when he finds out it was you?"

"Aldo erased all the security camera footage," I start, but my father doesn't let me finish.

"Yeah, from the mansion. But what about all the neighboring buildings? What about traffic cams? You think Constantine can't get his hands on all of that footage?"

"I was careful!" I plead with him.

"You were careful," he scoffs with a shake of his head. "You have no idea the trouble you're in right now. You have no idea what kind of danger you've just put your family in!" he practically screams, causing my sister to jump.

I look over at her, and she quickly steels her spine and meets my gaze for only a split second while she worries her bottom lip between her teeth. God, she looks like a younger version of our mother. They share all the same features even down to the same chestnut brown hair and amber eyes.

Renato stands stock-still at her side, not moving, not even looking like he's affected by my father's yelling. Hell, my father has probably yelled at him so much that it doesn't even bother him anymore.

My mother suddenly speaks up. "Now, Luca, Nico told us he had no choice in the matter when it came to Carbone's son," she says in an attempt to placate my father. She is the only one who can calm my dad down when he gets like this.

"I didn't," I explain to both of them. "He was hurting Selina. Who knows what would have happened if I hadn't intervened? He probably would have killed her." I can still remember the sounds of her sobs as Gino took his anger out on her in that room. Those sounds will haunt me for the rest of my life. "I did what I had to do," I tell him vehemently, standing my ground. "And I'd fucking do it again."

My father stops pacing and looks to me. "I just wish you would have waited. Going after any Carbone is dangerous."

"Too dangerous," Benito agrees from the corner, his large muscular arms crossed in front of his burly chest as he leans against the wall.

I knew he would take my father's side. I'm just glad he's not yelling at me too at this point. "I didn't have a choice," I tell them vehemently. "I just wish it would have been Constantine and not his son. That bastard needs to be taken down like the dog he is," I spit out, seething.

"Yes, in due time. But you can't just rush him without having an army prepared first. You could have been killed regardless of which Carbone you went after!" my father says in a deep rumble, his temper threatening to boil over.

The whole room is quiet while my father begins to pace the floor again. I swear he's going to make a hole in the carpet soon.

I know deep down it was a stupid idea going after Carbone on my own. It's just I've hated him for so long, given our family history with him, and I knew that party was my chance to finally do something for the greater good. I couldn't just take that opportunity for granted. My goal that night was to get intel on Constantine. What I didn't expect was his son to be in his place at that party, but I'm glad he was because the sequence of events all led me right to Selina.

And knowing now that Constantine must have had Selina in his clutches for a period of time infuriates me. When she's in her right mind, I'm going to have a lot of questions for her. I want to know exactly how she came to be under his radar and for how long. There are too many missing pieces of her puzzle, and I need to figure them all out to get a look at the bigger picture.

"Well, there's no going back now and changing things. We have to deal with what has been done," my father decides, stopping and then turning towards the rest of us. "Gino Carbone is dead. Constantine will no doubt find out who killed him and come for our family. We need to start preparing for the inevitable." He makes a point to look at my sister when he announces, "No one leaves the house without permission. And if you do leave, I want you to always have at least four guards. No exceptions."

Benito and my mother nod in agreement while Renato stays quiet.

Aria folds her arms across her chest and glares at me. "So, we have to change our entire lives because Nico screwed up?" she asks, fuming.

"Yes," my mother and father say at the same time.

"What about your connections with the feds?" I suggest. "Can't they do something about Constantine?"

"He was already released from prison on a technicality. We would need all new evidence to build a case against him again. Carbone has moved most of his operations overseas where the feds can't reach him." My father shakes his head. "No, there's nothing they can help us with at this point." He sighs and scrubs a hand down his face. "I wish you wouldn't have gotten involved in Carbone's business, son."

"Well, I don't regret what I did because I finally found Selina," I tell him with anger lacing my voice.

My mom puts a hand on my shoulder and pats gently, trying to calm me down. "I know you never stopped loving her," she says softly.

She's right about that. Not a day has gone by where I haven't thought about Lina. A void has been in my life for ten years. And having her back in my world seems like an impossible dream. One that I don't want to wake up from if she suddenly disappears again.

"How is she?" Mom asks.

"She's resting. She had some broken ribs, a punctured lung…" My voice trails off as my hands curl into fists at my sides. "There's a laundry list of things wrong with her," I say, my voice hoarse and weary. Fuck, I don't think I've slept more than a few hours since she arrived.

"Well, she's in a good place for recovery. With the doctors, nurses and therapists on staff here, I'm sure she'll be better in no time," she assures me.

Years ago, my parents turned their home into a compound complete with staff and top-of-the-line security. They have been involved with taking down a lot of human trafficking rings, and sometimes the feds couldn't place all the victims in homes or shelters. My parents took a lot of people in over the years, rehabilitated them, and made sure they had a much better chance at life by the time they left.

They are saints. Well, for the most part. I mean, my father is still a mafia boss and deals in illegal activities and routinely gets his hands dirty. And, you know, there's that whole pesky business of occasionally murdering people. But I think the good mostly outweighs the bad, to be honest.

They have saved a lot of people from terrible fates. Selina was just one of the many souls that they tried to save. And if it wouldn't have been for her mother, Selina would have stayed here and lived out her days in peace. We have no idea what happened after she left here, and that just adds to the never-ending pile of questions I have for Lina when she's feeling better and actually lucid.

"I'm glad Selina is safe now," my father says, even though he still looks and sounds grumpy as hell.

"Me too," I agree.

Just then, the heavy door swings open, banging against the wall. We all turn in unison as Selina stumbles into the room. I can hear the wheezing coming from her chest as she looks at me, her eyes narrowing as she accusingly spits out, "You!"

Before I can even react, she collapses onto the floor, gasping for breath. I rush to her side, but she's already unconscious. Her breathing is labored and the high-pitch wheeze coming from her mouth scares the hell out of me. "Call the doctor. I think her lung might have collapsed again," I tell them before picking her up in my arms.

With her limp body carefully cradled against my chest, I jog out of the room and up the steps. I race down the hallway with her in my arms. I spot the nurse, Sarah, coming out of a doorway with a caddy full of medical supplies in tow. She looks stunned to see us.

"What happened?" Sarah calls after me as I enter Selina's bedroom and carefully lay her down on the bed. "I didn't even see her walk out," she says with a shake of her head in disbelief. "She had pulled her IV out, and I was just getting some things to clean her up," she explains.

"It's not your fault," I assure her. Sarah is supposed to be taking care of Selina, not guarding her. "They're calling for the doctor. Try to keep her comfortable until she gets here," I inform Sarah, stepping back so that she can do her job.

My hands rake their way through my hair as I go to stand by the window. A million things are running through my mind as I pull at the ends in frustration.

The way Selina looked at me, it was as if she despised me. I mean, I did kill someone in front of her. I'm sure she fears me. But what if she never gets over that fear...or worse — what if she hates me?

She obviously has no idea who I am. Hell, she might not even remember me. Maybe I created some sort of fantasy in my head about our time together when, in all actuality, it meant nothing to her.

No.

I decide right then and there that none of that matters. I don't care if she doesn't remember me. I don't care if she even fucking hates me for a while. I will win her trust back no matter what it takes. I still love her. I never stopped loving her. And I'm not giving up on her.

CHAPTER 7

Selina

THE NEXT TIME I wake up I'm alone in the strange room again. My chest still hurts, but it's not an excruciating pain like last time. I try to sit up, but then I realize I can't move my arms. Panicked, I look down and see that my wrists are cuffed to the metal railings on the sides of the hospital bed.

I struggle to get free until I eventually wear myself out and give up. There's no way I'm getting out of these anytime soon, and I need to save my strength for when I really need it. For all I know, Constantine is waiting for me to get better so that he can beat me, torture me and kill me in retaliation for his son's death.

I will beg him for mercy, but I know it's only a matter of time before he kills me anyway. He's been distant lately, not like when I was younger and I was the most important thing in his world. In his own fucked-up and cruel way, I think he used to care for me.

The door to my room opens, and a nurse enters. I think it was the same one from... Wait, how many hours or days has it been? How long have I been here? My brain is so fuzzy. I grit my teeth as I try to concentrate. *I need my pills.*

The blue-eyed young woman looks at me and gives me a tentative smile. I probably got her in trouble last time for escaping. Hopefully Constantine didn't hurt her. I never handled it well when he would punish people for my faults and actions. He knew I hated that, and he would use it against me often. *Manipulative bastard.*

When the nurse comes over to replace my empty IV bag, I check her face and arms for visible bruises and feel relieved when I see none. "What is he giving me?" I ask. I have to know if he's drugging me. Is this some kind of new drug he's testing out on me first again?

"This is just saline," she informs me. "You're done with the antibiotics."

Saline? Antibiotics? What the hell is going on here? I think to myself.

"I need my pills," I tell her quickly. "He knows I need my benzos."

Her dark brows furrow before she goes to work replacing the bag of saline.

"Please," I beg her. I try to reach out, forgetting momentarily that I'm strapped to the bed. I huff with a resigned sigh. "I'll go crazy without my pills. I need them."

"I'm sorry," she says in a rush before finishing up and scurrying out of the room.

I scream in frustration, pulling at my restraints. I've never gone this long without being high. Not since I was a kid. Before I was with Constantine, who got me addicted to all kinds of shit to keep me calm and sedated and bending at his every will and demand. When he wasn't beating the defiance out of me, I was so high I couldn't protest against his evil ways even if I wanted to.

And now that his son is dead, his wrath will be magnified to unspeakable heights.

Tears fill my eyes and stream down my face as I desperately try to hold back a sob and fail miserably. The sound of my tortured cries fills the room.

Lying back on the bed, I close my eyes and force myself to think of the only happy point in my life. It's all hazy now — ten years and a lot of horrible memories and moments separating me from my happy place.

But I still remember him.

Nico.

The only boy I've ever cared for, and the only person in the entire world who truly cared about me.

The six months I stayed with his family was the happiest I've ever been. And then I was ripped away from that happiness by my mother...who turned around and sold me to Constantine. She needed the money for drugs. She was so addicted that she had no problems selling her own daughter not once, but *twice*. Nico's family never knew that my mother was the one who sold me in the first place before they rescued me and asked me to live with them.

I felt safe with them.

I felt loved.

God, I haven't felt loved in such a long time. I forget what that even feels like.

I should have told them that my mother was the one who sold me the previous time, but I was so scared to betray and disobey her. She beat that loyalty into me every damn day. And honestly, I never thought she would do that to me again.

I should have known better.

I was too young, too naïve, and too trusting. But over the years, I've come to the realization that you can't trust anyone but yourself. You gotta look out for number one, because no one else is there for you in the end. Not even your own goddamn mother.

The only relief I have is that she passed away not too long after I was sold to Constantine. I heard she died in her sleep, choking on her own vomit after overdosing. Her death wasn't punishment enough, but I'll take it. Just knowing the bitch was dead and couldn't hurt me anymore made me feel minutely better through the years.

Anger boils up inside of me suddenly, and like a volcano erupting, I scream at the top of my lungs. If Constantine is torturing me by making me wait, then I'm going to draw him out by being loud, the one thing I know he hates. He likes docile, quiet girls. Always seen, never heard...unless it's in the bedroom.

I scream again and again until it feels like my vocal cords are being ripped to shreds. Thrashing on the bed, I test my bonds, but they hold. And not being able to move just pisses me off even more.

Sweat trickles down my forehead as I squirm around in the bed, trying to slip out of the cuffs. But my efforts soon prove futile. The cuffs are very secure and tight against my skin. There's no wiggle room at all.

I need my pills. If I don't get my pills soon, then I'll be forced to face my horrendous past and all the things that happened to me. And that is not something I can do. I've done everything I could over the years to stay numb, to stay so far out of reality that I wasn't sure if I was awake or dreaming most days.

"I can't be here," I say out loud, a sob ripping from my chest. "I can't be here," I chant. "I can't be here."

If I don't get out of here soon, I don't know what will happen to me.

CHAPTER 8

Nicholas

I WINCE AT the sound of Selina's screams, and the pen in my hand suddenly drops. I was trying to read over some contracts, but I can't concentrate. She's been screaming for hours. Fortunately, at this time of evening, her and I are the only ones in this part of the compound. No one can hear her cries for help. Well, except for me.

Selina is not the girl I remember. Not at all. She's strung out, living in her own world. The doctor assured me her mind will clear over the next couple of days, and I'm trying to hold on to that promise and not drive myself insane with worry in the meantime.

They're slowly detoxing her, but fuck, it feels like it's taking forever. I don't want to talk to her until her mind is clear, but her screaming is driving me up the wall.

When she begins to cry out again, my legs are moving before my brain can even catch up. Frustrated, I leave my room, turn right down the hall and push open the door to Selina's room.

Selina startles when she sees me. "Where is he?" she yells, her voice hoarse. She pulls at her restraints, and I can see blood caked on the white cuffs around her wrists. The skin underneath is raw from her incessant struggling.

I move closer to her bed, gauging her reaction to me. I was hoping to see some sort of recognition in her eyes, but she simply stares at me like I'm a stranger. I mean, what did I truly expect? I haven't seen the girl in ten years, since we were kids. I'm sure I look a hell of a lot different now than when I was a teenager.

She sure as hell looks different. She looks so...grown up. Her face is still beautiful, just like I remember it, though. Heart-shaped with big doe eyes and full lips; the top one a little fuller than the bottom. I remember drawing her face many times after she left. I had etched it into my memory. I never wanted to forget how pretty she was, and I wanted to remember that she was *real*.

"Where is who?" I eventually ask even though I already know who she's talking about.

"Constantine," she asks in a hushed whisper as if she's afraid to speak his name any louder. "Is he coming for me?"

I can hear the fear in her voice, and it makes me want to kill that bastard with my goddamn bare hands. "He doesn't know where you are," I assure her, trying to keep my voice level. "You're safe here."

An almost crazed laugh escapes her lips, surprising me. "You have no idea what he's capable of. He will find me." Selina turns her pretty face towards the window and whispers, "He *always* finds me." She then pulls at her restraints, seemingly forgetting that she was bound, and begins to mumble incoherently to herself.

My brows furrow as I stare at her. The doctor told me the other day that the withdrawal symptoms will make her paranoid and delusional. She's almost clean. By this time tomorrow, she might actually be in her right mind. God, I fucking hope so. I don't know how much more of this I can fucking take.

"Everything is going to be okay," I say in an attempt to placate her.

She slowly turns her head, looking at me...*no*, looking straight *through* me. "You can't possibly know that," she says somberly.

"I promise."

"You...*promise*?" she scoffs, her voice cracking on the last word. "You don't know him like I do." Her face turns back to the window, and I can see she's lost in thought, perhaps recalling memories. "No one knows him like I do," she murmurs in a singsong voice.

My hands curl into fists at my sides. I hate the fact that Constantine had her under his control. I can't help but wonder how long she was with him. Was it the entire ten years or for only a brief period of time before I stumbled upon her and his son at the party? Did he steal her innocence away from her just like he's done with hundreds of other girls and women?

Feeling my anger trying to boil over, I quickly turn and leave the room without even telling her goodbye. Hell, she probably won't even remember me being there. The drug concoction Carbone had her on is taking a long time to work out of her system. Dr. Catalano is optimistic that there won't be any permanent brain damage, but there's no telling until she's completely clean.

I have a million different questions I want to ask Selina, but I will have to be patient and wait until she's clear-minded and in a state where she's able to finally answer me truthfully and honestly.

Instead of returning to my bedroom, I venture down the hall to a room I'd converted into an art studio years ago. When I open the door, the smell of fresh oils and acrylics welcomes me. After Selina disappeared without a trace, I spent months taking my anger and frustration out on everyone and everything around me. I turned into a brawler at school, fighting anyone who crossed my path or looked at me the wrong way. After getting kicked out of three private schools, my parents grew tired of my shit and sent me to a therapist.

Mr. Mackey had a way with words and zero tolerance for bullshit. He taught me how to channel some of my feelings into something more creative. And the very first time I put pen to paper, I was hooked. I could sit and draw for hours, forgetting the world around me, forgetting about all the problems I was so focused on before.

Pencils and ink soon turned to charcoal and then to oils and acrylics. It didn't matter what medium I used, I realized I loved to draw and paint. It was so effortless and natural that I imagine maybe I was a talented artist in a previous life.

As I stare around the room at the dozens of paintings and drawings, I can't help but remember how I felt during each and every one that I created. There are probably a hundred renderings of Selina in here. I drew her as I knew her and as I imagined she would become. I wanted to age us together even though I had no idea what she would actually look like. Even though she looks ethereal on canvas, none of those drawings or paintings even came close to the real-life woman. She's beautiful. No, more than beautiful. She's perfection. Prettier than I ever could have imagined.

A painting is simply just that — a painting. But having her here in the flesh, seeing her with my own two eyes is nothing short of magnificent.

When I look around the room, my obsession with her is evident. I've had my fair share of women in the past, but they were all one-night stands. No one could even hold a candle to my Lina, and I couldn't bear the thought of anyone else trying to fill that empty void inside of my chest where I knew only she could fit...and where only she belonged.

I stare at one of my recent paintings. It simply doesn't do her beauty justice, and I take it off the easel before replacing it with a blank canvas.

And as Selina's screams echo down the hallway, I paint her. I paint every detail from my memories over the past few days from the time I first saw her at the party until now. Her cries fuel my desire to get every little detail right, even down to the tiny freckles that are scattered across her nose.

Painting her is cathartic. And by the time I'm finished, it's nearly dawn, and Selina's screams have finally ceased.

CHAPTER 9

Selina

AFTER DAYS OF being...well, wherever the hell I am, I wake up feeling clear-minded for the first time in as long as I can remember. I glance down at my wrists, which were previously bound. They're now wrapped in gauze and bandages, and I'm no longer cuffed to the bed.

My brows furrow. Why is Constantine taking so much effort in nursing me back to health? Is he doing all of this so that I have my strength back before he beats me down into nothing once again?

I shudder at the thought. You never know with my captor. It's always a mind-fuck no matter which way you spin it. He's pretended to be nice in the past, only to break me almost beyond repair right after. Trusting him always led to some kind of punishment, but I had to learn that the hard way.

I glance down at my bandaged wrists and frown. I've had open wounds before, and I was always forced to take care of them myself with what little materials I had. He's never shown me an ounce of kindness, and I have no idea why he's doing this now. But, with knowing Constantine the way I do, there is always an ulterior motive. He's like a snake coiled up patiently in tall grass, waiting for the perfect opportunity to strike its next victim.

Lying back in my bed, I breathe in as deeply as I can and release that same breath, my chest still hurting. I have to prepare myself mentally for whatever is about to come my way. Without my pills, I'll have to face it head-on, and I don't know if I'm ready for that.

A soft knock has my eyes snapping open. I sit up quickly, maybe too quickly, because my head spins slightly before I'm able to focus on the dark figure coming through the doorway.

Dark hair. Steel gray eyes. Broad shoulders under a black, expensive, tailored suit with a black shirt and matching tie.

It's the man who kidnapped me. The man who killed Constantine's son right in front of my eyes. Even though I don't remember very many details from that night, I remember Gino's violent death vividly.

I draw my knees up to my chest and wrap my arms around them, protecting myself the only way I know how.

The man walks in slowly, like he's afraid to spook me. "It's good to see you awake...and lucid," he comments before stopping several feet from my bed.

I stay quiet. I've learned over the years that my mouth can get me in trouble. It's better to say nothing at all and wait to be prompted to speak.

"How are you feeling?" he asks, his voice deep and calm.

Again, I just simply stare at him. His dark hair and gray eyes look so familiar... Not just from that night, but like a distant memory that my brain just can't seem to touch upon. Maybe I've seen him in my past. I've seen so many men, unfortunately.

He's handsome, I'll give him that. But sometimes the most beautiful things in this world are the most toxic and poisonous. I've learned that firsthand the hard way.

Even though most women would probably throw themselves in front of a bus for just a chance to be with this guy, I can't say the same. I'm more frightened than attracted to the opposite sex. Men can't be trusted. They only want one thing. And if you don't want to give it to them, they'll just take it.

The man sighs and rakes a hand through his short, thick hair at my lack of conversation. I watch him closely, waiting for a sign that he's getting upset or mad at me. Because I know what will come after that point.

Abuse.

Pain.

"You can speak freely here," he assures me. "Nothing will happen to you."

I want to laugh in his face. That's what they all say. *Nothing will happen to you.* Liars. All of them.

"I'm sure you have a lot of questions," he offers. "Maybe we should start there. Do you have any questions for me?"

"You work for Constantine Carbone?" I mutter. It's not really a question, more of an accusation, but I don't care. I need to know. I need to know who and what I'm dealing with here.

"No," he scoffs as if it's the most absurd thing he's ever heard in his entire life. "I'm trying to take that bastard down," he says, seriousness clouding his features.

His words shock me to the point where I'm speechless. My hands clench around my knees, drawing them even closer to me. *Is that why you killed his son?* I desperately want to ask that question, but keep my mouth shut.

"I rescued you that night at the party, Selina," the stranger tells me, his gray eyes assessing me. He knows my name. I wonder what else he knows. "You're safe now."

A sob tries to bubble its way up my throat, but I swallow it down quickly as I slowly lie down on the bed. "I've been *safe* before," I mutter miserably. Tears fill my eyes as I stare up at the ceiling, the decorative pattern in the plaster blurring together the longer I stare. I squeeze my eyes shut, stray tears streaming down my temples. Memories of that horrific night in Italy bombard my mind. I've had drugs to help me cope before. But now that I'm sober, I have nothing stopping me from dwelling on my past, on my trauma.

No. I can't let myself even think about the man and his family that tried to help me. I don't want to go into that rabbit hole of horrors of what happened to them because of me.

Panic grips my throat, and it feels like a demon clawing its way up through my esophagus. Short bursts of air escape me in panicked breaths as my lungs threaten to lock up altogether.

It was my fault.

They're dead because of me.

"Selina!"

I hear my name being called, and it takes a few moments for me to come back to the present. The stranger is standing next to my bed, reaching out towards me. I quickly put my hand up to stop him, and to my surprise, he does.

"You're in a secure compound," he begins to explain. "Carbone would need an army to get to you."

His words should comfort me, but they don't. I've tried to escape Constantine before, and he has always found me. He told me once that the only way he would let me go was if one of us were dead. And I truly believe that. He has some kind of sick fascination and obsession with me. He always has, ever since I was first sold to him when I was a young girl. I was his *little pet*. My body begins to tremble at just the thought of his nickname for me.

"He'll come for me," I say resolutely with a heavy sigh. "It's only a matter of time."

"He'll have to kill me first," the man says with such resignation that I almost believe him.

I don't know who the hell this guy thinks he is, but if he thinks he's any match against Constantine, he's got another thing coming. That man is the devil himself, all-powerful. Nothing can stand in the way of him getting what he wants. And he wants me and revenge for his son's murder, I'm sure. It's only a matter of time before the guy standing before me is as good as dead.

"Considering you killed his son, I'm sure he will kill you first," I state matter-of-factly.

A smile appears on the handsome man's face. "I'd like to see him try."

Cocky. Confident. He won't be feeling so confident when Constantine is ripping him to shreds with his own bare hands for killing his son and for taking what's his.

"I'm tired," I lie, rolling over to my side and closing my eyes, effectively blocking out the stranger. The truth is, I just want to be left alone to process everything.

The man doesn't say anything. I hear his footsteps retreat as he leaves the room, closing the door behind him. I expect to hear a lock clicking in place, but there are no other sounds except his footfalls fading as he walks away, leaving me alone just like I wanted.

I breathe in deeply and let out a long sigh. Am I truly free of Constantine, or is this just simply another one of his tricks to test my allegiance to him?

Only time will tell I suppose. Until then, I'll keep my guard up and not allow my walls to come down for anything or anyone.

CHAPTER 10

Nicholas

AFTER SELINA HAD vanished without a trace, I grew cold and distant with everyone around me. Her disappearance changed me, molded me into the man I am today. The more time that passed, the harder my exterior became until I was just a shell of the former smiling, charming boy I once was. Her leaving left a black hole in my chest where my heart once was. I threw myself into work alongside my father, and that is when I learned about how truly cruel the world can be and oftentimes is.

I thought having Selina back would change...everything. I thought we would go back to how we were; that the past decade would somehow just erase itself. But it seems like we're at some sort of crossroads, and I'm having trouble figuring out which direction I should go to move forward.

I still haven't told her who I am. A part of me is still holding out hope that she will somehow just know it's me like I did when I first saw her. Granted, I don't have a distinguishable feature like she does with her heterochromia. Without her strange eye colors, would I have even known it was Lina in that hallway?

Probably not. We haven't seen each other since we were teenagers, and a lot has changed since then.

I do need to tell her the truth, though. I just have no idea how she's going to react to that news. Will she be sad, happy? Or will she be mad at me for not finding her sooner?

I want to tell her that we never stopped looking for her; that there hasn't been a single day where she hasn't crossed my mind. She has no idea of the lengths I have gone to to try and locate her. I've literally put my life on the line more times than I can fucking count, infiltrating numerous human trafficking rings to try to get some information on anything that would lead me to her whereabouts. And coming up empty so many damn times nearly broke me.

I guess the unknown is what's truly preventing me from confessing everything to her. That coupled with the fact that she keeps asking about Constantine, which makes me think he had her under his control for a large part of her life, maybe even the whole time that she was missing. I desperately want to know the answers, but I know I have to be patient when it comes to Selina. She's strong, but she's in a delicate state right now. I'm sure she's been through hell more times than anyone ever should, and I don't want to push her too hard, too fast, especially if she's not ready. I know the information I seek will come out eventually. And I can be a very patient man when I want to be.

Making my way into the large dining room on the other side of the compound, I find my parents, my sister and Benito already digging into a delicious-looking dinner. It's my father's favorite — spaghetti with homemade bread and salad.

"You're late," Aria chides me with a grin.

"I was busy," I mutter before taking a seat.

My mother smiles at me before passing me a large bowl. "How is Selina?"

"Better," I admit while scooping some of the salad onto my plate. I'm glad I can finally say that and not be totally lying. Seeing her sober and not under the influence of any kind of substance is refreshing, to say the least.

"Does she know who you are yet?" Aria chimes in.

"Not yet. But I'll tell her," I say with a frown.

"When?" Aria asks.

I roll my eyes at her. Aria has always been one to meddle in my affairs. She's the nosy, little, bratty sister I never wanted, but I honestly can't imagine life without her even though she's a pain in my ass most days. "Soon," I say vaguely.

She hums in disapproval and then turns her attention back to her meal.

I'm about to put the first bite of food in my mouth when my father tells me, "Constantine is in town. The funeral for his son is tomorrow." I open my mouth to speak, but he holds up a hand, stopping me. "Just so we're clear, Nico, we're not going anywhere near the funeral or the cemetery. Constantine will have eyes and ears everywhere, and we can't afford to draw any more unwanted attention to our family. I will not have anyone put in that vulnerable position and risk capture...or worse."

Even though we're missing out on an opportunity to track Constantine and gather intel, maybe even enough information to bring him and his empire down once and for all, I agree with my father. I already fucked things up for everyone, and now we all have to be on our toes if...no, *when* Constantine figures out it was me who killed his son.

"Selina was with Constantine for a period of time," I announce to the table. I hear Benito curse under his breath, but I continue. "He hurt her. I feel it in my gut. I don't know how long she was with him, but I know the bastard scared her to the point where she's afraid he's coming for her even now."

"It could explain why we never found her," my father suggests.

"We have barely been able to track Constantine over the years since he was released from jail."

I nod in agreement. If Selina was with him all this time, all the previous missing pieces of the puzzle would slowly fit together, creating a crystal-clear image. Constantine somehow got his hands on Selina and was keeping her on his yacht out in the middle of the ocean where the rules don't apply to people like him. He kept his distance from New York City and kept a low profile, still defiling women and probably Selina along the way without any consequences for his fucked-up actions.

The thing I can't figure out is how Selina got mixed up with the likes of him. How did their paths cross? I hope to fuck it wasn't because of our connection with her, but I don't feel like that's it. There's something else. A big part to this story is missing.

I push the salad around on my plate as I sit and stew in my thoughts. I thought bringing Selina back home would make everything better, but I know there's a long road ahead of us. She's slowly recovering, so all I can do is give her time at this point.

If she was with Constantine, I can only imagine the horrors she lived through and witnessed over the past decade. I shudder at the thought of them and her going through that living, breathing nightmare. The only solace I can muster is the fact that she's here with me now. She's finally home. It won't be an easy road ahead of us, but I'm going to be there with her every single step of the way. I'll never give up on Selina, because I know she would have done the same exact thing for me had the roles been reversed.

I've been a closed off, moody son-of-a-bitch since she disappeared, but I'll try to be a better person. For her. *Only* for her.

My humanity shut off a long time ago. When she left, my heart ceased beating, leaving a dark, empty hole in my chest. My entire world came to a halt. And now that she's back, I can feel that dark muscle beginning to beat again. She's slowly bringing me back to life, and she doesn't even realize it.

The only thing that will bring me more peace would be the feel of Constantine's neck in my hands as I squeeze the very life from him and watch the light in his eyes slowly fade away.

He hurt my girl. I can feel it deep in my soul. And his blood on my hands would make me rest a little easier. I'm sure it would help Selina immensely as well. Having her real-life boogeyman dead and unable to ever hurt her again would be a great gift to her; one I plan on giving.

"Everything all right, Nico?" my mother asks, bringing me out of my dark thoughts.

I look up at her and force a smile. "Not yet. But it will be," I assure her.

CHAPTER 11

Selina

I'VE BEEN IN this place for weeks, slowly recuperating from my injuries. Going through withdrawal from the concoction of benzos that I was on for years was unpleasant and mind-numbing. At least the breathing treatments are finally done — Dr. Catalano gave me the all-clear this morning. Small miracles, I suppose, since I was getting so tired of them.

I haven't seen a single sign of Constantine since I arrived here, which is alarming, to say the least. I don't know if he's just biding his time or if the man who murdered his son was telling the truth after all. Maybe I'm locked away someplace where Constantine actually can't find me. *Yet.*

He always finds me eventually, though, and I don't think this time will be any different. I think the only way I could truly escape him is if I left earth. I don't think there is a place on this planet that he wouldn't go to find me. He would never leave his *little pet* behind.

Just the memory of him saying those two little words to me sends a violent shiver of fear running down my spine.

"Are you cold?" Dr. Catalano asks, bringing me back to the present. She's been in my room for several minutes, silently evaluating me and making notes in a chart.

"No, I'm fine," I answer her in a hushed whisper.

She's an older woman with a no-nonsense attitude. But that's totally fine with me, because I like to hear the facts straight instead of someone trying to blow smoke up my ass. And this woman definitely doesn't beat around the bush. She tells it exactly how it is. And even though my countless requests to her for benzos fell on deaf ears, I'm almost glad now that she didn't give in to me. I don't remember the last time I was sober. It's almost like I'm seeing the world around me with a fresh pair of eyes. Even the food smells and tastes better. It's like I've been reborn in a way.

Dr. Catalano stands and says, "I'll let Mr. Vitale know that you're ready for physical therapy and —."

"Wait," I gasp, cutting her off, as my eyes snap up to meet hers. "D-did you say...Vi-Vitale?" I ask, stammering. My entire body begins to shake as the name alone brings back a flood of memories.

"Yes. Nicholas Vitale. He's the one who brought you here," she explains with a cocked brow. "Is something wrong, Selina?"

"No. I..." My voice trails off. There's a bitter shock coursing through my system at the fact that *Nico* killed Gino right in front of my eyes without an ounce of remorse. The young Nico I knew back then was sweet and kind. He would never *murder* anyone. "No, this can't be," I whisper. Suddenly, I throw the blanket off of me and swing my feet over the side of the bed. On unsteady legs, I slowly walk over to one of the windows.

I cover my mouth to silence my gasp when I look out over the vaguely familiar estate. It's daytime and sunny outside, so I can see a lot more details than the last time I was at this very window. Some things have changed around the property, but I remember the little things that haven't — like the color of the front gate, the layout of the garden.

"Sometimes I wondered if I'd only dreamt about this place," I whisper more to myself than to the doctor. "I wondered if *he* was even real."

Over the years, I've tried to forget my time here at the Vitale's home. At first, I held on so tightly to the six months of memories that I made here, reliving every happy moment over and over again in my mind. But eventually, it became too difficult to remember that kind of love and kindness when I was suffering every hour of every day. Holding on to the memories became more like a burden. My world was too cruel to believe any of it was real, and so I became more closed off and bitter as I grew older and no one rescued me.

Not that I expected them to actually come for me. Hell, I don't even know if they searched for me at all. I always assumed...or at least hoped that they did, however. That's just the kind of family Nico had.

But as time went on, I realized I needed to stop reliving the fairytale that had been those six months and move on with my new, cold and hard reality with Constantine.

The pills helped. They kept me from facing the truth. And without them now, I don't know what will happen to me. I can't face my past alone. It might just finally break me.

"I understand you were here when you were young?" the doctor inquires.

"Yes, when I was thirteen," I answer with a nod. "It was only for six months...but it was the best six months of my entire life," I confess with tears forming in my eyes. A sob threatens to escape, but I quickly hold a hand over my mouth as my eyes dart to the door. All I can think is that I don't want him to see me like this. *He can't see me like this.* But the truth of the matter is that Nico's already seen me at my worst at the party and in the days following. He probably already knows all the horrors that have happened to me. He knows that I'm dirty and used up. That I'm *broken*.

Oh my god, I need to get out of here.

My legs threaten to give out, and the doctor is quick to grab my arm and gently guide me back to bed. "Please, Selina, you need to rest. You've been through quite an ordeal." She grabs the manilla folder and scribbles some notes. "I have a physical therapy session set up for you tomorrow morning." She looks up at me after she's done writing. "The therapist's name is Dwayne, and he's wonderful, extremely kind and patient," she adds. "I'm also going to recommend that you speak with a psychiatrist. The Vitales have a fantastic doctor on call — Dr. Moira Graham."

I want to protest and tell the doctor I don't need any of those things because I won't be here long, but I keep my mouth shut. If I'm going to run away from here, I need to keep my plans to myself so that no one can lock me up or ruin them.

I can't stay with the Vitales. The longer I stay, the more danger I'm putting them in. I've seen what Constantine does to people who help me. And I refuse to let him harm anyone else because of me and his sick obsession.

The first chance I get, I'll escape from this place and leave this family behind for good. Anyone that helps me is as good as dead, and I won't let Constantine hurt them too.

CHAPTER 12

Nicholas

THE DOCTOR INFORMED me that she accidentally let the cat out of the bag earlier. Selina knows who I am now; knows where she is. I was worried for her to find out the truth and the consequences thereafter; but to be honest, I feel more relieved now than anything. Yes, I wanted to tell Selina myself, but I kept delaying the inevitable. Selina saw me as some sort of monster that killed a man in front of her, and I didn't want to confess that the boy she once cared for grew up to be that same monster.

But now that she knows, it makes all of this easier somehow. It feels like a great weight has been lifted from my shoulders. No more pretending. No more hiding.

Selina is in her room when I enter through the open door. The hospital bed she was in when she first arrived here was replaced with a big four-poster bed early this afternoon. And that's where she's currently sitting, her legs tucked under her as she quietly reads a book. She's still wearing a gown, however, but that's why I stopped by — to remedy that.

Upon catching a glimpse of me, she gently sets the book down and gives me a tentative smile. I could practically cut the tension in the room with a knife, and I hate that. I hate that we've become like this. I wish I could rewind ten years and get a do-over. But the truth is what happened, happened. There's no going back, and there's no changing it. The only thing we can do now is try to push forward and look towards the future, whatever that may be for her, for me, for *us*. Fuck, I hope there's an us.

"The doctor gave you the all-clear," I tell her, setting down a bag of clothes on the edge of the bed. The clothes are plain, most of them gently used donations that we give to all the women who temporarily stay here. "It's not much, but I'm sure you can go shopping soon," I explain.

She opens the bag and sorts through some of the clothes before a small grin graces her pretty face. "Thank you."

"And I brought you dessert," I explain before setting the bowl of mint chocolate chip ice cream down on the nightstand beside her.

Selina stares at it for a while before she whispers in astonishment, "You remembered."

When her unique eyes meet mine in a stare, I quickly clear my throat. "I might have remembered you eating mint chocolate chip ice cream by the gallon back then," I muse, my lips tilting up in a smile.

"I haven't had it since I lived here," she says, staring down at the bowl like it's so much more than just ice cream.

The sadness in her voice imbeds itself deep in my bones. If she couldn't even indulge in her favorite ice cream over the years, I wonder what else she missed out on. But before I even let myself go there and start thinking about that shit, I throw those thoughts right out the window. I can't dwell on that now, or I'll ruin this moment by getting angry. I'm barely holding it together as it is. I don't need to have a major outburst in front of Selina and scare her more than I have already.

"Well, there's a huge container of it in the freezer. So anytime you want it, it's yours," I offer.

She gently grips the bowl in her delicate hands and scoops a little bit of ice cream into her mouth. She closes her eyes as she sucks on the spoon, savoring the taste before letting out a long moan of satisfaction.

Fuck. My cock twitches inside of my pants from the sound coming from her throat. *Down boy*, I internally tell my dick as I cross the room and sit down in a chair by the window.

As soon as I'm seated, I hear Selina say, "I can't believe I didn't recognize you before. It's just...you look so *different*. So much older. Grown up."

"I don't know if I would have recognized you at that party either except for —."

"My eyes," she guesses.

"Yep."

"So you weren't a hundred-percent sure who I was when you saved me from Gino?"

I shake my head. "I knew he was hurting a woman. That's all that mattered in the moment, and that bastard deserved what he got," I explain, my voice dangerously low.

She flinches at my harsh words, perhaps recalling that night and what I did in order to protect her. I'm not the innocent, little boy she knew back then. I've changed a lot over the years. I just hope we can find a kinship again like before. And I hope she can overcome her obvious fear of me.

I work my jaw from side to side before continuing with, "I was hoping it was you after I bumped into you in the hallway, but I wasn't totally sure until I saw the birthmark on your neck after all was said and done."

She absently reaches up to touch her fingertips to the heart-shaped mark. "You remembered that too, huh?" she whispers.

"I remember everything about you, Lina."

My use of her nickname has her eyes growing wide with surprise.

I'm sure she hasn't been called that since she lived here, and it feels so damn good to be able to call her that once again.

"I tried so hard to forget you," she confesses in a rush. "Remembering you was like the sweetest torture. You were the only good thing in my life at one point, and it was hard to relive those moments in my mind, because I knew I would probably never see you again. But sometimes you were just the saving grace I needed, the only thing that got me through some of the most horrible times in my life."

I want to ask her where she's been, but I know she needs to do it on her own. She doesn't need me pressuring her to tell her story. And so I sit quietly in the chair, watching her slowly eat the ice cream and just enjoying being in the same room as her with everything out on the table and her actually sober and coherent for the first time since she arrived.

"Nico," she says softly, and I swear my heart stops beating. I haven't heard her say my name in ten fucking years, and it's like a distant memory unlocks deep inside of my mind. "How did you find me?" she questions.

"Pure luck," I confess. "When your mom took you and disappeared, we spent years trying to figure out where you went. It was like you just up and vanished. Like a ghost." My hands ball into fists on top of my knees when I think about what her mother did. To Selina. To my family. To me. To *us*.

"I should have told you the truth the day she came for me," she says before setting down the now empty bowl. Just knowing she has a belly full of her favorite ice cream brings me peace in some way. "My mother had already sold me once for drugs when your family rescued me. And then...she did it again."

"Shit," I hiss. I mean, it was one theory I had suspected all along, but to hear the cold, hard truth coming straight from Selina's mouth...

"She sold me to Constantine Carbone a few months after she took me from here," she says with anguish dripping from her tone.

My world suddenly stops spinning, everything coming to an abrupt halt. I have to force my mouth to form my next words, because I'm floored with this new information. "You were with him for the last ten years?"

She nods.

Fuck. I was hoping he had just recently gotten his claws into her, for her sake. But the fact that she was with him the entire time she was missing, while she was underage, only thirteen years old, so young and innocent...it makes my fucking blood boil. I can feel the anger seeping out from every pore in my body, my muscles vibrating with unreleased fury. "That son of a bitch," I murmur under my breath. Then, I look at her and demand, "Tell me everything." I can't wait a second longer. I need to know the truth. I need to know exactly what happened, so that I can scorch the earth and all that remains until I find that bastard and put him six feet under where he fucking belongs.

Selina slowly unfolds her legs and stands, turning her back on me as she begins to speak. It's as if she doesn't want to see my reaction to her story, and that's fine with me. I don't think I can hide my true feelings from her behind a poker face right now anyway. I'm only human.

"We stayed in the motel for only a few hours that night. My mother disappeared from the room, came back high as a kite and declared we were leaving just out of the blue. I tried to call you, but she pulled the phone cord out of the wall and hit me." Her hand slides up to her cheek as if she's remembering the pain. "Said she would kill me if I tried to contact you." She folds her arms protectively around herself. "She took the number you gave me and flushed it down the toilet to make sure I wouldn't have a way to reach you."

I always wondered why Selina never called, but I never imagined her mother could be so cruel and evil. Maybe I should have known or sensed it somehow, but I was just a dumb kid back then. I was still viewing the world through rose-colored glasses, not believing in true evil until later on in life when I saw it personally after I started working for my father.

"We lived out of the car for weeks," she continues. "My mom used all the money that your parents gave us for a little food and a lot of drugs. We couldn't even afford to go to a hotel," she says, shaking her head with disgust. "And then one day, while we were at a restaurant she was planning on dining and dashing at, she was watching the news on one of the TVs. Something about Constantine Carbone being acquitted of his charges and getting released from jail." She's pacing the floor now, and I can hear the tremor in her voice by just the mere mention of his name. "The look on my mom's face. I'll never forget it. She looked... relieved. Like she had just witnessed some kind of miracle."

I close my eyes and pinch the bridge of my nose between my thumb and forefinger. Fuck, her mother saw Constantine's release as a solution to her problems, some sort of breakthrough moment. She was willing to sell her own daughter just to get her next high. It's fucking incredible the lengths some people will ultimately go to to get what they want, especially when they're addicted to something.

"A few days later, she drove us back to New York City. I was so excited. I thought she had actually come to her senses and was going to let me stay with you and your family." Her shoulders sink as she sighs deeply.

I sit back in the chair and frown. I can just imagine how excited Selina would have been, thinking she was going to see me again. Little did she know her mother's plans for her.

Selina stops pacing and stands before me, staring at the floor, her eyes moving back and forth as if recalling a memory. "But she drove down to the docks. I was forced out of the car by two men. They roughed me up pretty bad, because I fought for my life. I didn't want to go with them. I screamed for her to help me, but I saw the look in her eyes. I had seen it before. It was the same look she gave me the first time she sold me."

I watch as she begins to pace again, wrapping her arms around her stomach as if the next words that are going to come out of her mouth are going to physically hurt her. My fingers dig into the fabric on the arms of the chair, bracing for the inevitable impact.

"The first time I met Constantine I knew he was the devil himself in an Armani suit. He said the sweetest things to me, called me his *little pet*." She sucks in a sharp intake of air as if it hurts to breathe. "He took my virginity by force that night. It was the worst day of my life. I just remember the pain…and the blood. So much blood," she whispers.

My entire body vibrates with an overwhelming sense of anger and disgust. I've never felt like this before. I want to yell. I want to scream. I want to go find Constantine and rip his fucking head off with my bare hands.

But I force myself to remain calm, for Selina's sake. I make myself stay in my seat and not act out even if it's going against every fiber of my fucking being right now. She's not even done with her story. I can tell she has more to talk about, and I have to let her continue. I owe her that much at least. The emotional dam has burst, and she's pouring her soul out to me. The best thing I can do is sit and listen to her as she gets it all out.

"We lived on his yacht in the middle of the ocean nine months out of the year. Sometimes we would dock in Italy or Spain and spend a few weeks on land. But he rarely returned to the United States. I know he was afraid of being caught again, of going to jail. That's his biggest fear." She goes to the bed and sits down, and I can tell that she's physically and mentally drained from telling her story. "I was with Gino that night. Constantine rarely let me leave the yacht, but Gino begged his father to let him have me for the night." She visibly tenses. "He was just like his father." A shiver runs through her. "I'm glad he's dead."

The room is silent for a few minutes, and I know that it's my turn to speak. My turn to tell her everything I've been dying to say for the past ten years. "We never stopped looking for you, Lina. The fucked-up thing is the fact that we couldn't find Constantine, and we were searching for him as well. If we would have found him, we would have found you. But he took every painstaking effort to not get caught again. And in doing that, he actually kept you hidden from us."

Her gaze meets mine. "I always wondered if you were searching for me. Sometimes, at night, I would look up at the moon, wondering if you were staring up at it as well. I always wished that you were safe...and happy. Even if I wasn't either of those things," she confesses in a soft tone.

Leaning up in the chair, I rest my elbows on my knees as I look at her and say, "We did everything we could to try to get you back. I want you to know that."

She nods slowly, taking in and processing all the information I'm giving her. I just hope she believes it.

Releasing a sigh, she looks up at the ceiling and says, "I just wish I could have gotten away from him sooner. I wish I would have been stronger."

I scoff at her words. "You're the strongest person I've ever met."

She turns her gaze back to me. "I don't know if I believe that," she says, her voice wavering with soul-breaking disbelief.

"Maybe not yet, but you will," I vow. She survived unspeakable hell and came through the other side. She's so much stronger than she gives herself credit for, and I will remind her of it every damn day if I have to. Her captor didn't break her. And he sure as hell didn't take away the fun, loveable girl I fell for ten years ago. I know she's still in there somewhere, and I'll be damned if I'm going to just let her go. Together, we will get her back.

"I'm going to let you get some sleep," I tell her as I stand up from the chair. It's probably going to have permanent imprints from my fingertips gripping it so damn hard.

Keeping my voice calm and level, I say, "Goodnight, Lina." My entire body is vibrating with pent-up frustration. Fuck, I'm going to have to get a late-night session in at the gym to get my frustrations out. I need to get rid of this rage before it ultimately consumes me.

"Goodnight, Nico," she whispers.

I leave her room, feeling like some progress was made instead of taking another ten steps back, like before. And as I'm walking to the gym, a thought suddenly occurs to me. All this time we've been trying to get close to Constantine, but Selina may just be the missing piece we've needed all along. She knows where he regularly docks his yacht and maybe even some secret locations we know nothing about.

Selina could be the key to finally taking that bastard down for good.

CHAPTER 13

Selina

I'VE NEVER HAD physical therapy before, so I'm a little apprehensive when I make my way into the gym on the lower level of the compound. But the moment I walk through the door and see a tall, handsome, young man waving me over with the biggest grin on his face that I've ever seen in my life, all the trepidation in my veins slowly melts away.

He has short brown hair and matching soft brown eyes. "You must be Selina. I'm Dwayne." He holds his hand out, and I take it. He shakes it, never losing his smile. "It's so nice to finally meet you. I've heard a lot about you from the Vitale family."

I don't even know what to say, but Dwayne doesn't even let a second of awkward silence get in between us. "Let's start with some light stretching," he offers.

We start out simple enough. I didn't realize how out of shape I was until we do some light exercises and I'm already out of breath.

Living on a yacht nine months out of a year makes it hard to get in normal exercise. And sometimes, if I wasn't a *good girl*, Constantine would lock me in a small utility closet for days or weeks at a time. Being confined and cramped for long periods of time obviously did a number on my muscles. I just didn't realize the damage that was done until today. Now I understand why the doctor recommended physical therapy in the first place.

From the start, I can tell Dwayne is very passionate about his job, and I love that about him. Our hour-long therapy session flies by because Dwayne is quite the talker. It turns out he's the nicest, kindest, purest soul on this earth, and I can see why the Vitales hired him. He spends the hour talking about everything under the sun, including gushing about his boyfriend of four years.

"So, do you think you guys will get married?" I ask him as I go through our final stretches.

An idle smile plays over his lips as he nods. "Oh, someday," he says before adding, "Hopefully sooner rather than later."

Standing, Dwayne asks me, "So, how do you feel?"

"Better," I confess. Even though I'm used to being confined to a room or small spaces, I would much rather be doing something like this with my time. "My muscles feel sore but good," I tell him.

He nods in understanding. "We'll keep building up your stamina until we can get some real workouts in," he tells me.

"That sounds great."

Glancing at his watch, he says, "It's almost time for your appointment with Dr. Graham. She's just down the hall and on the left in the library. I'm sure she'll have the door open for you, waiting."

My face falls. This is what I have been dreading as soon as Dr. Catalano had mentioned me speaking with a psychiatrist. I don't want anyone delving into my mind and trying to pluck out everything that's wrong with me. *God, what isn't wrong with me?*

"Don't worry, Selina. She won't bite. I promise," Dwayne assures me with a wink. "She really is the best. She's not one of those weird quacks."

Well, if Dwayne likes her, then I guess I can give her a chance. I mean, what other choice do I have really? If I want to stay here, even if it's not for much longer, then I need to do whatever the Vitales want me to do. And if they want me to see a psychiatrist, then that's what I'll do.

Besides, the psychiatrist might prescribe me some medication so that my brain can go offline again and I won't have to face the truth of my past or my demons that still haunt me. Deep down that's what I truly want — I want to be numb. I don't want to feel anything ever again.

∽

Dr. Moira Graham readies her pen on a notepad resting on her lap. She's short and plump with red hair, brown eyes and glasses that match her hair color.

She has a nice smile and soothing voice, which should make it easy for me to talk to her, but I've been shut up like a clam since the moment I walked in the door. She seems patient enough, though, not forcing me to bare my soul or talk about anything in particular, really.

"I notice you keep looking at the door, like you're afraid someone is going to step through it at any moment."

My eyes, which were locked on the door, suddenly avert to her face. *Shit. I didn't even know I was doing that.*

"Who are you picturing coming through that door, Selina?" she asks gently.

I swallow hard. Speaking his name out loud usually has dire consequences, so I keep my mouth shut and nervously wring my hands in my lap.

She watches my movements with hawk-eyed scrutiny. Then, she questions, "Do you not feel safe here?"

"No," I blurt out before I can stop myself.

"And why not, Selina?" she asks.

Shit. Why did I tell her no? No always leads to more questions.

Questions I don't want to answer, because then my deepest darkest secret will be out on the table, and I can't deal with remembering what happened that awful day.

"I'm never safe," I tell her simply.

"And why do you think that you're never safe?"

"Because he always finds me."

"Who finds you?" she presses.

"Constantine Carbone."

Saying his name out loud sends a shiver through me. It's like speaking the name of a demon and being afraid he'll appear at any given moment. I can see a change in the psychiatrist's face as well as she jots down some notes. God, I wish I could see what she's writing. Does she think I'm crazy? Does she think I asked for all of this? Does she blame me for putting her employer on Constantine's radar?

No, stop thinking that, I chide myself internally.

I've been battling horrible inner thoughts my entire life. I always expect the worst in every situation. Always. And it's only because the worst always seems to happen. I've never actually been happy and safe.

Well, except for when I lived here with the Vitales the first time.

My eyes drift to the wall of windows to the left of me. Thinking about my past here, in this house, causes a familiar ache to take center stage inside my chest. For the first time in a long time, I allow myself to remember. The memories I desperately locked away for many years come flooding back to me. I can almost smell the familiar grass and the way it used to feel on my feet as Nico and I would run through the yard, playing tag or kick ball. We were always outside or finding excuses to go outside.

"What are you thinking about?" the psychiatrist asks, bringing my gaze back to her.

"The past," I tell her simply.

"The past meaning when you were last here?"

I slowly nod. I wonder just how much the Vitale family told her about me. I'm assuming everything up until this point. She most likely knows my history, knows my past. Probably assumes some of the horrors I've been through but couldn't possibly understand them. No one can but me.

"Do your memories from here help you cope with the present and what happened to you when you were being held captive?"

A lump forms in my throat, and I struggle to swallow past it. It's like she can see right through me. Maybe she can. Maybe I'm as transparent as a ghost. I mean, I do feel like I've been dead for years. Never living; merely existing. "Yes," I whisper. Picking at an imaginary thread on the arm of the chair I'm sitting in, I ask her, "Do you... do you think you could prescribe me something?"

"May I ask what you would want the medicine to accomplish?"

"I...I just want to be numb," I confess. It's been difficult facing reality since I realized where I am and who I'm with. I don't want to see the looks of pity and disgust that I'll no doubt find sometime soon on Nico's face.

The psychiatrist glances up at me, her pen finally stopping. "I understand you were on a concoction of drugs when you arrived. Did they ever make you feel better?"

I consider her wording. Did they make me feel better? No, not really. They simply masked everything so that I could ultimately deal with it. I shake my head slowly, answering her honestly.

"I think dealing with past trauma sober would be a much better option than dealing with it while high or incoherent. Wouldn't you agree?"

I fidget in my chair and glance at the clock on the wall. God, it's only been thirty minutes. It feels like I've been in the hot seat for at least two hours.

"How about this?" she offers. "If you continue to see me and we continue to talk, I might be willing to prescribe you an anti-anxiety drug to help with your panic attacks you told me about. But I haven't been totally able to assess you on this first visit, Selina, so I don't feel comfortable just writing out scripts. Do you understand?"

I give her a small nod. I hate to think about trying to cope with all of this sober, but what else can I do? It's not like I have easy access to drugs like I did before.

"Are we done?" I ask.

"Do you want to be?" she questions.

I nod again.

"Then we can be done," she says simply. "Same time Wednesday?"

"Okay," I agree.

I can tell the doctor sees me as a tough nut to crack, and I don't know if she'll ever make her way through the hard exterior walls I've built up around me over the years. I spent a lot of time fortifying them so that nobody could get in. I don't even really remember the girl I was before Constantine took me and stole my innocence. Maybe she's in there somewhere, screaming to get out.

If anyone could find her again, it would be Nico. But I won't be here long enough for him to break her free. She's probably lost forever, drowning in an endless pit of sorrow, and I refuse to throw her a life vest. The old Selina is better off dead and gone forever.

CHAPTER 14

Selina

I WAKE UP from a nightmare, my body trembling under the blankets. I sit up slowly; and when I raise my hands in front of my face, I can still see the blood covering my skin. "Oh god, no!" I gasp as I desperately try to rub the red stains away. My nails scratch at my skin, tearing it open as I try to rid myself of the image.

Running to the bathroom, I turn on the hot water in the sink and scrub my skin until it's red and raw. I know their blood is just in my head, but I feel like it's still on me. The dream followed me into real life, and it's staining my very soul.

I can still hear their screams. I can still see their faces when they realized their fate...because of me. It was my fault. *It was all my fault. They're all dead because of me!*

Screaming, I lash out, my fist connecting with the mirror before me. The glass fissures, creating a distorted reflection of my face. My features look ugly, warped. And that's how I truly see myself — a fucking monster, a murderer. If I hadn't been so damn selfish that day, they would still be alive.

And now I'm bringing that same danger upon the Vitale family, who have only shown me love and compassion. The curse has followed me here, and I don't know how long it will be before I'll be wearing their blood too.

"No," I say out loud, shaking my head vehemently. I won't let that happen to them. I refuse to let Constantine harm them. He's taken everything from me. I won't let him take them from me too.

Fleeing from the bathroom, I go to the closet and pick out the darkest clothes I can — a pair of black yoga pants and a dark gray hooded sweatshirt. I dress quickly, scooping up a pair of black and white sneakers in the process and stepping into them before I slip out of my room.

The compound is quiet. I'm sure there are guards somewhere... maybe everywhere...but I don't care. I'm not a prisoner here. They have to let me leave whenever I want to. Right?

Even I don't know the answer to that question, but I'm bound and determined to find out.

My feet move quickly, carrying me down the hall. I glance back at Nico's room one last time, hating the thought of possibly never seeing him again. But I know it's for the best. I'm only endangering him and his entire family by staying here. And I'm sure he'd rather have his family alive and well with me gone than the opposite of what will happen if I stay.

I tread lightly down the steps. The compound is quiet and dark, save for a few dim security lights here and there.

I stare at the front door when I reach the bottom level, but I'm not that stupid. There has to be some kind of alarm associated with that entrance. Instead, I turn and go to the back of the house where I've seen the inground pool.

I stop at the sliding patio door and take a breath. My hand trembles as I grip the handle and test it, pulling it just an inch before stopping, hoping that a loud alarm will not sound, waking up the entire house.

I cringe, waiting, but nothing happens. Blowing out a sigh of relief, I open the door just enough to slip out before closing it behind me. I walk past the swimming pool, anxiety creeping up into my bones as I slink past the patio and make it to the yard.

Ducking down, I run through the large garden, the tall flowers and shrubs giving me cover. I shrink down by a bush and wait, panting. The night air is crisp and cool against my skin as I look back at the compound. Tears fill my eyes at the thought of leaving behind the only family who ever loved me, but I know it will be better this way. At least I will know that they won't have to suffer. I wouldn't be able to live with myself if anything happened to the Vitales because of me.

Steeling my nerves, I slip out of the garden and cross the yard. All of this seems...too easy, and I'm shocked by the lack of security. I'm beginning to wonder why Constantine hasn't attacked or come for me yet. If I can get out, that means he can get in. And that thought alone is what pushes me towards the fence. I grip the bars, and the metal is cold and unforgiving. The fence is tall, and I know it will not be easy, but my determination and sheer will might just work in my favor.

I grip the bars, preparing to try to pull myself up when I hear a deep, ragged voice call out, "Stop!"

My heart pounds against my ribcage as I stand still, not sure what to do. Should I stop? Should I run?

It only takes me a moment to make up my mind. Before the person behind me can make a move, I take off running.

Nicholas

In the middle of the night, I'm awoken by an alarm sounding on my phone. It's a strange sound, not one of my usual alerts, waking me up out of a dead sleep.

Unlocking my phone, I switch on my bedside lamp and read the messages popping up on my screen. The first text from Aldo asks what he should do. There's a photo attached to the message, so I open it up and stare at it. I'm confused at first, not exactly sure what I'm looking at. It's a photo captured from the motion detector cameras in the hallway. Zooming in, I see Selina sneaking out of her room. Normally that wouldn't raise alarm...except that she's fully clothed, dressed in all black with sneakers. The subsequent pictures are of her walking downstairs and then disappearing outside one of the side entrances.

Aldo's next text has my heart doubling in speed.

We've got a runner.

Fuck. Texting him quickly, I make sure he alerts the guards to stand down. I don't want anyone laying a finger on her. Not only would it drive me fucking crazy to see anyone touching her, but I know Selina might lose it if one of the guards manhandles her. They're trained to not let anyone in. But they're also trained to not let anyone out without permission first. Selina is not a prisoner here, by any means. It's simply a safety precaution.

With Carbone on the hunt for her, we cannot let her leave. If I had it my way, Selina would stay here indefinitely. But ultimately that decision is not up to me. It's hers and hers alone. However, she can never be allowed to leave until Constantine is either behind bars or dead. We can't risk him gaining access to her ever again. And the fact that he possessed her for an entire decade makes me think he desperately wants her back and would be willing to do anything to have her in his grasp again.

I run silently through the compound and out through the yard until I see her dark, lithe figure by the fence. As soon as she touches the bars, intending to try to hoist herself up and over the tall fence, I yell out, "Stop!" My voice sounds deep and desperate, and I wonder if she even realizes it's me.

It only takes her a few seconds to make a decision. And as soon as she darts off to the right, I know that decision was made. She doesn't want to stop. She wants to run. And my only choice is to run after her.

The adrenaline pumps in my veins as I chase her. She's fast. But I'm faster. I gain ground on her within the matter of a few seconds, and I gently grab her arm, bringing us to a stop, not wanting to hurt her.

But then she starts to fight. "Fuck," I curse as she elbows me in the ribs. Grabbing her tightly, I put her in a hold with her arms criss-crossed in front of her and her back tight up against my front. I don't want to hurt her. That's the last fucking thing I want to do. "Stop fighting me, Lina!" I order.

"No!" she cries out, kicking at my shins.

I hold her until she wears herself out, and then and only then do I finally release her. Panting, she takes a few steps away from me, glaring. And, fuck, if looks could kill, I would drop dead right here on the spot.

"What the hell is your problem? Why are you trying to leave?" I demand, desperately wanting to know the reason behind her sudden erratic behavior.

"I just need to leave, Nico. You couldn't understand," she says, her eyes tilting up to the night sky before she lets out a small sigh.

"I'm not letting you go for no goddamn reason," I tell her, growing angrier by the second. "Constantine is still out there. Maybe even waiting for you!" I yell, trying to get it through her head.

"I know! That's the point of me trying to get away from you. Don't you get it? I don't want him to hurt you too!" she cries. "I don't want you to end up dead like them!"

"Them? Who?" I ask.

Her eyes grow wide as she realizes she said something she didn't mean to. "Nothing. I didn't...never mind."

"No, tell me. I want to know," I insist.

"It's not safe for anyone, not you, not your family, if I'm here. He *always* finds me," she says resolutely.

"He'd need an army to get in here. Don't you get that? You're safe here, Lina. You're safer here than out on your own!" I say heatedly, trying to talk some sense into her.

She rolls her eyes at my words. "I've heard that before. You don't know him." She wraps her arms around herself. "No one knows him like I do. No one knows what he's truly capable of."

"Enlighten me then," I suggest. "I want to know what you're so afraid of that you want to leave the safest place on the planet for you right now!"

She swallows hard and doesn't speak for so long that I begin to wonder if she'll ever tell me. But then she finally starts with, "When I was fifteen, I got away from Constantine. They had docked his yacht in this little Italian village. Constantine wanted to go sightseeing or something. I don't really remember." She shakes her head. "I just know I was able to slip past him and his security guards. I ran until I couldn't run anymore." She shivers at the memory, wrapping her arms tighter around herself. "I found a house at the end of an alleyway. It was a family of five. The mother and father were so delightful, and their three small children were beautiful and kind." She takes a moment to release a shaky breath. "The father knew a little English, and I explained to him the situation I was in. They agreed to help me."

I listen to her story carefully; and even though I don't know the ending, I think I know where this story is going. If it haunts her this much so many years later, it must be horrifically brutal. It obviously scarred her soul deeply.

"Constantine found me an hour later." Tears fill her eyes, but she doesn't let a single drop fall. "He killed them. Even the kids. He killed them all in front of me." She closes her eyes, and a single tear sneaks out and trails down her porcelain cheek. "I was covered in their blood. Constantine didn't let me shower for weeks. I wore their blood on my skin, on my clothes. He told me it was my lesson to learn — that it would happen anytime anyone tried to help me." Her eyes flutter open and she gazes up at me. "I don't want that happening to you and your family, Nico. I don't want you to get hurt!" she exclaims, her voice wavering with despair.

I take a step closer to her. Slowly, wanting her to know my true intentions, I gently raise my hand and cup her cheek in my palm. Her breath catches in her throat as my thumb wipes away the stray tear from her cheek, and then she looks up at me with those haunting eyes of hers. Fuck, she's never looked more beautiful. "He can't hurt me, Lina. Only you can. By leaving," I explain. "Constantine can't get to you here. I promise you that. He wouldn't get within ten miles of this place without us knowing."

Selina scoffs like she doesn't believe me, pulling away from my touch and taking a few steps backwards. So I tell her, "Come. Let me show you." And then I turn and wait for her.

She stares at me, uncertainty written all over her face. But she eventually starts to walk and begins to follow me. I'm going to ease her mind and take her to the control room, as we call it. Because then, and only then, will she see how truly safe she is here.

CHAPTER 15

Selina

THE CONTROL ROOM, as Nico explained on the way down here, is an underground bunker of sorts with so many computers and technical gadgets that it's almost mind blowing. The room is buzzing with people and the smell of coffee.

We walk up to one man in particular with dark hair and brown eyes behind black glasses. I can tell he must be in charge based on the number of keyboards, monitors, and equipment at his large desk. He has so much more than the average person in here. And when he sees us approaching, a small smile graces his lips.

Nico claps him on the back and asks, "Aldo, can you please explain to Lina how safe she is here?"

Aldo seems to light up inside. "Sure thing," he says, turning in his chair to face his multiple computer screens. This is his expertise, and I can tell he likes to show off.

He begins clicking the mouse with his right hand, and multiple camera angles begin popping up on one of the monitors. "We have twenty-four-seven surveillance inside and outside of the compound," he explains. "No one gets in without a keycard and facial recognition. Numerous guards are on various shifts throughout the day with rotating schedules, so that they are unpredictable to an outsider. There are also infrared drones that run routine patrols over the perimeter every few hours. And that's not counting the hundreds of cameras, most equipped with thermal and motion detection on the outskirts of the property."

My shoulders slump in relief after he's finished, and I feel like a thousand pounds have been lifted from them. "Wow," is all I can manage to say.

A dimple appears as the corner of Aldo's mouth rises. "Yeah. Pretty impressive." He turns in his seat to face us once again. "This place is like Fort Knox. No one is getting in without us knowing far in advance. And if anyone would happen to get inside the gate, they would never make it to the front door without us stopping them first."

"Do you understand now when I tell you it's safe here?" Nico asks me.

I give him a nod. "Fort Knox. Got it."

"Thanks, Aldo."

"Anytime."

Nico leads me out of the control room and back to the compound. When we reach the hallway for our rooms, I stop outside my door and turn to Nico. "Thank you," I tell him. He has no idea how much he helped me today. I was driving myself insane with fear of Constantine barging in here and taking me or worse — hurting them all right in front of my eyes.

"You're welcome. Try to get some sleep. Then we'll do lunch together later?" he suggests.

"Sure," I reply with a nod. I go into my room and close the door. My brain is still processing all of the information I just learned. Thinking I'm too wired to sleep, I lie down on the bed, never intending on sleeping. But it doesn't take long for me to drift under, because I think, for the first time ever, I actually feel protected from Constantine.

∼

It's almost noon by the time I wake up, and I shower and get dressed for the day before making my way downstairs to meet Nico for lunch. I'm hoping he's still there, and I'm pleasantly surprised when I see him sitting in the kitchen, looking like he's waiting for me.

He's dressed in a navy-blue t-shirt and gray joggers, which hang loose on his hips. I have to force my eyes to his, and I can tell right away that he looks drained. It's written all over his face. I just figured he went back to bed like I did, but now I'm thinking he didn't. I just hope I wasn't the reason he couldn't sleep, but what else could it have been?

He flashes me a grin when I walk in and sit down on a barstool at the kitchen island. I wait quietly while he rummages through the fridge. "There's some leftover chicken salad if you'd like," he offers.

"Sure."

I watch him closely as he makes us a couple of sandwiches. He's so meticulous in the way he does every little thing. It's fascinating to watch.

He sets a plate in front of me, and I waste no time digging in. I haven't had something as simple as a chicken salad sandwich in a long time. Sometimes I would get five-course meals, and sometimes I wouldn't eat for days at a time. It all depended on Constantine's mood and if I was being a "bad girl" or not. Most of the time I would choose almost starving to death over pleasing him, so I learned to eat whatever was put in front of me, because I never knew when my next meal would be.

Nico sits beside me and cradles his sandwich in his large hand before taking a big bite. I smile as I surreptitiously watch him eat.

"What?" he asks when he finally catches me staring.

"Nothing. You just...you have some mayonnaise on your face."

He grins sheepishly. "Sorry." He grabs a napkin and wipes his mouth. "I didn't eat all day, and my workout this morning kicked my ass."

Ah, so that's why he looks so tired. He didn't go back to bed after all. He chose to work out instead. My eyes roam across the island, and I can't help but notice his biceps straining against his shirt sleeves. Nico definitely filled out over the years, and I find myself staring often at his body, which is more like a work of art than anything else. I can't remember the last time I ever checked out a man or even felt...*attracted* to one. "Do you work out every day?" I ask, then take a small bite of my sandwich.

"Yeah. Or at least I try to anyway. Sometimes shit comes up, but I try to stick with a routine. And I train with Renato and Benito a few times a week as well."

I pick at my sandwich, debating in my head whether to ask my next question or not. "Could I...could I work out with you sometime?" I ask.

"Sure. The gym is open to you anytime, Lina. You don't have to ask permission."

Nodding, I tell him, "Okay. Thanks." I've always thought of myself as weak, and I'd like to start building some muscle mass...just in case. I hate to think of being in Constantine's clutches ever again, but it could happen. Anything could happen. I just want to be ready for him this time.

"If you want some help training, I could help you," he offers, as if he's reading my mind.

"Training? What sort of training?" I question with furrowed brows.

"Hand-to-hand combat and self-defense," he explains.

I instantly perk up at his offering. "Can we start right now?" I ask eagerly.

The corners of his lips tilt up. "Uh, sure. Maybe after we eat?" he suggests.

I smile and nod in agreement. Being able to handle myself against someone attacking me is exactly what I need. For far too long I've been a victim, and I'm tired of it. I want to be able to fight back. With Constantine, I always felt weak and powerless. Now it's time to take back some of my power.

CHAPTER 16

◈

Nicholas

SELINA IS A quick learner. I only have to show her certain moves once or twice, and she masters them on the second or third try. Pretty soon she'll be kicking ass and taking names, and I couldn't be prouder.

We started out easy, but now we're gradually getting into harder moves, like her breaking out of my holds from the front and behind. We're both sweating and exerting all of our energy on this as if our lives depend on it, and perhaps in a way they do. I don't want her to ever be in a vulnerable position again in her life.

I can't protect her twenty-four seven, even though I'd like to. There could come a time when someone could try to take her away from me again, and I want her to be able to fight them off and at least have a chance to escape.

Just the thought of someone trying to steal her from me has me pushing her harder and harder. I want her ready for anything and everything.

"And if I come up behind you and grab you like this?" I ask, grasping her and holding her in a tight grip.

"Elbow," she says before bringing it down gently into my side. "Slide my arms up. Drop to the ground."

I watch as she falls to the ground out of my grip. "And then?"

"And then I run."

"Good. Very good." I pace the mats in the gym where we've been training for what feels like hours. "If you can get a kick or punch to the vulnerable parts of their body, then you do that." I stop and motion to my face. "Eyes." And then I point lower. "Balls."

"Eyes and balls," she says with an eager nod.

I chuckle, and then Lina smiles sheepishly. While this all seems like fun and games for now, I want her to be serious when someone actually does attack her. And so, when she starts walking away to reach for a bottle of water, I suddenly move up behind her silently... and then I grab her.

At first, she doesn't do anything, and I'm worried. But then, she suddenly juts her elbow right into my ribs, causing a rush of air to escape my lungs. She drops faster than I can blink, and she's out of my grip in a second.

"Shit," I say with a strained grin while grabbing my side.

"I didn't hurt you, did I?" she asks, stepping closer with a concerned look on her face.

Her hands reach out to gingerly inspect my ribs, and I suck in a breath at the unexpected touch. *Fuck, I should let her hit me in the ribs more often,* I can't help but think to myself.

Her fingers suddenly freeze as if she just realized what she's doing, and she takes a quick step back. "Sorry," she whispers as a blush creeps up her neck to her cheeks.

I'm not sure if she's telling me she's sorry for hitting me or for touching me, but I hope it's not for the latter, because I want her to do it more. "I'll be fine," I reassure her. "You did good today, Lina. We can keep practicing a few times a week if you want to."

"I want to," she says in a rush, and I can't help but smile.

People might underestimate Selina considering all the terrible shit she's gone through, but I know she's a fighter. No one can break my girl — not even one of the most powerful men on the planet. She's fucking indestructible.

∼

After a nice hot shower, I slip on a white t-shirt and a pair of dark blue sweats and am about ready to crawl into bed when I hear screaming. My first instinct is to check my phone for alarms that I might have missed while I was showering. If the compound was breached, an alert would be on my phone.

But when I find no such evidence on there, I quickly run out of my room and stop in the hall, waiting, listening. My heart is threatening to pound out of my chest as I wait impatiently for any signs of distress.

"No! Help me!" Selina screams from her room.

My bare feet pound against the wooden floors as I race to her. Even though it's next to impossible, maybe someone slipped in undetected by our security system. Her screams are heart-wrenching, like she's being murdered, and I expect the worst as I slam open the door to her room.

The lamp on the nightstand by her bed is on, and I quickly search the room for an intruder. No one is here...except for Selina... who is in her bed, sleeping.

She cries out again, and I suddenly realize she's having a dream. No. A fucking *nightmare*.

Her face is scrunched in pain, and I can see sweat beads running down her temples as she fights against imaginary demons. I don't know if she would want me in her bedroom, let alone her bed, but I can't just let her suffer in the nightmare. I climb onto the mattress beside her and gently shake her shoulder, trying to rouse her out of sleep. Selina recoils from my touch and a muffled sob escapes her lips. "Shit," I mutter under my breath. I'm only making it worse.

"Lina," I say softly. Then louder, "Lina, wake up." She doesn't open her eyes, and my frustration grows as her breathing picks up faster like she's going to hyperventilate at any given moment. "Lina!" I yell, shaking her.

Her eyes snap open, and she immediately goes into defense mode, clawing and kicking and screaming.

I grab her, holding her tight and saving herself and myself from any more harm. "It's all right. It's me. It's Nico. It's all right, I'm here, I'm right here," I tell her in rapid succession to try to calm her down.

"Nico?" she asks as she slowly wakes up fully and becomes aware of her surroundings.

"Yes. You were having a nightmare," I explain before releasing her and climbing off her bed. I stand at the edge, waiting while my jaw tightens. I don't know what she was dreaming about, but I can guess. I hate that she can't even sleep without being haunted by her past. If I could, I would erase all those bad memories from her mind so she would never have to relive them ever again.

"A...a nightmare," she repeats. "I-I'm sorry." Her voice cracks with soft-spoken guilt as her peculiar eyes focus on me. A little gasp comes from her mouth before her fingertips touch her lips, a look of horror on her face. "Did I hurt you?"

"No," I say with a shake of my head. She's always so damn afraid of hurting me. The very thought causes a grin to tug on my lips, but I quickly school my expression and ask her, "Do you want to tell me what your nightmare was about?"

She hesitates, and I figure she won't tell me since she rarely opens up to me, but then she surprises me by saying, "It was about them. That family. Talking about what happened to them today must have trigged another nightmare."

"It's okay to talk about them...or anything, Lina. I'm here to listen anytime you need me," I tell her seriously.

My words seem to have a calming effect. "Thank you," she whispers, and I can hear the emotion in her voice.

Sometimes I wonder how she survived all those years all alone with nobody to confide in or to vent her frustrations to. She only had herself to rely on. Even though she's so damn strong, I'm afraid if she keeps bottling up everything inside, one day she's going to just… burst. Lucky for her, I'll be there if or when she finally does.

I get up, ready to return to my room to try to get some sleep when I feel her hand grasping mine in a quick, firm grip. I stare down at our connection, her hand looking so damn tiny in mine.

"Nico?" she asks, and her voice sounds so small, so innocent.

My gaze meets hers. *Blue and green…like the ocean.* "Yeah?"

"Will you…will you stay with me tonight?" she asks, biting her lower lip nervously.

"Uh," I start. Damn, I know I should just go back to bed because she might regret this in the morning; but for some reason, I can't say no to her. And definitely not when she's looking at me with those big puppy dog eyes and begging me to sleep next to her and keep her safe. "Sure," I say, relenting.

She lets go of my hand and crawls under the covers, watching me cautiously as I sit down on the bed over the blankets and lean my back against the headboard.

She turns on her side, facing me, and I watch as her eyelids grow heavy until she can no longer keep them open. When her breathing evens out, I slowly reach down and run my fingers through her long, silky hair. "Go to sleep, *cuore mio*. I'll be here to slay all the monsters that try to get into your dreams," I promise her.

CHAPTER 17

Selina

I VENTURE OUTSIDE in the early afternoon, wanting to escape the confines of my room and any reminders of bad dreams. The sun is shining brightly, not a cloud in sight. The sun glinting off the water in the pool blinds me for a second as I hear a voice call out, "Hey, Selina!"

I put my hand up to shield my eyes from the glare as I see Aria in a bikini sitting at the edge of the pool with her feet dangling in the water. Her skin is perfect, tan and smooth, and her long, chestnut brown hair cascades down her back, looking like perfect beach waves even though I doubt she even took the time to fix it today. She's just one of those natural beauties. She was beautiful as a child too. I can remember seeing her for the first time and wondering how someone could be so perfect in real life. If anything, her beauty only magnified as she aged.

Even though I've only seen her around her compound on a few

occasions and we haven't spoken much other than to say hello and goodbye, I would love to spend some time with her. We got along great when we were kids. Aria was like the little sister I never had and would always tag along with Nico and I wherever we went, wanting to be with us no matter what we were doing or where we were going.

Aria flashes me a warm smile and says, "Water feels great. Want to join me?"

Suddenly, the baggy clothes I'm wearing feel out of place and strange. Nervously, I pull at the cuff of one of my long sleeves.

"I probably have a bathing suit you could borrow," she offers, standing up and walking towards me. "Come on. Let's go see." She grabs a towel on the way, drying her legs and feet off quickly before we walk to her room.

I follow her even though I never technically agreed to get in the pool. I haven't been swimming in a long time; but on an unseasonably hot day like today, it would be almost a sin not to enjoy the water.

Aria digs in the back of her walk-in closet before she finds a bathing suit. It's a two-piece, not terribly revealing, but not something I would pick out for myself to wear around the Vitale home.

I change in her bathroom and step out, shyly covering my midsection with my hands. "Do you have anything less..." I pause, trying to find the right word.

"Less revealing?" she suggests.

"Yeah," I say with a soft chuckle.

"I think I may have a one piece in here somewhere, but I haven't worn one since I was, like, twelve." Her voice trails off as she roots around in her closet.

I remove my hands from my stomach and stare at my reflection in the mirror. My stomach is flat and toned, but there are numerous visible scars. Most of my body is covered in scars, and it makes me sick to look at the reminders of my days being held captive and the horrific tortures I had to endure. There's a roadmap right on my skin of what I went through. There's no hiding, no denying it.

Suddenly, Aria appears at my side. She stares at the marks on my body, and I watch her face with bated breath, waiting for it to morph into disgust. But instead of the reaction I'm fearful of, she locks eyes with me in the mirror and...smiles. "You look like a fucking warrior, Selina. You survived hell and back, and you lived to tell the tale. Not many can say that. Wear those battle scars with pride, girl. You're absolutely killing it," she says, shocking me to my very soul.

I've never had a female figure in my life ever praise me or lift me up before. My bitch of a mother was always worried I was eating too much, getting too fat or that I wasn't pretty enough. And then when I was sold, I always felt wanted for all the wrong reasons.

"Thank you, Aria," I tell her, my voice unsteady. Tears burn the back of my eyes before I quickly blink them away.

"Anytime," she responds with a smile. "Now, let's go swimming before the clouds decide to make an appearance and ruin our day."

We go back downstairs and out to the patio. Aria perches on the edge again, and I get in, enjoying the warm water. When we lived on Constantine's yacht, I used to go swimming in the ocean whenever I got the chance. I felt a sense of freedom, even if it was short-lived. Sometimes I would find myself wishing that I wasn't such a strong swimmer and that the ocean would swallow me up and take me away from that life.

But today, I don't feel that overwhelming sense of dread at all.

"Cannonball!" someone yells before I hear a huge splash at the other end of the pool by Aria.

A huge wave of water crashes over Aria, soaking her from top to bottom. "You're a jerk, Renato!" Aria yells as she flips him off.

He laughs heartily and begins to swim laps around the pool. I make my way over to Aria in the water and stare back at Renato. He's around my age and handsome enough with light brown hair, green eyes and more muscles than I can count — I swear he has an eight-pack instead of a six-pack.

The way they interact with each other every time I see them together makes them appear as more than friends, but I could be totally wrong. Looks can be deceiving. But curiosity gets the better of me, and I just have to ask, "So, what's up with you and Renato? Is he your boyfriend?"

"He wishes," Aria scoffs as she wrings water out of her wet hair. "He pines over me, and I let him," she says with a shrug and a sassy grin. "Besides, my father would murder him if he touched me," she confesses, her smile faltering a bit.

I frown at that. So, maybe Aria likes Renato more than she's letting on, but she keeps her distance because her parents wouldn't approve. That would be a tough spot to be in. Pining over someone and never being able to actually have them. I can tell Renato really likes Aria. Maybe even loves her.

"If it's meant to be, it will be," I tell her.

She hums in agreement and nods. "I think I'm going to go get something to eat. I'm starving." She pulls herself out of the pool and stands up, her wet feet padding along the patio while she goes to a chair with a big, fluffy towel. "You know, we should go shopping sometime," she throws over her shoulder.

"I would like that," I tell her sincerely.

She flashes me a toothy grin and then disappears into the house. A few seconds later, I see Renato climbing out of the water and running after her, and I can only laugh. He's like a lost puppy when it comes to that girl.

I stay in the pool for another hour, enjoying the hot sun and warm water until my skin starts to turn a bright shade of pink. Not wanting to get sunburnt, I climb out of the pool, water sluicing down my body as I walk over to where the towels are. Quickly, I dry off my legs and arms before using the towel to get the excess water out of my long hair. My swimsuit is still pretty wet when I walk inside the house, but I plan on hanging it up and jumping in the shower anyway when I get back to my room. As soon as I turn the corner, I run smackdab into what can only be described as the hardest chest in the history of chests.

Firm, gentle hands catch my arms, holding my elbows before I go stumbling backwards. And then I look up into the familiar, steel gray eyes I've grown so accustomed to.

When I glance down, I realize I've soaked the front of Nico's white t-shirt with my wet bathing suit. My eyes roam over his muscular pecs and rock-hard abs, which are now visible through the damp material, and I swallow hard.

"I'm guessing you were just in the pool," Nico muses as his lips tilt up into a strained smirk.

"Sorry," I manage to whisper.

After my nightmare last night, Nico stayed with me. He slept on top of the blankets, never once trying to cross any boundaries. He was there to help me, to comfort me. Just as a friend...

But the heat I'm feeling from his body now and the way his hands are gripping my arms makes my heart skip a beat. Something deep inside of me awakens, and it's hard to place the exact emotion since I've never felt it before in my entire life.

When I woke up this morning, Nico was gone, and I half wondered if I dreamt about him too after the nightmare. However, when I rolled over, I could smell him on the pillow; his scent of citrus and sandalwood warming my soul.

I didn't leave my room this morning, too embarrassed to run into him at breakfast and reliving the way that I asked him to stay with me last night like a desperate child afraid of the monster under her bed.

"Is everything okay?" his deep voice snaps me back to the present, and I stare up at him.

My lips suddenly feel dry, and my tongue darts out to lick them. Nico's eyes darken as he watches the movement. My stomach clenches as warmth races down to my core, and I suddenly feel too close, too hot, too...I don't know. Stepping back suddenly, I pull out of his grasp. "I-I'm fine. I'm sorry again about your shirt," I tell him as

I wrap the oversized towel around me and cinch it tight, desperately needing the barrier between us.

"It's fine. I'm on the way to the gym to work out with Renato anyway," he explains.

I simply give him a nod, unable to speak with the words sticking in my dry throat.

"I'll see you later, Lina," Nico promises.

And as he walks away, I know what the foreign emotion is now that I was feeling. It's *desire*.

CHAPTER 18

Selina

WEDNESDAY MORNING'S APPOINTMENT with Dr. Graham went just about as well as I expected it to go. She asked an ungodly amount of questions, and I refused to answer ninety-nine-point-nine percent of them. And then we continued the tedious back and forth of her asking and me evading for nearly an hour until she finally relented and sent me away with a notebook so that I could "journal my feelings" or whatever.

The notebook feels heavy in my hand as I carry it back to my room. I've never discussed my feelings with anyone let alone had enough guts to write them down on paper. Dr. Graham thinks it will be good for me to journal whatever is on my mind, but she has no idea of the appalling things I've seen or what goes on inside of my head. I'm just thankful that she nor anyone in this house can read minds.

Lying down on the bed, I sigh as I flip open to the first blank page in the notebook. I put the tip of my ballpoint pen to the paper, but my hand just rests there. I force myself to write something, *anything*, but the words just aren't coming out how I want them to. The sentences look jumbled and messy.

It's not like I don't have things to talk about. It's just that it feels like if I put them on paper, then that makes them all *real*. The torture and agony I endured feels like an ongoing nightmare in my mind. But if I start to write them down, I'll be forced to face the truth and fixate on them over and over again.

Blowing out a frustrated breath, I rip out the page, ball it up and toss it into the nearby trashcan. Staring at the fresh empty page, an idea comes to me. At the top of the paper on the blue line, I write *Things I Want to Do*.

It will be like my own sort of bucket list, but this is for the immediate future and just little things, nothing like traveling the world or doing something spectacular before I die. This is more of a wish list for the present; short-term goals that I'd like to accomplish while I'm staying here.

Number one on the list is to get my GED. I've already started working on it, thanks to the Vitale family. I'm supposed to be taking a placement test soon, so that I can begin studying and focusing on everything I need to work on. And even though I'm extremely nervous, I'm excited at the same time.

School was never a priority to my mother. Well, I guess, neither was I really. I was young when she pulled me out of public school, bragging to the superintendent that I would be homeschooled with the best tutors money could buy. She loved to put on airs even though every single person we met could see right through her bullshit. Too bad it took me years to figure her out.

Frowning, I return my attention back to the notebook. I chew on the end of the pen while I think for a few minutes. *Drive a car* ends up on the list next. I've never even been in the driver's seat of a car before. I've always wondered what it would be like to just take off on a carefree ride to anywhere you want to go with the windows down and the music blaring. It seems like it would be liberating.

Go surfing. Nico and I used to go surfing a lot when I lived here. There is nothing quite like the power of the ocean and catching the perfect wave. We used to spend the whole day from sunup to sundown out on the water, and I never grew tired of it. Not even for a second. I found a passion in that pastime that I have never been able to find again.

I twirl my long hair around my finger as I try to think about what else I want to put on the list. Staring down at my split ends, I know exactly what I want to write next.

Cut my hair.

Constantine never allowed me to cut my hair. He told me once that the long hair made me look younger. A violent shiver runs through me as I recall that memory. I hate thinking about him. The sad thing is, he was a huge part of my childhood. Some children fear the boogeyman or the monster under the bed. I actually lived with mine. He was real. He *is* real.

"You're still not safe," I tell myself out loud. I need to keep reminding myself of that. I'll never be safe until he's dead.

And that's why the next thing on my list I write is...*Kill Constantine Carbone.*

I stare at the words, unable to tear my eyes away from them. I will them to come true somehow. I want the man who assaulted and raped me for years to be brought to his own fair justice. Death might be too lenient for him, however. I want him to suffer. I want him to suffer for all of his victims' lives, not just mine.

A knock sounds on my door, and I call out for Nico to come in.

Nico doesn't open the door, however. It's Aria. She looks just like a miniature version of her own mother — pretty and petite with long, dark curls and amber eyes. She's dressed in a shimmery beige summer dress with sandals. God, she always looks like she just stepped out of a fashion magazine. I don't know how someone can be that well put together all the time when I'm over here just trying to not get any more stains on my shirt.

"I'm bored," Aria says with a pout. "Want to go shopping?" she asks with a hopeful expression.

"Sure, I'd love to go shopping," I tell her.

Aria's face instantly lights up. "Okay, great. I'll see you downstairs in five," she says before leaving my room.

After our pool day together, I feel like Aria and I could be really great friends. We always got along when I lived here the first time, but the age gap made it difficult for us to bond over anything since she was really into Barbies and I had already outgrown them. But I do remember the time we spent together playing outside with Nico and having movie and game nights as a family.

Now that we're older, we have all new things to try to bond over. Clearly, she likes to shop as I haven't seen her wear the same thing twice since I arrived. She's always in the cutest clothes and dresses, and I definitely could use her help in that department.

Aria couldn't have picked a better time to ask me. Sighing, I glance down at my outfit — a pair of black yoga pants and a plain shirt. It's the best I have at the moment, and I'm definitely in need of a change.

~

Nicholas

Aldo and I spent the day examining some of the intel Selina provided us with. We've been holed up in the control room; and as I walk back to the house, I relish in the feel of the sun on my skin and the fresh air in my lungs. Even though we were really starting to make some progress, I needed a break to go see my girl. I miss the fuck out of her.

Like an addict without his fix, I need to just see her to tide me over until my next hit.

On the way to her room, I think about the information she gave us that we were diligently working on. Constantine supposedly has been taking girls and women to an island somewhere and auctioning their virginity off to very rich and powerful men. Selina could only tell us what she overheard Constantine talking about; she hasn't actually been to the island. Fuck, if we could find it, we could save so many young women.

Aldo promised to keep searching until we find it, so hopefully he can come up with something soon. The odds are stacked against us, though; because if the most powerful men in the world go there, I'm sure it's well hidden and kept secret to only those who attend the auctions.

The sick fucks.

I shake out my arms, trying to relieve some of the tension in my body before I knock on Selina's bedroom door. As I wait, I try to think of a reason to tell her as to why I'm here. Maybe I'll offer to work out with her again or ask what she wants for dinner. Any excuse to talk to her is fine with me. The door is open a few inches; and when she doesn't answer after a minute, I peek my head inside. The room is empty, and I frown.

Where could she be?

I didn't see her outside or downstairs on the way here. Worry starts to gnaw at my gut. What if she tried to leave again? She wouldn't do that, though, would she?

Pushing the door open, I walk in. There's a notebook in the middle of her bed that grabs my attention, and my heart squeezes inside my chest. Did she leave me a note? A fucking goodbye letter?

The first page is open with the pen still resting against it and there are words scrawled neatly down the page. I know I should respect her privacy and not look, but I need to make sure she didn't run off. If she did, I might still have a chance to find her and bring her back before anything happens.

I only plan on taking a glance, but then I realize it's a list. My curiosity gets the best of me, and I move closer, reading the list and memorizing it.

Get my GED.

Drive a car.

Go surfing.

Cut my hair.

The last one gives me pause. *Kill Constantine Carbone.* I can't help the grin forming on my lips when I read over the last item over and over again. Carbone didn't break my Lina. No, he only made her stronger, reinforced her will, spirit and determination. She just needs to be reminded of that now and then. And I want to be the person who helps her realize her strength.

Relieved that it's not a goodbye note, I leave her room after that and go to seek her out. If she wants to accomplish those things on her list, I want to be the one helping her through each and every one. I want to be by her side and watch her accomplish all of her goals. I want to be there for her through everything she has to deal with, the ups and downs and everything in between.

The sun doesn't rise or set unless she's with me. She's my whole world now.

I run into Renato in the main room of the compound. "The girls went shopping," he informs me, as if reading my mind.

"Ah, okay," I say with a grin. I'm glad Selina could get out of the house. I know she's been anxious to go shopping too, but I haven't taken her because I'm terrible with that sort of thing. I'm glad my sister is making an effort. I know both of them could really use a friend, so it's kind of perfect.

"Want to train with me today while they're gone?" Renato suggests.

"Sure," I tell him. I've been meaning to take my frustrations out on something one way or another.

"Fists or knives?" he asks.

"Knives," I tell him with a salacious grin. "Definitely knives."

CHAPTER 19

Selina

I STARE AT myself in the mirror of the dressing room and can't stop scowling. I feel so strange in these clothes.

"How does it look?" Aria calls from outside the door.

I frown as I glimpse at the short but modest, pretty floral dress and jeweled sandals. "I look like an idiot," I call back, being brutally honest.

"I'm sure you don't, Selina," she huffs. "Just...just let me see you."

My frown deepens. I haven't showed her the past fifteen or so outfits she forced me to try on, so I guess I'll show her this one. *Just to shut her up*, I tell myself mentally.

When I push my way out of the thick curtain for the lavish changing room, Aria actually gasps loudly.

"Oh, that's the one!" she says with a huge smile, as if we just chose my perfect wedding dress or something.

"You don't think it's too..."

"Too?" she prompts.

"I don't know," I say with a frustrated huff. I want to say *too normal*, but I refrain. When I was under Constantine's rule, I either wore next to nothing or the skimpiest, sexiest dress money could buy. If I wasn't almost naked, I looked like a hooker. There was no in between. There was definitely nothing like *this*.

"It's perfect for your figure." She grips my shoulders and leads me over to the bright lights over a wall of mirrors. "You can see better out here. Those dressing room mirrors are shit," she assures me.

I stare at myself in my many reflections, but only for a moment before my eyes automatically go to the floor. Biting my lip, I shake my head solemnly. I can't even look at myself without feeling a myriad of emotions, and that makes me sad, depressed, angry — hell, all of the above and then some.

"I wish I had your long legs," Aria comments with a sigh as she sits in a nearby chair, swinging her shorter legs in the air since her feet don't touch the ground.

Aria is petite, almost a foot shorter than me. But her height doesn't do anything to take away from her beauty. Just like Nico took after his father in the looks department, Aria is an exact replica of her mother. I always thought her mother was the most beautiful woman I've ever seen. Even as Verona has aged over the years, she's still stunning.

My eyes slowly glance over my outfit in the mirror until I meet my own gaze. Aria voicing her insecurities about her height makes me realize that everyone has insecurities, even the people who appear to be flawless and perfect on the outside. I need to stop over-analyzing every little thing wrong with me and just focus on *living*. I just spent a whole day of shopping without a care in the world, and I never thought I'd be able to do something like that. My life is moving forward and changing for the better, and I need to just jump on and enjoy the ride.

"So, do you like it?" Aria asks, and I can tell she's on the edge of her seat, waiting for my answer.

"I do," I tell her. "You were right — the dressing room mirrors *are* shit. The dress looks so much better out here."

Aria smiles widely and nods in agreement. "Told you." She hops up out of her seat and tells one of the retail workers that I'll be wearing my outfit home.

"Yes, of course, Ms. Vitale. I'll ring everything up right away," the woman says before walking away.

I'm still scrutinizing myself in the mirror when Aria tells me, "Nico's gonna love it."

Her comment catches me off-guard. The thought of Nico seeing me dressed up has butterflies taking flight inside my stomach. I like him. I *really* like him. But for some reason, I keep pushing him away. I don't ever let our small touches go anywhere even though sometimes I really want them to. Maybe it's because I don't want him tainted.

I'm dirty.

Used up.

Broken.

Sighing heavily, I try to shake the bad thoughts out of my head. Glancing over my shoulder, I watch as Aria hands over a few bags to one of the nearby bodyguards, who accepts them without question, before taking a few steps back away from us.

"Do you ever get tired of them being around?" I ask her in a hushed whisper.

She shrugs her right shoulder. "I'm used to it. It's been like this my whole life. I guess I don't know any other way," she confesses.

From what Nico has told me and from what I've seen, it's almost like Aria is a prisoner in her own home. Her parents never let her leave the house on her own. And I can't help but wonder if Mr. and Mrs. Vitale tightened their grip on their daughter after I was taken not once, but twice.

I can't fully blame them for being overprotective, however. My life would have been completely different if I would have been blessed with a helicopter parent instead of the terrible person who gave birth to me. I was sold by my own mother...twice. And if my own mother can do something so heinous, then anything could happen to Aria. I'm just happy she never had to go through what I did. Even if that means being locked up inside an ivory tower, I would take that fate over mine any day.

"My brother is different with you," Aria says, breaking me out of my thoughts.

"What do you mean?" I ask, turning to her.

"He's always so moody and closed off. Been like that for as long as I can remember. But when you're around, I can see a light breaking out inside all of that darkness. He's so patient and gentle with you," she explains.

I want to ask her why she thinks that is, but I'm afraid of her answer. I think deep down Nico loves me...or at least maybe thinks he does. But a big part of me wishes he would just get over me and move on with a normal girl. Someone who isn't so messed up. Someone who can make him happy. Someone without so many issues. He deserves so much better than me, so much more than I can offer him.

Aria comes up from behind me, and I watch her reflection in the mirror. She takes a lock of my long blonde hair and curls it around her finger. Looking up at me, she asks, "What do you think about going to the hair salon next?"

My eyes meet my own in the reflection. A smile twitches at the corner of my mouth as I nod emphatically. I've been wanting to cut my hair for years, and now I have no one standing in the way of my decision. No one telling me what I can or cannot do. This is the sense of freedom that I've been craving. And I so desperately want to be free.

CHAPTER 20

Nicholas

"YOU'RE NOT CONCENTRATING," Renato sneers as he shoves the blade of his knife towards me.

I barely move out of the way in time. I can hear the *snick* of the blade cutting the air as I dodge it at the very last second.

Training has always been a way of life for me ever since I was a little kid. My father taught me to always be ready. For anything.

I started doing the knives training years ago, because it gives the boring wrestling and fighting an element of danger that really gets my adrenaline going. I can tangle with my father's men all day and take all of them on. But when you add a real, dangerous weapon into the mix...well, anything can happen.

I grip the hilt of my knife harder and thrust it towards him as we do a dangerous dance around the outdoor training area. He dodges it easily, as always. Renato is in top shape. All of my father's men have to be in order to carry out what he expects from them. Just because

Renato is closer to my age doesn't mean anyone goes easier on him. If anything, they expect more. And he knows it.

Sweat drips down my bare back as the sun beats down on it. It feels like the hot rays are trying to peel my flesh off my bones. "It's hot as fuck today," I comment before moving to the side quickly as Renato tries his best to cut me.

"It was your idea," he says with a grin as he steps back and bounces on his heels. "Girl trouble?"

"You know that's what it is," I tell him with an eye roll. "Fuck, some days I feel like I'm making some real progress with her. And then the next, it feels like I'm back to square one."

"Time."

"What?"

"Give it time. Time heals all wounds, or whatever the fuck it is that people say."

Renato comes at me again, and this time I follow through with the attack and have his ass flat on the ground in a split second. He squints up at me through the bright sun with a shit-eating grin on his face. "You think I will ever beat you?"

"Never," I tell him with a smirk as I reach down to offer my hand to help him up. We both return to our designated standing spots, and he motions for me to come at him again.

"I dunno. That girl has your mind all fucked up. I think now's my chance," he says with a dark chuckle.

"Maybe," I agree. I take a stance before charging him. He not so easily discharges my weapon and tackles me to the ground. When he puts his arm around my neck and we're wrestling, I instantly tap out. If Renato is good at anything, it's putting someone in a chokehold and making them take a long nap in record time.

"Giving up so soon?" he taunts.

I gather my knife from the grass and go back to position. "Not sleepy," I quip.

My comment has him howling with laughter. Then, he lifts up

his arms and poses, making his larger-than-life biceps bulge. "No one can stay awake with these babies wrapped around their throat."

"Just because the sun's out doesn't mean your guns should be out."

He nods in agreement. "Yeah, I better put these things away before your girlfriend sees them and decides to come to my room tonight." And then he emphasizes that bullshit spiel with a wink.

I know his insult is all in jest to rile me up, but it has my blood boiling in two-point-five seconds. "The fuck you say?" I ask through gritted teeth.

Renato must notice my change in disposition because he quickly says with a grin, "Ah, there you are. I've been looking for you all day." He lifts his hand and motions with his fingers. "Come at me, bro."

And I do.

My blade nicks him twice as we fight and wrestle to the ground. And only when I'm on top of him and my knife is threatening to cut into his jugular does he call it, tapping out.

"Giving up so soon?" I ask, repeating his earlier taunt.

"Fuck, you can be ruthless when you want to be," he says, wiping the thin lines of blood from his side and stomach with his earlier discarded white t-shirt. After he's cleaned up, he tosses the shirt aside, and I can see the glint of anger in his eyes. He hates to lose. And me getting the best of him even once feels like losing to him. "No more pussyfooting around," he grinds out.

I can't help but laugh at his comment. Most men wouldn't last one round in the ring with us even if we weren't technically going full bore earlier.

I'm getting into my stance, ready to take on Renato when I get a glimpse of blonde hair. It's not the long hair I've become accustomed to seeing, but a shoulder-length bob style. And I'm so caught off-guard when her peculiar eyes meet mine that I never even hear or see Renato coming at me.

I feel the blade of his knife slicing through my skin as he tackles me to the ground. "Ah, fuck!" I cry out as he comes down on me hard with all of his weight, effectively knocking the wind right out of my lungs.

"Oh, shit!" Renato yelps as he realizes what he's done. He quickly scrambles off of me and stands up. "You looked ready, man. I thought you were ready!"

I can hear the panic in his voice. I don't know if he's more concerned that he might have seriously injured me or what my father will do to him if he finds out about it.

I'm still struggling to breathe when Selina comes running up to us. I can see the apprehension and fear in her eyes. "Are you okay?" her timid voice asks.

She looks...different. Not just her shorter hair, but *everything*. She's in a short floral dress and cute sandals. And fuck, I can't stop staring at her long legs as I try to recover from the hit. I'm such a sucker for long legs.

My sister runs up behind her, and I realize Aria must have made Selina her project today, giving her a complete makeover.

When my lungs are no longer on fire and I can finally speak, I tell them, "I'm fine."

Renato offers me a hand up, and then looks down to my stomach and says, "Oh fuck."

I glance down and see blood flowing out of the open wound. It's already soaked through the waistband of my gray sweatpants. "It was my fault," I tell him assuredly. "I wasn't paying attention."

"Selina, will you take Nico up to the nurse?" Aria asks.

Lina slowly nods, her wide eyes focused on my wound. *Fuck.* I know she hates the sight of blood based on what happened to her in the past.

"Please, hurry," Aria says, gently shaking Lina's shoulder.

The urgency in Aria's voice seems to have its intended effect, and Lina finally snaps out of her odd trance. Grabbing my hand, Lina pulls me towards the house. I walk in a fog, staring down at our joined hands. Her hand feels so small and delicate in mine as she leads me upstairs to the nurse's room.

She knocks on the door with her free hand, refusing to let me go, and I can't help but smile. I know I shouldn't be excited about holding hands with a girl like a prepubescent teen, but this is the most Lina has touched me since she arrived here. Every little step is a giant one with her, and I'm thankful for every single one.

Sarah opens the door and takes one look at me before she says with a heavy sigh, "Come in. Lay on the table."

I do as she says as she walks over to the sink to wash her hands. I expect Lina to let go of my hand, but she grips it even tighter as she sits down on a chair next to the exam table.

"What happened this time?" Sarah asks with a frown as she puts on a pair of blue latex gloves.

"Knife fighting with Renato."

"Hmm, usually he's the one up here, not you," she admits while she cleans my lower stomach with antiseptic.

"There's a first time for everything," I say with a heavy sigh.

Sarah fills a needle and comes to me. "I'm going to numb the area first, because it looks like you're going to need a number of stitches."

I grit my teeth and breathe out slowly as the needle enters my skin, and I hold Lina's hand a little tighter. Fuck, it feels good to have her here with me.

Sarah walks over to the cabinets and begins opening and closing drawers, collecting what she's going to use. "So, Renato is normally the one I'm stitching up after one of your knife fights." She glances over her shoulder and flashes me a toothy grin. "Don't tell me he finally got the better of you?"

I let out a soft laugh and shake my head. "I was...distracted."

Lina grips my hand a little tighter, and I gently squeeze hers back for reassurance. None of this is her fault. She's just so damn beautiful that I couldn't look away from her. When her eyes meet mine, she whispers, "I'm sorry."

"Not your fault, sweetheart," I whisper back.

My term of endearment has her cheeks flushing with a pink

blush, driving me crazy. Fuck, I love that she's shy with me sometimes.

Sarah turns around with a metal tray full of what will ultimately mean pain for me. Having missed our whispered conversation, she asks, "So, what distracted you?"

"The most beautiful woman I've ever seen in my life," I answer before glancing over at Selina. Her pink blush is slowly turning into a deep red.

Sarah grins, her eyes moving back and forth between Selina and me. "Ah," she utters, her smile growing wider. "Selina, how about you distract Nico again while I stitch him up?"

Selina gives her a nod, but I can tell she's still feeling guilty. I squeeze her hand until her attention is on me. Then I say, "You cut your hair."

"Uh, yeah," she says while touching the shorter ends with her free hand. "Do you like it?" she asks, her eyes peeking through some of the stray strands at me.

"Yeah, it's —." I stop myself from saying how hot it is. She looks smoking hot with that new haircut. She looks older too. But instead, I find myself telling her, "It suits you."

She smiles at my comment.

"Holy shit!" I holler as one of the sutures goes deep.

Sarah apologizes. "Maybe this will make you think twice about fighting with knives. You and Renato have better things to do than have a pissing contest every few days, don't you?" she scolds me.

I grit my teeth and hiss through another deep suture. "No more knives. Got it," I agree halfheartedly.

A few minutes later, Sarah is done stitching me up. I'm probably going to have an ugly scar on my lower stomach, but I'll just add it to my ever-growing collection of training battle scars.

Lina pulls her hand from mine, and instantly I miss her touch. It felt so good to feel her skin next to mine. "I think I'm going to go read in my room," she tells me before walking out.

I stare down at my empty hand and curse inwardly.

Sarah comes back over with some gauze and tape. "Try to keep this dry for a couple of days. And then you can take off the gauze and let it breathe. Don't scrub too hard when you do shower."

She fires out instructions, but I barely hear her. I'm too caught up in my own thoughts.

"Hey," Sarah says, snapping her fingers in front of my face to get my attention. "Did you hear anything I said?"

"Keep it dry. Let it breathe. Don't scrub too hard."

She rolls her eyes and grins. "Good enough. Just come to me if any of the stitches open up. Okay?"

"Sure," I tell her before hopping off the table.

"Take it easy," she warns.

"Sure," I repeat, causing her to roll her eyes again.

Then she asks, "Hey, how is Selina doing anyway?"

"Good. I think," I say, my brows furrowing. "Honestly, she doesn't tell me much. I just know she's in a better place than where she was. And that's all that matters at this point."

Sarah nods in agreement.

"See you later," I tell her before leaving. My feet carry me straight to Selina's room. I knock, and after I hear her tell me it's okay to come in, I peek my head around the door. She's curled up on her bed with a book. "Wanna do something fun?" I ask her.

I can see the apprehension in her gaze, but she nods anyway and says, "Okay."

"See you downstairs in five," I tell her. I have an idea. I just hope Selina likes it.

CHAPTER 21

Nicholas

I LEAD SELINA outside and to the enormous garage that houses all of our vehicles. "Take your pick," I tell her.

Selina's brows furrow as she glances up at me. "What...what do you mean?"

"Which one would you like to drive today?"

"Drive?" she says, her eyes widening. "Nico, I don't know how—."

"I know. I'd like to teach you," I explain to her quickly. I know it was on her list of things she wants to do, and I'd love to help her achieve all of them...especially the last one. Having Constantine Carbone dead and gone forever where he can never hurt another living soul sounds just fine to me.

"That one," I hear her say, and I follow the direction that she's pointing.

It's a silver BMW M5. "Definitely a safe option," I tell her, rubbing my chin with my finger and thumb.

"Which one do you like to drive?" she asks.

"This one," I tell her, bringing her over to my dark blue McLaren 720S. "But since it's your first time, maybe we should take the BMW just to be safe." Honestly, if Selina would have an accident in my car, I wouldn't freak out. That's what insurance is for. It would hurt my soul for a quick instant, but I would get over it. As long as Selina's safe and not hurt, that's all that really matters.

She walks over to the BMW. "Maybe you should drive us someplace first," she suggests.

"I know just the place," I tell her. Then, I make a phone call to one of the bodyguards and tell him to get a team ready to follow us. Selina seems to visibly relax when she realizes we're going to have guards with us. "Can't be too careful," I explain, and she nods in agreement.

∽

I drive us out to an abandoned airport. There are roads leading in and out, stop signs, and parking places that she can practice in; the whole nine yards.

The guards stay at the entrance, waiting for us, while I park in the middle of the huge parking lot. The pavement is cracked and overgrown in places, but it will be perfect for teaching Selina how to drive.

We switch seats, and I can feel the nervousness coming off of her in waves as she grips the steering wheel.

"Gas is on the right. Brake is on the left." I position her hands so that they are at a more comfortable angle. "There."

"There are so many...*things*," she says, her eyes darting over the dashboard, and I can hear the uncertainty in her voice.

"Don't worry about all the *things*," I tell her, trying hard to suppress a smile but failing miserably. "Just focus on the road ahead of you and steering. You only have to worry about the gas and the brake today. We'll have you listening to some good tunes and checking out the other gadgets soon enough, but I want you to concentrate today on just the driving aspect."

She releases a nervous laugh. "Okay. I think I'm ready."

"Good. Now, put your foot on the brake, and put the car in drive down here," I instruct her, helping her locate the gearshift. "Great. Now, gently release the brake and put your foot on the gas—."

Selina mashes her foot on the gas, sending us careening forward. A scream releases from her lips before I holler, "Brake, brake, brake!"

She switches her foot over to the brake and tamps it down, causing the car to come to a squealing stop and us to rock hard against our seatbelts.

"Shit!" she cries out.

I'm afraid to look over at her, scared that I messed this whole thing up by not easing her into it more gently. But I'm shocked when I hear laughter coming from her side of the car. Peering over at her, I look at her face, which is lit up like the sun, grinning and laughing. She looks like she's having the time of her life. She looks…fucking *happy*.

"That was exhilarating!" she exclaims suddenly as a fit of giggles escape her.

I can't help but join in her laughter. Fuck, her laugh is like a siren's call. So cute and genuine. My girl likes danger. I can tell already. And I'm totally okay with that. As long as I can keep her safe, she can have all the danger she wants.

"Okay, Evel Knievel, let's try that again. But slower this time," I warn.

She gives me a serious nod and bites her lower lip as she concentrates, driving me insane. My cock instantly hardens at the sight.

Selina is so fucking sexy without even trying. She's completely irresistible. And I can't stop staring at her, taking in every little detail — like how her eyes grow wide with delight when she does something right or the little crease she gets between her brows when she's really concentrating.

We spend the next few hours driving around the abandoned airport. I teach Selina how to drive on the main roads leading in, stopping at all the necessary signs, and how to use her turn signal. She picks everything up quickly, and I couldn't be prouder of her. She really wants to learn. I can tell. And that makes me want to teach her even more.

When she finally puts the car in park, I tell her, "Now you can cross driving a car off your list."

Her smile falls off her face, and I know instantly that I fucked up. "You...you saw my list?" she asks quietly.

I grimace. *Shit.* I really hope she doesn't hate me for invading her privacy. "It was by accident, but yeah," I tell her. "I went to your room, and the notebook was laying open on your bed, and I just kind of looked." Internally, I facepalm myself as I quickly add, "I'm sorry."

"So you saw...the last thing on my list?" she asks, her voice barely above a whisper, as she stares straight ahead over the steering wheel.

Kill Constantine Carbone. How could I forget? "Yes."

"And what do you think about that?" Her eyes finally meet mine.

I don't break our eye contact even for a second when I tell her, "I want him dead just as much as you do. And I'm going to make sure it happens."

Selina visibly relaxes, and it's like an invisible weight has been lifted off of her shoulders. Maybe she was afraid I would think less of her for wanting to kill someone...or perhaps my affirmation of her revenge is something she's needed all along. Either way, I'm happy to see some of the ever-present tension dissipate a little.

I watch in amusement as Selina reaches down and puts the car in gear. "Can I drive around the parking lot again?" she asks eagerly with an easy, carefree smile on her face for the first time ever that lights up my whole fucking world.

"Yes, of course. Let's go, speed racer," I tell her with a laugh.

CHAPTER 22

Selina

WE RETURN TO the Vitale compound late that night. Nico and I are still laughing and joking by the time we walk through the front door.

"Looks like you two had a good time," Aria says with a smirk as she crosses through the foyer on her way to the kitchen.

"Lina learned how to drive," Nico says with a grin.

I've never seen him smile this much. He would probably say the same thing about me, but ever since I got here, Nico has been serious and broody. It's nice to know that if I let go a little, he can too.

His words stop Aria in her tracks. "Really? That's awesome," she says with a smile, but it doesn't touch her eyes. "I never learned how to drive," she confesses with a one-shoulder shrug. "But I always have someone driving me around, so I guess there's not really a need," she adds, but I can hear the sadness in her voice.

Aria really is sheltered, but I'm sure Luca and Verona had their reasons for doing so. I mean, they've seen so many children sold into human trafficking, they probably have a hard time sleeping at night if they don't know where their children are at all times. And I can't say I really blame them. If I ever have kids, and that's a *huge* if, I would never let them out of my sight. I hate to think about living in fear all the time, but I know that's exactly what it would be like. I know what can happen. And I wouldn't wish that upon my worst enemy, let alone an innocent child.

"Well, you kids have fun," Aria tells us with a wave. "I'm going to get some snacks for a movie night with Renato."

"Wear protection!" Nico calls after her, which earns him a glare and the middle finger from his sister.

When Aria disappears into the kitchen, I ask Nico, "Are her and Renato...?" I know I had asked Aria about their relationship before when we were in the pool, but she was very coy about the whole thing, making it seem like Renato just has a crush on her and she entertains it.

Nico shrugs. "I know Renato is in love with my sister. I've caught them making out before, but I have no idea what they've done or haven't done." He grimaces before adding, "And I don't wanna know."

I chuckle at his discomfort. "So...a movie night sounds like fun," I tell Nico.

He looks at me, searching my face before he says, "Yeah? You want me to ask Aria if we can crash?"

Nervously, I wring my hands together. "Or we could have our own," I ask, forcing my voice not to break.

"S-sure," Nico says. Then he clears his throat. "I have Netflix in my room, or we can watch a movie in the —."

"No, your room is fine," I assure him. I know he's trying to give me an out to make me feel more comfortable. And while I love that about Nico, how he never pressures me into anything and how he always puts my feelings first, I just want to feel normal for once in my life. And a movie night with him alone in his room sounds great... and *normal* to me.

"Okay. I'll grab us some snacks if you want to go pick out a movie?" he suggests.

"Sure. See you soon," I throw over my shoulder before I walk upstairs towards his room.

∽

Nicholas

While the popcorn is in the microwave, I go over and pull out two sodas from the fridge and a few boxes of candy. I have no idea what Lina will like, so I'm just trying to cover all the bases.

After the popcorn is done, I juggle everything in my arms and take it upstairs to my room where Lina is waiting patiently for me on my bed.

She's stretched out on her stomach with her long legs on display. Fuck, she's gorgeous. I take a mental snapshot of her looking so relaxed and carefree, wanting to paint it later.

When she looks up at me, she has a grin on her face as she eyes all the snacks. "Wow, did you raid the pantry?" she asks.

"Pretty much," I answer with a chuckle. "Didn't know what you'd like, so..."

"Well, I love popcorn, and that's a must-have with a movie, so you did good." She sits up and helps me with everything.

And with her on her knees before me, fuck, all my blood rushes right to my cock. Cursing under my breath, I grab the boxes of candy and walk over to my desk to set them down. With my back towards her, I will the beast behind my zipper to calm the fuck down. Even though I would love to fuck Selina, I know she's not ready for that.

Hell, I would settle for a heavy make-out session or even a kiss at this point, but I can't rush anything with her. *And I won't.*

And it's not because I think she's too fragile or weak. No, fuck that. She's the strongest person that I know. It's simply because I don't want to scare her off or change anything between us. Our friendship is too important to me to lose just because my dick wants to get wet. Instead, I'm going to wait and let things progress slowly at their own pace. I don't know how long it will take before she's ready to move to the next level, but I'm willing to wait. I'll wait for ten more years, if that's what it takes. I would wait forever for her...

"You okay?" Selina asks, and I realize I've been standing over here for far too long, not moving, not talking.

"Uh, yeah, just trying to decide what I want." I pick up a box of *Junior Mints* and take it back to the bed. I sit on the mattress with my back against the headboard while she lies down on her stomach again, facing the TV.

My hand creeps to my hard cock, and I press my hand against it. Fuck, she drives me crazy with those long legs. Snapping my eyes shut, I try to think of anything but Selina and her sexy body.

"Are you sure you're okay?" Selina asks, startling me.

When I open my eyes, she's next to me on her fucking knees again, looking concerned. And that makes me feel like the world's biggest asshole for all the dirty thoughts running through my mind. What can I say? I'm not a fucking saint, and I'm definitely not a monk. I have urges, and right now I have the urge to spread those long legs of hers and bury my face between her thighs until she's crying out my name and coming all over my face...

"Um, yeah." Trying to take the attention away from my awkwardness, I quickly change the subject. "What movie did you pick out?" I ask, and even I can hear how weird my voice sounds. She probably thinks I'm losing my mind.

"It's about a zombie apocalypse," she answers with a grin.

My lips tilt up. "Nice!" Leave it to Selina to not pick something generic like a rom-com. I totally would have watched a sappy romance movie, though. Hell, I'd do almost anything to make her happy.

She eventually lays back down and starts the movie. My eyes keep drifting to her sexy legs and plump backside, but I force myself to chew on the candy and keep myself in check. I have no idea what the movie is about besides zombies...oh, and an apocalypse. I can't even hear the actors' voices anymore. I'm having an internal battle with my cock, who won't fucking listen no matter what I say.

Grabbing one of the pillows, I put it over my lap. I feel like a fucking teenager who can't control his hormones on a first date.

When the movie is finally over, I almost groan out loud with relief. If I have to stay in this room with her alone for another second, I might just spontaneously combust.

Selina stands up, glances at me with a pillow over my lap and cocks her head to the side. Does she know I'm trying very hard not to come in my pants right now? *Oh fuck.*

"That was fun," she says, nervously wringing her hands in front of her.

"Yeah, we'll have to do it again sometime," I tell her with an uneasy grin.

"Well, goodnight," Selina mutters before walking out of my room and closing the door.

"Fuck," I breathe out in a long sigh before hanging my head in shame. That was awkward as fuck because I've been a walking boner for the past hour and a half. Standing, I make my way into the bathroom. It's been a while since I've jacked off, and I need to take care of business so that shit doesn't happen again next time I'm around Selina.

CHAPTER 23

Selina

I PACE MY bedroom floor. For some reason, the entire movie night with Nico felt awkward. I'm not sure if he felt it too, but I desperately want to know. I need to make sure I didn't do anything to offend him or make him feel uncomfortable.

Before I can change my mind, I leave my room and make my way down the hall. I timidly knock on Nico's door and wait. I stand in my pajamas, nervously shifting from foot to foot, but he doesn't answer. Maybe he's in bed already?

Gnawing nervously on my lip, I put my hand on the doorknob and turn, carefully pushing the door open. A lamp illuminates the room, and I see that he's not in bed.

Water running from the en-suite bathroom catches my attention, and so my feet pad across the hardwood floors to the door that's ajar. The water is louder now, and I can tell that he's showering instead of just washing his hands, like I first thought.

I tell myself to walk away, to not look, but it's almost like I can't help myself. Instead, I step into the space where the door is open and peer into the spacious bathroom. Inside the walk-in shower, which is made up of tall glass, I see Nico. His naked body is dripping wet from the water raining down upon him. My heart begins to beat faster at the sight of him — his muscles and abs on full display. My eyes lower to where his hand is fisting his cock. It's thick, long and hard, *perfect*, just like him.

He slaps a hand against the wet tile and groans out, "Lina."

Oh my god, he's thinking about me while he's getting off. Long streams of cum erupt from his cock, and I can't help the gasp of surprise coming from my lips. It must have been louder than I thought because next thing I know, Nico's eyes are meeting mine. We stare at each other, and I can see the surprise and confusion lacing his handsome face before he's saying my name again.

I'm not even conscious of my next move; I just know I have to get the hell out of there. I was caught watching him. I'm embarrassed more than anything, but also...turned on. I don't stop running until I'm safe inside my room with the door closed. With my back against the wood, my right hand covers my heart that's threatening to beat out of my chest.

My fingers clench and unclench, and then they involuntarily move on their own accord down my body and under my pajama bottoms. Biting my lip, I slip my fingers into my panties and rub my already wet slit. It feels so wrong, but so damn good. I close my eyes and picture Nico in the shower just as I saw him — wet and hard, stroking his cock and calling out my name.

I get close to the edge in no time, but I can't seem to cross that fine line of the edge. Gritting my teeth, the bad thoughts start assaulting me left and right, and I can almost hear Constantine's voice in my ear...

"Don't you dare come, little pet."

Trembling, my eyes snap open, almost expecting to see him standing before me. I'm terrified of pleasure, because with pleasure always comes pain. My body has been conditioned to accept that, and I fight it until I can't fight it any longer. My fingers eventually stop trying, and I know I've already checked out mentally. That moment full of lust is gone with no relief in sight.

Blowing out a frustrated breath, I pull my hand from my panties as tears fill my eyes. I feel embarrassed. *Dirty.* It was wrong what I did. And I can't stop the tears from falling or the sobs that follow, wracking my body as I collapse to the floor. Pulling my knees up to my chest, I curl into a ball on the floor and give over to my emotions.

A knock is at my door, and my spine goes rigid. "Lina," I hear Nico's deep, gentle voice call from beyond the door.

I can't face him right now. Not in this state that I'm in. So I leave his pleas unanswered, and I go to bed to face my demons alone.

～

The psychiatrist clears her throat. I snap out of my daydream and force myself to meet her eyes. "Sorry," I mutter under my breath.

"Where were you just now?" Dr. Graham asks.

"I was just thinking," I admit. And if the doc was talking just now, I didn't hear a word of what she just said.

"Can I ask what you were thinking about?"

My cheeks instantly warm at the question. I'm curled up in the leather chair by the window, and I pull my knees closer to my chest. "I was thinking about…Nico," I tell her, my voice barely above a whisper. I don't want to open up to her, by any means, but I desperately need someone to talk to about everything that happened.

Dr. Graham seems pleased by my answer. She's probably thrilled that we're actually making some progress for once instead of me shutting down and refusing to answer her questions. "Were you thinking about something in particular? A memory or something more recent perhaps?" she asks.

"Something that happened last night," I confess. God, I've been ignoring Nico since it happened. When he came to my door after I caught him, I couldn't even face him. I felt like the world's biggest jerk for turning him away, but I was too embarrassed to confront him about what happened. And also a big part of me was worried that I would give in and do something stupid like kiss him or...more. I even refused to go downstairs for breakfast where we've been eating together every morning for the past few days, making me feel even worse about everything.

"And what happened last night, Selina?" she presses.

"Nico and I watched a movie together in his room."

"That sounds like fun," she says with a sincere smile. "Did anything else happen besides the movie?"

"No. I mean yes."

"You don't sound so sure," she says gently. Her voice is so soothing and controlled. No wonder she got into this profession. Sometimes I feel like I could tell her anything, and there are times when I do tell her some things. A lot more than I've ever told anyone.

"I went back to Nico's room to talk to him after the movie, but he was..." My voice trails off. "I saw Nico...in the shower." I bury my face against my knees, trying desperately to hide my face, which I'm sure is red as a beet right now. I'm still embarrassed over the whole thing. But even more so...I'm still aroused.

"Do you want to talk about it?" she asks while pushing her red glasses up the bridge of her nose.

I'm tempted to tell her no, but in a way, I do want to talk about it. I want to know if what I felt is normal. I have no idea what normal is anymore. "He was...touching himself. And I couldn't look away. I watched him." Closing my eyes, I admit, "He called out my name when he came."

After a brief hesitation, she finally asks, "And how did that make you feel?"

I open my eyes and stare out the window once again. "It...it turned me on," I confess, feeling absolutely horrible as soon as the words come out of my mouth.

"Well, that's a normal reaction, Selina," Dr. Graham assures me.

"I can tell by the look on your face that you don't agree with that, though."

"It's wrong," I say adamantly, and I don't know who I'm trying to convince more — the doctor or myself.

"Why is it wrong?"

"I shouldn't be thinking that way about him."

"And why not?" she prompts.

"Because he...because he's Nico!" I exclaim, not even understanding my own answer.

"Because he's your friend, and you don't want him to be more than your friend?" she suggests.

"Yeah, I guess," I tell her, but that doesn't sound right to me. Nico is my friend, but I think we deeply loved each other when we were kids; before we even knew what love really was. But so much has changed since then. I could never expect him to want me the same as he once did.

"Are you attracted to him?" she asks.

"Yes," I answer without hesitation. "Nico is beautiful, inside and out. He's...perfect. And I..." I stop from voicing my negative thoughts out loud.

"And you're what, Selina?" After a long hesitation when I don't answer her, Dr. Graham asks again, "You're what, Selina?" she prompts.

"I'm anything but perfect. I'm broken. I'm used up," I blurt out with tears quickly filling my eyes and spilling out over my blazing hot cheeks. I'm not used to talking about my feelings at all. No one has ever cared enough in the past ten years to ask how I felt about *anything*.

"You're not any of those things, Selina," Dr. Graham assures me. "Remember that negative thoughts don't help us cope with real problems. They only tear us apart instead of healing, which is what we really need." She makes a few notes before saying, "Tell me how you're feeling right now, Selina. Use your words."

"I feel embarrassed. I feel stupid," I grit out while angrily wiping away my tears. God, I haven't cried this much in years. And all of a sudden, I get here, and the floodgates are always opening. Maybe it's because deep down I know I won't get punished for showing emotion, for crying.

"Don't feel embarrassed or stupid. Anything you say here stays between us. Think of me like your own diary, but in human form. You can talk to me about anything, and your words will be locked away just like in a journal for your eyes only."

I nod, trying to absorb her words. I've never opened up to anyone in my entire life before...well, except for Nico. He knew the real me, but that was back then when I wasn't so messed up. Hell, I was messed up even back then, but not as fucked up as I eventually became after being sold to Constantine.

"Everything you feel is normal, Selina. You know that, right? Nothing you feel is wrong. I promise," she ensures me.

I nod in agreement even though I'm not sure I completely believe that. "After I left his bathroom, I went back to my room and...touched myself." My neck and cheeks warm again. I don't know why this is so difficult to talk about. I'm sure a lot of people talk openly about sex, especially with doctors.

"Did you enjoy yourself?"

"I couldn't..." I shake my head, not being able to voice the embarrassing words out loud.

Dr. Graham clears her throat. "You had mentioned before that you were never allowed to enjoy yourself during sexual encounters with your captor."

I squeeze my eyes shut. I can still hear Constantine's words while he forced me to have sex with one of his friends.

Don't come. Don't you dare come, you little whore! If you come for him, I will beat you until you're dead!

"Selina! Selina!" Dr. Graham calls out to me, but it sounds like her voice is a million miles away right now.

I open my eyes and stare up at her in confusion. At some point, I must have climbed out of my chair and huddled into the corner of the room.

"It's okay, Selina." She offers me her hand, but I refuse to take it. "No one is going to hurt you here," she tells me. It's the same thing she always tells me, but I've been told that before, and look what happened — my mother sold me for the second time and I was ripped away from this happy home.

Suddenly, pure and undiluted panic violently rips through me as my body begins to tremble uncontrollably. I quickly wrap my arms tightly around my knees and curl up into a fetal position on the floor. I lay there for what feels like an eternity with my eyes closed, blocking out everything else in the world and sobbing in the darkness until I hear Nico's deep voice calling for me.

My eyes slowly open, and the moment I see Nico on his knees beside me, I suddenly crawl to him and thrust myself into his open arms. He holds me tightly, rubbing his hand up and down my back while whispering soothing things into my ear.

"Don't let me go," I whisper to him frantically, my entire body shaking with fear.

"Never," he promises. And that one word makes me feel infinitely better all at once. It makes me finally feel *safe*.

CHAPTER 24

Nicholas

AFTER I TUCK a mentally and physically exhausted Lina into her bed, I leave her room and go outside. I need to get some fucking air. When the psychiatrist called me, telling me that she couldn't get through to Lina and that I was probably the only person that could, my heart sank into my fucking stomach.

Not only was I worried for her and the mental state she was in, but I was also pretty sure that Lina wouldn't come out of that state because of me. She's been pushing me away ever since she arrived, and it's been killing me slowly day by day.

Last night was a low point for both of us. She caught me in the shower. Fuck, I just couldn't help myself. I had a moment of weakness, and she witnessed it. She even heard me calling out her name while I came. And when I saw her standing there in the doorway...it felt like my world was crashing down around me. I know I need to take things slow with her, and that was not fucking slow, by any means.

She ran out of my room like her ass was on fire, and she refused to open her door when I tried to confront her to talk about what had happened. And having Selina ignore me all of last night and this morning, when she refused to come to breakfast to eat with me, fucking tore me up inside.

But there's no way I'm giving up on her. I refuse to give up. She's my girl. She's always been mine. The universe put us together not only once but twice for a reason. And I'm never letting her go again.

The fact that I got through to her just moments ago, when the psychiatrist couldn't, gives me some semblance of hope. Selina and I share an unspeakable and unbreakable bond. I think deep down she knows that I would never harm her or let anyone else hurt her again.

I know that my old Lina is in there somewhere, waiting to be set free. And I want to be the one who gives her that freedom, no matter what it takes.

When I walk to the backyard of the compound, I see Benito in the outside gym, landing punches on a bag. When he looks up and sees me, he smiles. But as soon as he sees the look on my face, his smile drops off his face, and his expression grows very serious.

"What happened?" he asks when I get closer.

"Nothing," I tell him. And then I immediately say, "Everything."

"Fuck. Okay," he says with a nod. "Let's work it out," he tells me.

Benito is the one who taught me how to channel my anger and feelings through working out. It's almost like landing punches on an inanimate object helps me release what I'm trying to bottle up inside. Sure, painting and drawing helps with some of my anger, but sometimes it gets to the point where I feel like a volcano inside, waiting to erupt into a fit of rage...or worse. Without Benito, I probably would have just kept bottling everything up with no release, and the consequences of that wouldn't have been pretty.

He tapes up my hands as I silently watch him. I feel so fucking drained and lost.

"Talk to me, Nico," he says as he holds up a big mitt, which I strike with my right fist.

It feels good to hit something. I punch a few more times before I finally open up. "Just when I think I'm getting somewhere with Selina, something happens, and then I feel like we're taking ten steps back." Sighing, I land a weak punch with my left and then throw my hands up in frustration. "I don't know how to fix it. To move on."

"Tell me what's been happening so far."

And so I do. I tell him about seeing her list, about taking her driving, about the movie night in my room. I leave out the part where she fucking caught me in the shower; too embarrassed to regale him with that particular tale. And then I tell him about a few hours ago when she was having a panic attack in the psychiatrist's office.

"The doctor couldn't get through to her?" he questions.

"Nope."

"But you did."

"Yep."

"But. You. Did," he says, punctuating every word. I stare at him, and he gives me a slow nod. "I know you want everything in the fast lane, but life doesn't work like that, kiddo. You just gotta give her all the time she needs, no matter how long that takes." He throws down the mitt and points a finger at me. "Let me ask you a question. If she disappeared from here tomorrow, would you wait another ten years for her?"

"I would wait a fucking lifetime," I confess in a rush.

"Then there's your answer. You can wait. You have it in you to wait. Your dick is just trying to tell your brain a different kind of story. Think with your head," he says, pointing up. "And not with your…other head," he says, pointing lower.

I can't help but chuckle at his logic and advice. "Thanks," I huff.

"You'll get there with her. I promise you that. Baby steps, Nico."

"Baby steps," I agree.

I stare up at the sky that's beginning to darken. There's a storm rolling in. But in the distance is a ray of sunshine beaming down to earth. I guess there's always light to contradict the darkness in every situation.

Benito is right. Even if it doesn't seem like I'm making progress with Selina, every day is a push forward towards the future, to a better place for us. I need to remind myself of that every time I think we're taking a step back or anytime I feel frustrated. We're still farther than we were the day before.

"Thanks, Benny," I tell him as I clap him on the shoulder.

"Any time, kiddo. Any time."

CHAPTER 25

Selina

"TAKE AS MUCH time as you need, Selina. This is just a placement test. It will give me a better understanding of where we should begin with your studies for your GED test," the teacher explains. She's older with gray hair and kind, blue eyes. I swear every single person the Vitales hire are nice, amazing and patient. But considering the type of women and children who stay here and the horrific things they've been through, I'm sure most of them need people like that in their lives. I know I definitely do.

I sit at the desk and stare down at the paper, gripping a number two pencil in my hand. I've never had trouble reading. I've read enough books to fill a library in my lifetime. At times, books were my only escape from the real world, and I was happy that Constantine at least gave me that one solace. Although, taking my prized books away from me was one of the ways he was able to punish me or manipulate me into doing bad things for him.

Pushing those thoughts aside, I focus on the questions before me. They start out easy enough, and I think they're going by grade level, getting harder as they go along. The first few I answer quickly. It's very basic, identifying shapes and colors.

About ten questions down is a math question. My eyes squint as I try to understand the problem. I don't even remember taking math in elementary school, and so the numbers just run together until they blur.

Feeling frustrated, I skip that question and continue on. But the complexity of the questions keeps growing. I can feel a hot blush creeping up my chest and cheeks as I skip question after question. Soon, there aren't any I can answer. The words blur from the tears quickly filling my eyes, and I slam my pencil down on the desk in annoyance.

"Selina, are you all right?" the teacher asks.

"I don't... I can't..." My voice trails off as my mouth suddenly goes dry.

"It's okay. It's simply for placement, so that we have a starting point for you. A baseline."

An angry tear leaks out of the corner of my eye and cascades down my burning cheek. God, I can't even remember the last time I cried over something as stupid as this, and that makes me feel even worse.

I can't even answer a simple math question...or most of these questions. Constantine stole my life from me. And I never went to school past the third grade, thanks to my mother, who only pretended to home school me when I was a little girl. They kept me from having a normal childhood.

I hate them both.

I hate what they've done to me.

And I hate who I've become because of it.

Standing quickly, the small room fills with the screeching sound of my chair scraping against the tile floor. I grip the test in my hands and begin tearing it apart into little pieces. I don't remember being this angry before. I've been so numb for so many years thanks to the drugs. It's hard to remember what real emotions, like anger, truly feel like.

A scream comes from somewhere in the room. It's feral and deafening. And it takes me a moment to realize the sound is coming from my own mouth.

My vision darkens around the corners, and my hands grip the corner of the desk I was sitting at. Suddenly, I flip it over. A small sense of satisfaction comes from that. But it's not enough.

It will never be enough.

Because I have so much repressed resentment inside of me that I'll never be able to release all of it. And I'm afraid it will end up consuming me and swallowing me whole.

Nicholas

It's late in the afternoon when I get an emergency alert on my phone. My stomach drops when I realize it's about Selina. Racing out of my room and down the hall, I run to the other side of the compound in record time.

There's a room that we use for a makeshift school when children are staying here in the compound so that they don't fall behind in their classwork until they're returned to their families or placed into foster care.

I can hear her angry screams filling the hallway before I even reach the door. Swinging the door open, I catch Selina just as she's flipping over a desk. Numerous desks are flipped over, and I can only assume she did that to all of them.

The teacher stands at the front of the room, giving me a nervous glance when I barge in.

Running over to Selina, I grab her before she can flip another desk. She fights me at first, but I force her to stop. Then, I put my hand under her chin and force her to meet my eyes. "Hey, hey, hey," I tell her. Her eyes are unfocused, and she looks so damn lost that it makes my chest ache for her. My thumb strokes her soft cheek as she slowly comes back to her senses, her eyes finally clearing as she focuses on me. "Talk to me, Lina. What's going on?" I whisper to her.

"I can't do it! I can't. I can't," she says, shaking her head repeatedly.

I give her a nod that I understand her even though I truly don't. She's clearly angry about something and taking that anger out on whatever is nearby. I've never seen her this upset before, and clearly she needs to get some frustration out. Taking her by the hand, I pull her towards the door. "Come with me," I tell her.

She digs in her heels and pulls her hand from mine. "Where are we going?" she asks warily.

I stop and turn to her. I can see the fear in her eyes, and I hate that someone put that there. "Do you trust me?" The words are out of my mouth before I can stop them. *Fuck, what if she says no?* But I feel extremely relieved when she nods her head yes. "Okay. Then, follow me." I leave the room first, and I'm pleased when I hear her right behind me on my heels. I lead her through the compound to where the gym is housed.

Thankfully, no one is in here at this time of the day, so we have the place to ourselves. When the door shuts behind us, I explain, "I didn't tell you the first time we were in here, but this room is soundproof. So if you need to yell, kick and scream, you can do all of that in here."

She arches a blonde brow at me.

"You can't just keep your emotions locked up inside, Lina. Eventually, the pressure becomes too much. Luckily, I know just the right outlet for you. I'm going to let you channel your anger on something positive." I lead her to the side of the gym where I proceed to grab a roll of sports tape. "Give me your hand," I tell her.

She hesitates but only for a second before reaching out towards me. I take her hand in mine and begin to wrap her hand and wrist with some sports tape. When I'm done, I do the other until she's all nicely wrapped up and ready to go. Then, I stick two punching gloves on her hands over the tape. "All set," I tell her.

Leading her to a long, heavy punching bag hanging in the corner of the room, I stand behind it and tell her, "Okay, start punching."

Lina throws a right hook and then a left. I can see the tension in her muscles and know she's not letting go. Not yet anyway.

"You can imagine this bag is anyone you want to take your anger out on," I remind her.

Then, instead of the dainty punches she was landing before, her fists become weapons, her strikes hitting harder and harder until all you can hear in the entire gym is her punching the fuck out of the bag. *That's my girl.*

She cries out, lashing out on the bag, and I just know she's picturing Constantine. She never got a chance to take her anger out on him before, and the release she's feeling is probably cathartic.

She lands several more direct, harder punches until she stumbles back, panting.

"How does that feel?" I ask her.

"Good. It feels good," she says with a shaky sigh. "I want to keep going."

I step back and let her do her thing, taking her anger out on the inanimate object until she's too tired to keep going. When she's finally done, I take her to sit down on a bench while I take off the gloves and unwrap the tape around her hands. I inspect them for any damage, but I don't see a mark on them.

"You can come in here and do this anytime you want," I tell her, meeting her gaze. "But make sure you wrap your hands and put on gloves. Otherwise, you could really injure yourself."

She gives me a nod but doesn't say a word.

"Do you want to talk about what happened earlier with the teacher?" I ask softly.

Lina worries her bottom lip between her teeth. "I was taking a placement test to see how much work I need to do before trying to get my GED." She frowns as she tells me, "I could barely get through ten questions before they got too difficult to answer."

I want to tell her that I'll help her study, that we'll get through this, but I keep my mouth shut. She doesn't need my reassurances right now. Right now she needs to vent, get all of her feelings out.

"I guess I just realized how much of my life Constantine and my mother stole from me. I never had an ordinary childhood. I never experienced the usual stuff teenagers do." She looks up at me, her blue and green eyes meeting mine. "The only time I ever felt normal and safe was when I lived here with you and your family. But that was so brief..." Her voice trails off as her eyes grow sad.

"Fuck the placement test," I tell her, which earns me a small smile. Fuck, that little grin can light up my entire world in an instant. "We can start to study every night if you want. We'll study anything and everything. And after you feel more comfortable, then you can take the test again. Okay?"

"Okay," she says, her smile growing. "Could you...could you help me with math?" she asks, and I can tell she's embarrassed by asking.

"Of course! I got straight A's in math in school. Math is easy if you have me as your teacher," I tell her with a wink.

She lets out a soft giggle, and I can't believe I got a smile *and* a laugh out of her today.

Progress.

Baby steps, just like Benito told me the other day.

Slow and steady.

This isn't a race when it comes to Selina. This is a fucking marathon. And I'm in it for the long haul. I'm here for her whenever she needs me and for whatever the reason.

CHAPTER 26

Nicholas

WE START OUT easy enough with math. We cover all the basics — addition, subtraction, multiplication, division. And once Selina has those down pat, then we work on the tougher stuff.

I have her doing mathematical equations during breakfast, and then I give her tests at night based on what we learned that morning. Selina passes with flying colors, of course.

And after a few days of running through exercises and tests, she's ready to take the placement test again.

Nervously, I pace outside of the classroom, waiting for her to finish...or waiting for her to begin throwing desks again.

But when everything remains quiet and calm inside for an hour, I'm satisfied that Selina won't be having another meltdown. Not that I can even blame her for acting out. Hell, if someone stole my childhood from me, I would be angry too. No, more than angry. I would be hellbent on having a murderous rage, scorching the fucking earth until no one who hurt me remained.

Fuck, I'm sure that's how she really feels deep down inside. And it makes me so proud to know how strong she is. She keeps it together every single fucking day, not breaking down when so many would.

When the door opens, I stop pacing and look up to see Selina walking out of the room. She stops in front of me, her eyes to the floor, not giving anything away. But when she raises her head and I see the smile on her lips, I know she did well, obviously much better than the first time around.

"How did it go?" I ask her.

"Great. Thanks to you," she says. "Thank you for helping me."

"No problem," I tell her. In all honesty, the time we've spent together studying has been amazing. Just being close to her makes me happy, and I haven't been this happy in a long time.

"The teacher is going to grade the placement test," Selina explains, "and then we're going to focus my schoolwork on what my weaknesses are and go from there. She's confident I'll be able to take my GED in about a month."

"That's amazing, Lina. And when you pass, we'll have to celebrate."

"*If* I pass," she corrects me.

"No. *When* you pass," I say confidently.

"Okay. When I pass," she counters, her smile widening. The watch on her wrist beeps, and she glances at it. "Oh, it's time for my physical therapy appointment."

"Okay, I'll see you later," I tell her, hating that I don't get to spend any more time with her right now and that I have to share her with someone else again. I watch her walk away, not blinking until she disappears around the corner and out of my sight.

Some people would probably tell me to get over my little obsession I have for her, but I know that will never happen.

Selina

It's early in the afternoon when Dwayne and I are finishing up my physical therapy session. I feel stronger already, like I can conquer the world. And it's all thanks to Nico and his family. I was living in fear and a deep depression for so long that I forgot what it felt like to just be normal; to be content and comfortable. And I do feel comfortable here. I've been to some of the most beautiful countries in the world and seen things a lot of people never get to see in their lifetimes, but I wouldn't want to be anywhere else right now.

I think I could actually be happy here. I think this could very easily be considered *home* to me someday.

"So, what kind of physical activities are you into?" Dwayne asks, breaking me out of my thoughts. "Hiking, biking, swimming, walking?"

I give him a small shrug. "I used to surf with Nico," I suggest.

"Surfing? Oh god, you couldn't get me out on the water, but more power to you," he says with a soft chuckle. "Surfing is great exercise, though."

"Do you think she's ready for it?" Nico asks, causing my head to spin in his direction.

"Oh, definitely," Dwayne tells him.

I didn't even realize Nico had entered the gym, and it makes me wonder how long he's been standing there, watching us. He's wearing a tight, white t-shirt and gray sweatpants. Damn, those sweatpants should be illegal. And I can't even stop my eyes from dropping to the outline of his...

"What do you think, Selina?" he asks, snapping me out of my trance.

My eyes immediately flash to Nico's face, and I watch as he cocks his head to the side and his lips tilt up in a knowing grin. Oh god, he just caught me staring.

"Uh," I stammer as a hot blush floods my cheek. *What was the question?*

Dwayne says, "As long as you don't go too crazy on your first day, you should be fine, Selina."

Oh, yes, surfing. We're talking about surfing.

"You're in great shape already," Dwayne comments, tapping me on the leg in a friendly gesture.

I watch Nico's eyes narrow on Dwayne, and I have to stifle a grin. Is Nico...*jealous*? I think he is. And why does a huge part of me want him to be?

"We can go surfing this afternoon if you want to, Lina," Nico suggests.

"Sure. That sounds like fun," I tell him with a smile.

"Great. I'm sure you could borrow Aria's board. I don't think she's ever used it since Mom and Dad bought her surfing gear as a Christmas gift a few years back."

"Then it's a date," Dwayne announces with a huge grin. He stands and tells us, "I'm going home for the day. You kids have fun!"

We watch him leave, and then the tension that always seems to be there between Nico and I slowly begins to drift into the room, thickening the air until I find it hard to take in a full breath.

Perhaps noticing the change, Nico clears his throat and says, "I'll go get everything ready. Meet you in the driveway in twenty?" he suggests.

"Yeah, sure," I say, my voice sounding throaty and hoarse like I've been chewing on gravel.

I watch Nico turn and walk away. And only when he's gone from the room do I feel like I can breathe again. I don't know why there's always so much tension between us, but I'm going to try to remedy that. I want Nico and I to be friends. Okay, maybe more than friends.

God, I don't even know what I want. But I do know I want things to just be easy and not so difficult.

I decide to head upstairs and take a shower. Every step of the way I can't help but think about the way he looked in the gym...and those sweatpants hanging so low on his hips.

Okay, so maybe a *cold* shower is just the thing I need.

CHAPTER 27

Nicholas

IT'S THE OFF-SEASON, so the beach isn't crowded, save for a few guys with fishing poles and one or two surfers out in the water. Even though the air is cool, the ocean is still warm, perfect for surfing.

I change first in the back of the van. I hop out, zipping up my wetsuit in the process while I motion for Selina to do the same. We bought her a suit at a little shop on the way. Once she's inside the van, I close the door and wait for her to change.

Three familiar SUVs are parked not that far away from us, and I give a nod to one of the bodyguards sitting in the front seat of the closest vehicle. Can't be too careful, especially with Constantine so close and creeping around in New York City right after the funeral of his son.

Aldo has been keeping tabs on the bastard, and everyone except me is stumped as to why he's staying in NYC. I know why he's not leaving. He's hoping to get his claws back in Selina. I can feel it deep down in my gut. Constantine doesn't like to lose, and he fucking lost the most beautiful girl in the world. He'll never get to have her again. At least not unless he's prying her from my cold, dead hands.

The side door on the van clicks just then and Selina steps out. "Uh, could you help me?" she asks, turning around. There is a gap in the back where she couldn't reach, so I grab the zipper and begin to pull it up. My fingertips graze her soft skin as I zip her up, and I feel her shiver from my touch. *Fuck.* Clearing my throat, I tell her, "There. All set."

When she turns back to face me, all the breath leaves my lungs. She looks so fucking pretty like this. We used to spend so much time out here on the water, surfing, laughing and talking. God, we would talk for hours. Surfing with Lina is one of my fondest memories from my teenage years.

"Race you to the sand!" she calls out before grabbing her board and taking off running.

Shit! I grab my board and take off after her. I almost forgot that we always used to race down to the beach, and whoever won got to catch the first wave. *I can't believe she remembered.*

She beats me down to the sand by a few seconds, and I blame it on trying to manhandle my board and her getting a head start.

"Looks like I'm up first," she says, practically beaming.

Chuckling, I tell her, "Okay, fine."

We paddle out together into the water with our boards. The feel of the saltwater washing over me brings back memories of Selina and I surfing together. Fuck, it's been too long since I've been out here. I missed it immensely. I've been surfing solo now and again over the past ten years, but it never felt the same. I never enjoyed it as much as I did when I was with her, so I pretty much gave it up.

"Are you good?" I yell to her when she starts swimming out to catch her first wave.

When she gets to the lineup, Selina simply looks back and smiles, and I know she's got this. Hopefully surfing is just like riding a bike;

something you never forget. But if she gets hurt out there, I'll lose my goddamn mind.

"Be careful!" I call after her, but she's too far out in the water to hear me now. I watch her swimming faster and faster until her graceful form suddenly pops up on her board and rides out a small surge. The wave wasn't spectacular, but it was special. Her first one since she's been freed.

"Your turn!" she says as she coasts in towards the beach and slides off her board and into the water.

I paddle out to the lineup, waiting for the perfect wave, which is the third one. Popping up on my board, I cruise along the water, the rushing sound of the ocean almost euphoric as I use my lower body to cut my board along the wave. I'm one with the ocean at that moment, and it's an amazing feeling. You feel powerful when you catch a big barreling wave; almost like you're controlling nature or just in the presence of something truly remarkable.

"Nice!" Selina calls out to me as I come swimming back towards her.

We take a few more turns catching waves, and I am growing obsessed with the smile on Selina's face. I haven't seen her smile this much since she arrived at the compound. A guy could get used to this.

Exhausted, I paddle back to the beach and crash on the sand. I'm watching Selina in the distance. She's gearing up to catch a perfect wave. The water crests, and she positions herself beautifully. But just as she begins gliding over the water, I notice movement out of the corner of my eye. Another surfer is breaking through the other end, trying to take Selina's wave. They're going to collide in the middle if they both keep going.

Waving my hands frantically, I yell, "Watch out!"

But it's too late.

The two boards hit each other, knocking both surfers off and into the water. Hard.

Selina goes under, and I lose track of her for several seconds.

With all of my strength against the waves, I swim as fast as I can out towards her. "Lina! Lina!" I call out, searching the murky water for a sign of her blonde hair.

Every second without her feels like a fucking eternity, and I'm beside myself, wading in the water and crying out her name.

Finally, she breaks through the surface, gasping for air. I swim over to her, dragging my board, which is still attached to my ankle by the leash, behind me, and gather her in my arms. "Are you okay?" I ask, checking her head for injuries.

"Yeah," she tells me, her eyes wide with lingering fear.

I know that probably scared the hell out of her. It scared the hell out of me too. I pull her close, holding her to me. "It's okay. You're okay," I tell her. "Can you swim back to shore with me?" I ask.

She gives me an unsteady nod.

On the way back, I see the surfer who crashed into her coming out of the water. "She had the right of way, dickhead!" I call out to him.

"Sorry, man! Didn't see her!" he calls back with his hands up in apology.

Muttering curses under my breath, I try to calm myself down. He's lucky we're on a public beach with witnesses. He might be losing a limb...or two if we were somewhere private. Hell, if I had my gun right now, I'd shoot the bastard right between the eyes. Looking up at the parking lot, I start to wonder if I can get a gun from one of the guards and make it back here in time.

"It's fine, Nico. I'm fine," Selina says, grabbing my face in her hands and forcing me to look at her. "Don't worry. I'm not hurt."

I stare into her blue and green eyes as my anger slowly begins to recede. "That guy would be dead right now if you were hurt," I confess to her fervently.

My words seem to affect her, but I can't read the expression on her face. "Just forget about him," she whispers before lowering her hands. And, fuck, if I don't miss her touch already. "I had fun. Even when I thought I was dying," she says with a grin.

I grimace at her words and then a dark chuckle erupts deep inside my chest. "You really are a little daredevil," I tell her. "First with the car and now with this." I'm starting to think she might enjoy the thrill a little too much. Fuck, I feel as if I aged ten years between today and the day she learned how to drive.

A sly grin slides onto her pretty face. Then she surprises the hell out of me by saying, "Give me, like, five minutes, and then we can go out again."

"You want to...go out again?" I ask, completely positive that I didn't hear her right somehow.

"Yeah, we still have a few hours before the sun sets," she says. "We always used to stay until sunset, remember?"

I nod slowly. Of course I remember. We would watch the sunset on the beach together after we spent hours surfing. Those days were some of the most magical moments of my life.

"Okay," I tell her. "We'll keep going if you feel up to it."

"I do," she says with a smile that lights up my whole fucking world.

I keep forgetting how strong my girl is. She's been through hell twice and back and fucking survived. Not many can say that.

We spend the rest of the afternoon riding wave after wave until we're both too tired to go back in the water. And when we watch the sun setting across the ocean, it feels like my life is finally complete and full of something other than despair, tragedy...and longing.

It's when we're climbing back in the van that I get an eerie feeling, like she's going to disappear again. The thought of her being ripped from my arms again has my chest aching and my stomach tying up in knots. I try to shake off the feeling, because I know if anyone tries to take her from me again, I will hunt them down and kill them with my own fucking bare hands.

Selina and I deserve some happiness in our lives. And I'm only happy when I'm with her. I just hope someday she feels the same way.

CHAPTER 28

Nicholas

ALDO ALERTS US early Saturday morning about a possible human trafficking situation not too far from here, and I make my way down into the control room. Thousands of servers line two of the walls in the back. There are several computer stations with multiple monitors, jammers, and all the other high-tech equipment and hardware that our resident hackers need to help us on our quest to hunt down the bad guys and bring them to justice.

Not that we aren't bad guys too in our own right. We are just doing some good to help balance out some of the bad.

I go to where Aldo is seated in front of five monitors. His skin is pale and his eyes look bloodshot behind his glasses. I would tell him he needs to get out more, but we both know he has no interest in the outside world. Aldo has been a loner for as long as I've known him. My dad hired him when he was young, probably around the age I am now. And he's been a real asset to the team in bringing down the seedy criminals who deal in the flesh trade while simultaneously protecting everyone staying here along with my family.

My father may have several drug rings and do his fair share of gunrunning, but he would never sell a human being for profit. That's where he draws the line. That's where we all draw the line. And since the bastards get away with selling young women and children more often than not, we have made it our lives' work to stop as many of them as we can. The government certainly can't stop them, and the police are usually being paid off to look the other way. So someone has to step up and bring these bastards down.

"What did you find?" I ask, taking a seat next to Aldo.

He runs a hand through his dark hair before he begins typing so fast I lose track of the movement of his fingers. "One of our drones caught some suspicious activity in this old, abandoned hospital. It's supposed to be empty and guarded, but it looks like it might be holding girls until their next shipment. Perhaps whoever is doing this paid off the regular security guard to keep quiet about it."

I stare at one of the monitors while he brings up feed from one of the drones. That's the great thing about technology. You can have eyes everywhere and all at once. It's crazy how the world is evolving so quickly. You just gotta try and keep up, and Aldo is always on top of the latest technological advances and gadgets.

At first, there's just grainy footage. But with a few keystrokes, Aldo has the video enhanced and zoomed in. Some big, bald guy is dragging a couple of young women into the decrepit building with boarded up windows. When the man emerges again, he locks the door behind him and leaves in a black, nondescript van.

"I'm going to send in a drone with infrared sensors to see how many heat signatures we can pick up inside. Most of the hospital is made of thick concrete and brick, so we probably won't get an exact number," he explains.

"But it's better than nothing." *And better than going in blind and risk being ambushed*, I think to myself.

"Exactly," he agrees. "We'll know a lot more in about twenty minutes or so," he tells me.

Just then, the door to the control room opens and in walks my father. While Aldo does his thing, I decide to fill my dad in on what's going on.

"We'll wait for the thermal info before we do anything," My dad suggests after I'm done talking.

"I want to lead the team," I tell him confidently.

He hesitates, his gray eyes pinning my own. "I don't know if you're in the right headspace right now, Nico. You know, with everything happening with Selina."

"It'll be good for me to get out and do this," I offer.

My father considers it for several seconds before giving me the go ahead. I've watched him lead a hundred different teams before, and now it's my turn. I know what is expected of me, and I know the danger that's involved. Extraction of these women won't be easy, by any means; and there's a good chance that someone will end up hurt…or worse.

But the reward always outweighs the risk. We're saving innocent lives. Nothing can surpass that.

∽

The abandoned hospital sits on the western end of the Rockaway peninsula in Queens. The beach that the hospital fronts is dead at this time of night, so we drive right over the sand and to one of the side gates with our vehicles packed full of our best men and enough firepower to take down whatever and whoever we find inside.

The fence is easily breeched; and once we're inside, all is quiet. Everyone knows what is expected of them from this point forward. We always plan ahead for every possible situation and outcome. But no matter how hard you prepare; something is always bound to go awry. I just hope that tonight is not one of those times.

Aldo sends me a text the moment we are inside the fence. I can faintly hear the drone above us, so I know he's searching for any potential hazards in the area as well as scanning for how many bodies are inside the hospital.

His text reads: **At least eight inside.**

Most of them are going to be helpless, scared women. But we won't know how many guards are here until we get in the building.

I hold up eight fingers, signaling the number of people to everyone before I motion for us to get ready to move in. Aldo didn't spot any motion detection cameras stationed anywhere on the property, so we have the element of surprise on our side. These fuckers won't know what hit them until it's too late.

I grab my Glock from behind my back and hold it steady in my right hand before we move to the back door of the main building.

Miner takes the lead, standing in front of the old, rusted door with his gun cocked. I've known Lance Miner since I was a teenager. He's a huge guy, ex-military and a total bad ass. He lives for missions like this. After his sister was sold into human trafficking and murdered, he dedicated his life to protect girls just like her. That's how he came under the employ of my father.

We became instant friends. Both of us were affected by the flesh trade when someone we loved was taken, and it changed our outlook on life. It changed us more than we let on. And tonight, he is the perfect person to lead this mission with me.

I hold up my fingers, counting down silently to my team.

Three...

Two...

One...

And after that, Miner kicks in the door and pushes through as he makes his way into the abandoned hospital.

The breach didn't seem to trigger any alarms, and we move silently through the dark hallway towards a light source and faint voices.

The closer we get, the louder the cries and voices grow.

"Please!" a woman calls out before I hear something that sounds like a fist hitting flesh.

The loud, tortured cry that follows the hit has my feet moving faster. The group moves with me fluidly like we're one entity. Our footsteps are silent. Our breathing is steady and slow.

When we reach the end of the hall, there is a large open room that looks like it used to be a waiting room. From our point of view, we can see two guards surrounding six women, who are tied to various chairs in the room. One of the guards is currently assaulting one of the girls, who is crying hysterically.

And when he raises his hand to strike her again, I take the shot without even second-guessing my decision.

The man's hand explodes in mid-air, and he screams out in agony. He reaches for a gun with his other hand, but it's too late. Miner is already on him, tackling him down to the ground.

My men take out the other man before he even has a chance to react. Two of them haul him outside, getting him away from the women.

"We need bolt cutters," Miner urgently requests from one of our men, who is carrying a backpack of tools. We didn't know what we would need, so we packed all the essentials.

When Samson hands Miner the bolt cutters, he begins working on the chains around one of the women who is bound to a chair near him.

The man whose hand was blown off begins to bellow in distress from the corner of the room. "Shut him the fuck up," I tell Samson, who in turns drives the butt of his gun into the man's face, effectively knocking him out cold.

The only sounds filtering through the room now are some muted cries from the women and the chains rattling as they're unceremoniously cut off. We work on freeing three of the women who look to be in bad shape, much worse than the others. Several of us carefully carry them out to an awaiting van while the others are left in the room momentarily.

Once the three women are safely in the van, Miner offers, "I'll go back in and secure the rest of the women."

I give him a nod. "I'll be there in a minute. Be careful," I tell him.

"Always," he says to me before disappearing into the dark building.

I'm sending a status update to Aldo on my phone when loud cackling from my right catches my attention. One of the men we captured is grinning and laughing, almost in full hysterics now as one of my guards searches his pants pockets.

"What the fuck are you laughing about?" I growl at him, taking a few steps closer.

That's when I see the man raise his hand. I only have a split second to react when I see the detonator tightly grasped in his palm. "Miner!" I scream, but it's too late.

There is a faint beeping sound before the entire building trembles and explodes, erupting into smoke and fire. The blast hits me, knocking me off my feet and throwing me into the side of the van where the women are. I vaguely hear their terrified screams as I fall to my hands and knees, the wind knocked out of my lungs.

Quickly, I try to recover and gather my wits. Glancing over at my men, I see that all of them are lying on the ground, but they all seem to be alive. My head is still spinning as I stand, and I quickly assess my body for damage. When I find no visible wounds, I run into the rubble that used to be the hospital. "Miner!" I call out, hoping to hear a response.

Someone follows behind me with a flashlight, the beam of light reflecting off the carnage. The three women are dead, their lifeless bodies covered in blood.

"Fuck," I grind out.

I hear someone grunting in pain, and I turn to see Miner under some rubble, his legs pinned and his chest moving in a weird rhythm as he stares up at the ceiling with wide eyes.

Kneeling down by his side, he reaches out for me, and I grip his hand in mine, holding it tightly. "You're gonna be okay," I grind out, but even I know his chances of leaving this place are not good.

His breathing is ragged and panicked. I can see fear in his eyes for the first time ever. He was always so damn strong and confident. His brown eyes slowly find my face and momentarily focus. "Take care…of my mom," he tells me as blood trickles from his mouth.

"I will," I give him my word.

He takes one last long gasp, and then his eyes go unfocused, the life slowly filtering out of them, and I know he's gone.

"Fuck," I hiss out between clenched teeth before reluctantly releasing his hand. Even though I know they're dead, I go to each of the women and check them for a pulse. I don't find a single heartbeat.

I'm covered in my friend's blood when I finally emerge from the hospital.

"Miner?" someone asks.

I shake my head solemnly. "Didn't make it. Neither did the rest of the women." I swallow hard. That is a jagged fucking pill to swallow. Not only did I lose my friend, but I also lost three innocent women I was in charge of protecting. They thought they were safe, and I let them down. They deserved so much better than this.

My hands curl into fists at my sides as I glance around, looking for one person in particular. And when my search comes up empty, I can feel my blood fucking boiling inside my veins. "Where is the man with the detonator?" I demand in a sneer.

"He escaped during the explosion," one of my men tell me, unable to even look me in the fucking eye.

"Find him," I tell several of the guards. "And don't you dare fucking come back to the compound without him."

I get a few affirmative nods before four of them take off running behind the building and two get in vehicles, the tires squealing as they fly down the road.

I hear sirens in the distance, and I know we have to move. The women that survived are our only concern now. I can't turn back time. I can't take back what was. I can't change anything. The only thing I can do now is move on and survive and make sure these women are okay.

We pack everything up and get in the van. I tell the driver, "Nearest hospital. Hurry!"

Once I make sure the women are safe at the hospital, then I'll return home. I don't know how to deal with what happened tonight. I'm so used to violence and death that it doesn't affect me as it once did; but Miner was a close friend of mine, and those women were innocent. This means more to me. Their deaths require vengeance. And I want to be the grim fucking reaper that brings them justice.

CHAPTER 29

Selina

IT'S LATE WHEN we get word that Nico and his men are on their way back to the compound. I've been holed up in my room all night with nothing but my nervous anticipation the only thing keeping me company. I worried for hours about so many things — about Nico risking his life for those poor women he was so desperate to save; and about the fact that he could be vulnerable from an attack from Constantine.

Even though I've kept my distance from Nico and made it some kind of mission to not taint him, I can't help my feelings for him. I loved him once. Maybe I can love him again. Sometimes I think I don't even know what love is anymore. The world has been cruel and unfair and full of monsters.

And a huge part of me thinks that he deserves better than what I can offer him. He deserves to be happy and with someone *normal*.

Sighing, I untuck my knees from my chest at the first sound of footsteps in the hall. My heartbeat stutters with every step. But when Nico passes by my open door without so much as a glance inside, the grin I had plastered on my face instantly falls.

Moving before I can even second-guess my decision, I follow him into his bedroom. He's standing in the middle of the room, unmoving, barely breathing, and I know something is horribly wrong.

"Nico?" I whisper his name before stepping around him to see his face.

The first thing I notice is the blood. *He's covered in blood.* My entire world starts to tilt on its axis, sending me into a tailspin as the memory of me drenched in *their* blood comes rushing back.

No, no, no, no.

I can't allow myself to break down right now. I need to help him. Yes, I must focus on that and only that one thing right now.

"Are you hurt?" I ask, my voice breaking.

He gives me an almost imperceptible shake of his head.

Okay, so it's not his blood. I swallow hard as I finally meet his eyes. The blank, distant look I see reflected in them scares me. He obviously had something terrible happen to him tonight.

Taking his hand in mine, I pull him towards me. He resists at first until I whisper, "Please, Nico." He finally relents, his feet moving slowly across the hardwood floor as I lead him to his en-suite bathroom.

Tears fill my eyes as I slowly undress him, the blood making his clothes sticky and crunchy. When he's completely naked, I go over to the shower and turn on the faucet, testing the water to make sure it's hot enough before I go back and coax him inside the stall.

Leaving him under the spray of water, I take off my clothes, piling them on the floor beside his before joining him in the large walk-in shower.

The water is tinged red from the blood as I gently wash his hands first. He stares down at the copper-colored water swirling in the drain, and I whisper to him, "It's okay. I'm here with you. I'm right here."

God, I wish I would have had someone back then to take care of me after Constantine made me wear the blood of the family he murdered like some kind of fucked-up trophy and grim reminder of what happened. I didn't have Nico back then, but he has me here now. And I'm going to help him through this.

I grab the bottle of shampoo from a recessed shelf and squirt some in my hands before lathering up his hair. I scrub his scalp gently, and he closes his eyes.

I help him rinse his hair then, wiping the water from his face. His gray eyes blink open and focus on me then. "I couldn't...I couldn't save them," he says, his voice just above a whisper, so soft I almost don't hear it.

"I'm sure you did everything you could," I tell him even though I don't know the whole story. All I have to go on is the devastated look on his face, and that's enough for now. I know he tried his best even without him telling me anything.

"There was a bomb," he says, and my heart skips a beat. "Miner went back in. I let him go back in." He shakes his head and squeezes his eyes shut. "I should have gone back in. It should have been me, not him."

I grab his face in my hands and force him to look at me. "No, Nico. Then *you* would be dead." I can't even imagine a world without Nico in it. In fact, the thought terrifies me so much that I find myself shaking under the hot water. It might as well be ice cold on my skin.

Nico doesn't speak any more while I continue to wash him until every speck of blood is gone. When we're done, I pull him from the shower and dry him off first before myself.

I wrap a towel around my body and grab his hand, leading him into his bedroom. He's so despondent, it's scary. I've never seen Nico this way before.

Pulling back the blankets on his bed, I coax him under them before covering him up. And then I go to the other side and crawl under with him. He rolls over onto his side, facing away from me, and

I curl up against his back, wrapping my arms around him and holding him. He's tense at first, his muscles bunching up from my touch, but they slowly start to relax when he realizes I'm not going anywhere.

"Try to sleep," I whisper into the darkness. I know it will be hard, but I'm sure he's mentally exhausted after what he went through tonight.

It takes hours, but I finally feel his breathing even out. And only when I'm sure he's asleep do I allow myself to drift off too.

CHAPTER 30

Nicholas

I WAKE UP the next morning alone. Selina is nowhere to be found in my room, and it almost seems like it was all a dream. But I specifically remember her making me shower before putting me to bed and curling up behind me. Feeling her arms around me made me feel so good...and loved. And after everything that happened, she somehow knew exactly what I needed.

Just then my door opens, and my dream girl walks in with a tray full of breakfast food. "Good morning," she says, her soft, pink lips teased into a little grin. "I figured we could eat breakfast in your room."

She sets the tray down at the foot of the bed and watches me carefully. She sets a glass of orange juice on the nightstand beside me, and I reach out and grab her hand. "Thank you for last night," I tell her vehemently.

"It's not a big deal," she says, playing it off before slowly pulling away and wringing her hands nervously in front of her.

"Yes, it is, Lina."

"You would have done the same thing for me back then if you could have," she says with a small shrug.

Her words hit me like a thousand bricks. Back then, when Constantine murdered that family in front of her. Oh fuck, no wonder she knew just what I needed. She went through the same fucking thing almost. *Except she was all alone.*

I throw the blankets off and curse when I realize I'm naked. Walking over to my dresser, I slip on a pair of boxer briefs and sweats before returning to the bed where she's currently sitting.

She picks up a croissant and tears it apart with her delicate fingers as she eats it slowly. I stare at the food and a part of me wonders if I can even eat. After last night, I feel like my world has been turned upside down. We lost one of our best men, and those poor women...

Fuck.

I squeeze my eyes shut.

I feel Lina's hand over mine, bringing me out of my torturous thoughts. And when I open my eyes, she's staring at me with a worried expression on her face.

"Your mother talked to me this morning about last night," she says softly. "None of what happened is your fault," she tells me fervently.

Slowly, I nod my head, but I don't know if I totally feel that way. I was leading the team, so technically everything that happens falls on me. None of us could have predicted that outcome, however. Not even Aldo detected the danger, and he's usually on top of everything. He's probably blaming himself even more than I am at this point.

"Here," she says. I look down at the fresh croissant in her other hand as she waves it towards me. "Please eat."

I take it and bite off a chunk before chewing and swallowing. After Lina finishes hers, I watch her stand and walk to one of the windows. She perches on the ledge and stares outside, closing her eyes now and then, and I wish I could crawl into her mind right now. I want to know all of her thoughts and feelings, her secrets. I desperately want to be able to figure her out.

I take a few swigs of orange juice and pick at the rest of the breakfast tray before giving up. I'm just not hungry, but I think I ate enough to pacify Lina. When I focus my attention back on her, she's not at the window anymore, but instead looking at a small charcoal drawing in a frame on the wall. That was the first drawing I did after she was taken.

"Is this...me?" she questions.

I try to gauge her reaction before I answer, but she gives me absolutely nothing as she turns her head and blinks at me. "Yes," I finally tell her.

"Do you have any more?" she asks.

Swallowing hard, I give her a nod.

"Show me."

Standing, I walk out of the room. I hear her soft footfalls behind me, so I continue down the hall. I set up my studio in this wing years ago. It was my mother's idea really. I think we both knew how therapeutic it was for me after Selina was taken.

I open the door and allow Selina to walk in first. I hear her small gasp and inwardly cringe. Fuck, I hope she doesn't think I'm some sort of creep.

Walking in behind her, I try to imagine the room through her eyes.

Hundreds of sketches and charcoal drawings, even paintings of her face are scattered through the small space. Most of them are from when she was younger. Some of them are what I imagined she would look like as she grew older. She's beautiful, but the paintings don't hold a candle to the real thing. Lina is so much more stunning in real life.

"I tried to imagine what you would look like as you aged alongside of me," I explain to her. My hand rubs the back of my neck nervously as I wait for her to say something...*anything*.

She takes her time, walking through the room and looking at each and every drawing and painting. Not all of them are of her face, though. No, some are of animals, landscapes, or ocean waves at sunset. "Nico, these are...incredible," she finally says.

It feels like I can suddenly breathe again, and I blow out a sigh of relief. "Thank you," I tell her.

"May I ask why you painted so many portraits of me?"

I hesitate before answering. "It's because I missed you so much, Lina. And I...I didn't want to ever forget you." My mom only managed to take a few photos of Selina while she lived here, but the photos weren't enough. I needed *more*. And painting her made her seem more real. Sometimes it felt like she was only a dream while she was here.

She turns to me as I walk over to her. I stare down at her beautiful face. "When you disappeared, I wanted your memory to live on, not only with me but with everyone who saw my art. I never wanted the world to forget how wonderful you were and how special you were to me."

Tears fill her pretty eyes as she stares up at me. Before I can stop myself, I cup her soft cheek with the palm of my hand. My thumb slowly caresses her bottom lip. It's so soft and delicate. Fuck, I want to kiss her. I'm so fucking desperate to kiss her, to touch her. But I need her permission first. I don't want to ever just *take* anything from her. And even more than that, I want her to trust me enough to give me her consent.

It feels like a strong magnetic pull unlike anything I've ever felt before bringing us closer as she rises up on her tiptoes, her mouth so close to mine that I can feel her breath on my lips. Just as her mouth gently brushes against mine, my phone rings, ruining the moment. And as if we were both caught in some sort of trance, which suddenly broke, she goes back down on her heels and takes a step back, worrying her bottom lip between her teeth.

"Sorry," I mutter quickly. Cursing, I pull my phone out of my pocket and answer it. I listen to my father on the other end of the call.

"Nico, meet us in the basement. We found the man responsible for the bomb last night."

"I'll be right there," I tell him before ending the call. Turning to Selina, I frown. She looks so damn beautiful it physically hurts. "I have to go."

"It's okay," she tells me with a forced smile. I can tell she was just as affected by our intimate contact as I was. "Is it all right if I stay here a little while longer?" she asks, surprising me.

"Sure. You can stay as long as you'd like." With one last look at her, I turn and leave. I hate to leave her alone right now after the moment we just shared, but a more pressing matter is present now. All of the pent-up anger I've been having as of late is about to be released…and I can't wait to get my revenge.

CHAPTER 31

Nicholas

BELOW THE CONTROL room is a deeper, darker, soundproofed basement that my father had created for his "extracurricular" activities. As soon as I open the hatch for the stairs, I can hear a man screaming. A satisfied grin appears on my face as I go down the steps, taking my time and relishing in the sounds of a man getting his justice.

There are a few separate concrete rooms with a drain in the center of each. It makes cleanup a little easier with being able to hose down the blood...and other stuff. When I round the corner, I see that Benito and my father are in the room with the man. I move my head from side to side, cracking my neck, ready to take over. My father narrows his eyes on me when I walk in, but he knows I'm old enough for this shit. I don't let them baby me like they do with Aria. This isn't my first time dealing with scum, and it certainly won't be my last.

"Has he talked yet?" I ask my father, who, in turn, shakes his head.

"Your mother and I are going to the hospital to check on the surviving women. We'll be back later." He clasps a hand on my shoulder and gives it a strong squeeze. He doesn't say another word, but I know he's silently asking me to get the information we want...no matter what needs to happen.

Once he leaves, I turn to the guy, who is strung up in the center of the room. His pale skin is covered in a sheen of sweat, and his eyes dart around the room anxiously.

I go over to the corner of the room where all of my usual instruments are. I select a pair of rusty pliers first before returning to our captive. "What's your name?" I ask him.

"Trey," he offers easily enough through chattering teeth.

"Well, Trey, it looks like you and I are going to be spending a lot of time together down here," I tell him nonchalantly before I reach for one of his feet. The sickening sound of his toenail being ripped off by the pliers numbs my soul as he unleashes a horrendous scream. "What we need from you is simple," I tell him before ripping off another nail. "We want to know who you work for. We want to know the location of their operations, and we want to know anything else you feel obligated to tell us." I stare him in the eye as I grip another toenail in the pliers. "And I will keep going until I get all of the above information."

"Please!" he begs as I tear off another toenail.

Once all five are gone, I start on the other foot. It becomes a methodical process now, and I tune out his screams until I'm finished with both feet.

Returning the pliers to the table, I search the instruments of torture for something that will make him squeal. My eyes land on an object that always worked in the past, and mind made up, I pick it up.

The electric drill whirls, the large masonry drill bit spinning wildly when I push the button and turn to Trey whose eyes widen.

"No, man. No, no, no, no. Please!" he begs as I step closer to him.

"It doesn't have to be like this, Trey," I tell him simply. "Tell me who you work for, and this can all be over quickly."

Trey trembles all over, his body violently shaking as his bloody toes drag across the concrete floor. "I can't! He'll kill me!"

"*I'll* kill you!" I tell him through gritted teeth. "I don't think you fully understand your predicament here, Trey."

He shakes his head back and forth vehemently. He's not ready to talk yet. But he will be. Soon.

The drill whirs, and I choose his thigh to start inflicting the damage. If he begins to bleed out too much, we can always cut off limbs and cauterize them to stop the bleeding. I wouldn't want his life ending too soon...or too easily. And I will not let him perish before I get everything I want out of this man.

The large drill bit digs into his meaty thigh, and he cries out in anguish as it goes straight down to the bone.

I'm quick and precise as I drill a few more gaping holes into his body. And when Trey's screams suddenly stop, I realize he passed out.

"Throw some water on him," I tell Benito, who nods at my request. "I want Trey awake for every fucking minute of this."

He's going to suffer until I get what I want. And then I'm going to torture him even after that, because I know that's what Miner would have done for me had it been the other way around.

~

Selina is waiting in the hallway for me, surprising the fuck out of me. It's well after midnight, and she should have been sound asleep in her bed. She's perched on the edge of a chair, which she must have dragged into the hall, with a worried look on her face. I've been gone for hours...or, hell, maybe even a whole day or more. I don't know for sure. Without any windows or clocks, it's easy to lose track of time down there.

"Who...whose blood is that?" she questions with a concerned look on her face.

Fuck, that's twice now she's seen me covered in someone else's blood. I know it brings back bad memories for her, but I honestly thought she'd be in bed by now. I didn't think I would even see her on the way back to my room, but she must have decided to wait for me. And I don't even know how I feel about that in this moment. I'm still shaken up, still angry...still *everything* other than what I should be in her presence.

"Go to bed, Lina," I growl at her. I'm not in the mood to pacify her right now. Adrenaline is still rushing through my body after I just killed a man. And even though he suffered greatly, I still feel like his death was too merciful, too quick. My revenge hasn't been sated, and it courses through my veins like poison. I'm still full of anger and hate, and I refuse to take any of those emotions out on her. She doesn't fucking deserve that.

"Nico, wait." She chases me down the hall and stops me before I can make it to my bedroom door. "Don't shut me out," she pleads.

"I'm not shutting you out," I tell her with a sigh. Closing my eyes, I grit out, "I just want to take a shower and go the fuck to bed."

"Did you murder the man who killed those women and your friend?" she questions in a whisper.

"Yes," I growl without an ounce of remorse for his death. And then I open my eyes and focus on her beautiful face. "Even though I do some good things in my life, Lina, I'm still the bad guy. Never forget that," I tell her before pushing past her into my room.

She doesn't follow me into the bathroom, and for that I'm grateful. I shower quickly and thoroughly, scrubbing off the dead man's blood from my skin. He was hard to crack, but everyone cracks eventually in the end. When you realize you have nothing left to lose and feel your life slipping away before your eyes, then the skeletons hiding in your closet begin to slowly pour out of your fucking soul.

We got the information we needed. With Constantine Carbone really no longer a threat here in New York since he started his affairs overseas, there is a new, up-and-coming mob boss dipping his toes into the flesh trade waters. We're sending one of his men back to him in pieces as a message that we're not going to tolerate this shit in our city. We're cutting the head off the fucking snake before it can slither its way into the dark underground and try to establish a good, solid position before striking.

I've made it my mission in life to save girls like Selina from the monsters in this world, and I'll be damned if anyone deals in human trafficking in this city while I'm living and breathing.

While I was hard at work making that man suffer, we got word that the girls at the hospital are now all in stable condition. That almost makes all of this horror show worth it, but then I think about the ones we couldn't save, and Miner. They shouldn't have died like that. I should have been able to save them all. I was head of that team, so the responsibility of their wellbeing falls on my shoulders. It's my fucking fault, and I will carry the burden of their untimely deaths for the rest of my life.

When I'm done showering, I climb out, dry off and wrap a towel around my waist. Selina is standing in my bedroom, waiting.

I'm about to open my mouth to tell her to go back to bed, but she quickly asks, "Did that man suffer before you killed him?"

"Yes," I tell her simply. "He suffered...immensely," I say with a sickening satisfaction that I gave some semblance of justice to the innocent people he killed.

"Good," she responds, surprising the hell out of me. Coming closer until she's standing right in front of me, she leans up on her tiptoes and places a soft kiss on my cheek. "You did good, Nico," she tells me before leaving my room.

I release a breath I didn't know I was holding, still reeling from the touch of her lips against my skin. For some reason, having Selina's affirmation makes me feel better, even if only minutely. I wanted to save them all, but what's done is done. At least I can help the ones that survived. We can give them a better life, a future. And for that, I am grateful. And because of Selina, it feels like a great weight has been lifted off my chest and that I can breathe again.

Lina always did have that effect on me — even on the darkest of days, she would be the tiny ray of sunshine that I needed to make it through. She's like this beacon of light guiding me home even when I'm feeling so far gone and lost that I don't know if I'll ever make it back on my own.

CHAPTER 32

Selina

A FEW DAYS after the rescue mission went awry, Mrs. Vitale suggested that I go to the hospital with her to speak to the three women who survived. I was reluctant at first, but I ultimately agreed to go. I don't know how well I'll be able to help anyone, considering I can barely help myself most days, but I just can't say no to Nico's family after all they've done for me. If Verona Vitale wanted me to jump off a bridge, I would probably do it because I owe them so much. I feel indebted to them. I truly owe them my life. And since she's not asking me to do something impossible or dangerous, I can, at the very least, do this for her.

Two of the women are being housed in a room together on the tenth floor of the hospital while another is still in the ICU. The elevator ride is quiet, and I glance over at Nico several times. He insisted on coming, and I feel a bit calmer knowing he's here with me. He's wearing a dark blue tailored suit, and he looks devastatingly handsome.

Reaching out, I grab his hand, and the reassuring squeeze I feel in response gives me all the strength I need to get through today. "You've got this," he tells me, his lips tilting up.

Verona went on ahead of us to the tenth floor, wanting to speak with the two women first while Nico and I go to the ICU on the fourth.

"The woman in the ICU suffered longer and endured a lot more than the others," Nico explains to me. I can see now why Verona wanted me to speak with her specifically. "Her name is Lauren. She's currently under twenty-four-seven surveillance in a room, because she keeps trying to harm herself."

I cringe at his words. Lauren clearly doesn't want to be in this world any longer. I can relate with that feeling all too well, and it takes me back to a time when I was in that kind of desperate state. *I never want to feel like that again,* I think to myself as a shudder runs through me.

"If you're uncomfortable, you know you don't have to do this, Lina," Nico assures me.

But I refuse to let my dark, painful memories drag me down into a deep pit of despair. Instead, I square my shoulders, hold my head up high and tell him, "I want to talk to her."

"That's my girl," he says with a smile.

The elevator beeps, and the doors slowly open up to the fourth floor. We step out together, and I grip Nico's hand even tighter in mine, not wanting to let go. I need his strength right now to get me through this. Dealing with Lauren's trauma will no doubt bring my own memories roaring back to life.

We walk down the hall and stop in front of the room that Lauren is currently in. Nico turns to me. "You can do this," he tells me confidently before pulling me close and placing a kiss on my forehead, his hands flexing at my waist as he holds me.

My breath catches in my throat. He's so close, but I want to pull him impossibly closer, crawl inside of him and never leave. If I've learned anything over the past several weeks I've been free from Constantine, it's that Nico is the only man I have ever trusted and probably the only one I ever will.

"I'll be right down the hall if you need me," he says before slowly releasing me and walking away.

Taking several deep breaths, I steel my nerves before I gently knock on the doorframe and then proceed into the room. I take note of the security camera mounted to the ceiling, watching Lauren's every move. Right now she's lying in bed, staring out the window. Her curly brown hair is up in a messy ponytail, and she looks thin, malnourished. She's breathing so shallowly that for a moment I think she might not even be taking air into her lungs.

"Hello," I say softly, not wanting to spook her just in case she didn't hear my knock. "My name is Selina."

"They told me you were coming to talk to me today," she utters.

"What else did they tell you?" I ask, curiosity getting the better of me.

"They said you would understand what I'm going through." She turns to me then, and I stare at the bruises littering her pretty face. I school my features quickly and move a little closer before taking a seat near her bed. "Do you?" she asks.

"Yes. I know exactly what you are going through right now," I tell her honestly. "I was held captive for ten years by a human trafficker who bought me," I confess. God, when I say those words out loud, it sounds crazy, but that is my story. I'm just grateful I can talk about it in the past tense now.

"Ten years," she says in astonishment. "I was only gone for six or seven months. I can't even imagine that long," she says with a shake of her head. "So you *do* understand," she says with finality, like maybe she initially thought I wouldn't. I get where she's coming from. Not many women have been in our shoes.

"I'm here to talk or just to listen," I offer. And then I quickly add,

"Only if you want to." I don't want to pressure her into doing anything she doesn't want to do.

Her eyes close momentarily. "The things they did to me..." Her voice trails off as she stares out the window with a vacant look in her eyes.

Surprising even myself, I cover Lauren's hand with mine gently, coaxing her back to the present. She glances towards me again, blinking her eyes. "You're safe now. Things will get better. I promise," I tell her confidently.

"It feels like the darkness is just going to swallow me whole," she tells me with tears in her eyes before pulling her hand away from mine to curl into herself. "And sometimes...I want to let it. I want to disappear," she whispers, her voice full of sadness and grief.

"I'm not going to let that happen. I won't let you disappear," I tell her adamantly. "There is a light at the end of that very dark tunnel, Lauren, trust me. I was lost, just like you. I wanted to die every single day when I was with my captor. But I held on. For what? I didn't know at the time. But now I know. I held on so that I could be here, with people that I care for, with people that...love me." It's hard to say the L word, but I manage to get it past the lump forming in my throat. For so long, I felt unwanted, unloved. And it's hard to imagine a world in which people care about me, maybe even love me for just being *me*.

The girl releases a sob from her lips. "I would like to see my grandma again. She was always so sweet to me. I don't know why I ran away from home. I'm sure I broke her heart," she says, her bottom lip trembling as she stifles her cries. "I don't think she'll ever forgive me for running away."

My heart breaks for the young woman. "Would you forgive your grandmother if she had been the one to run away?" I ask her.

Lauren pauses, and I can see her expression morph from sadness to understanding. "I would forgive her for anything," she whispers.

"Then don't you think she would forgive you too?" Her face crumbles, but this time I can see the joy behind her tears. I press forward. "I think she would be happy to see you again, Lauren. Don't you?"

The girl breaks down then. "She would be so happy."

"See? There is always a light at the end of that tunnel. Keep that in mind."

The girl reaches her hand out towards me, and I take it, gripping it gently. We sit in silence for a while before Lauren finally speaks. She tells me story after story about her and her grandmother, and I hang on to every word, listening with rapt attention.

"Do you...do you think someone could call her for me? To let her know that I'm here. That I'm okay."

"Of course," I tell her without hesitation. The two of them clearly had an unspeakable bond, and I can't wait to see the two of them reunited.

After writing down her grandmother's number, Lauren seems calmer, like she's been able to alleviate most of the stress and anguish that had been weighing her down. And later, when she falls asleep peacefully, I finally leave her room. Instantly, I feel different. Lighter. Like I'm floating. I believe I really made Lauren feel better; that I actually helped someone who has gone through some of the same things I have.

Just like my words had comforted Lauren, they comforted me as well. And in that moment, something inside of me changes. I'm tired of running away. I'm tired of not living.

Like I told Lauren, there is always a light at the end of the tunnel, no matter how dark or endless it seems. Nico is my light. And I'm drawn to him just like a moth is drawn to a flame. I don't even care if I catch fire when I reach my destination. I just want to be as close to him as possible, basking in his warmth, in his glow. And I know I can trust him to keep me from burning up. Nico would protect me at all costs. I know that now.

Nicholas

In the security room, I watched the entire interaction Selina had with Lauren. I was enamored by the way she brought the girl from the edge of darkness and back into the light. Selina is the strongest woman I know, by far, and today definitely proved it.

Just like my mother told me earlier, this is Selina's calling, her true purpose in life. She can help these women that we rescue just by being a kindred soul to them; someone they can look up to and trust. Selina knows exactly what they've gone through, and there aren't many therapists or doctors who can relate to their patients on that kind of level.

"You did great today, Lina," I tell her when we get back to the compound.

"You really did," my mom agrees. "Those girls have something they didn't have before."

"What's that?" Lina questions.

"Hope. Hope for a better future, for a better life. They want to make your success story their story too."

"I hope they can achieve everything they dream of and more," Lina says fervently.

"We'll make sure of it. I want you to help me make sure of it," my mother offers.

Lina gives her an emphatic nod. "I want that too."

When we get inside, Lina says, "Even though it's getting late, I would like to call Lauren's grandmother for her."

"Sure thing." I lead her into the library and then pull my cell phone out of my pocket and hand it to her.

She stares at it with trepidation, like she's looking at a foreign object, and I realize my mistake. Lina hasn't had much experience with cell phones, especially not the latest technology. I doubt if Constantine ever let her use a phone, let alone even get close to one.

Pulling my cell back to me, I ask her, "What's the number? I'll dial it for you."

A relieved look is on Lina's face as she recites the number on the piece of paper, which she holds tightly in her hands like a little lifeline. I know she's going to be nervous to call Lauren's grandmother, but I'm hopeful that the conversation goes well, not only for Lauren's sake, but also for Lina. I can see the optimism in her eyes, and I don't want anything to ruin that.

I hand the phone to Lina when it starts to ring, and she holds it up to ear, nervously gnawing on her bottom lip as she waits for an answer.

Someone on the other end finally picks up, and I hear a faint voice before Lina asks, "Is this Gloria?" A smile graces Lina's beautiful face, and my own face mirrors her expression. "You don't know me, but I know your granddaughter." She pauses. "Yes, Lauren. I spoke with Lauren this afternoon, and she's in the hospital —."

I can hear the grandmother's worried, erratic voice on the other end, and Lina pulls the phone away from her ear for a moment. After the grandmother calms down a bit, Lina continues. "Lauren would love to speak with you, maybe even see you."

"We can arrange the meeting," I whisper to her, and Lina relays my words to Gloria.

"Okay, great. I'll be in touch. Yes, yes, I'll call you first thing tomorrow," she says with a wide grin. She hands the phone back to me, and I end the call.

"It sounds like it went well," I tell her.

"Very well. I can't wait to see the two of them reunited. I really think Lauren will be in much better spirits after she sees her grandmother."

"I think so too." Tucking my cell phone away in my pocket, I walk over to Lina and put my hands on her upper arms, gently squeezing. "You did good, Lina," I tell her, mimicking the words she said to me just the other night. "No, fuck that. You did amazing today," I say, which earns me an ear-splitting grin.

"Your mom mentioned me helping out with the paperwork for the women and trying to help them get reunited with their families. I think I would really like to do that," she says while tucking a piece of hair behind her ear.

"And I think you would be perfect for the job." I can't think of anything better for Selina to do. I really do think this is her calling in life, and she's going to be amazing at it.

CHAPTER 33

Nicholas

I'M IN THE kitchen with my father when I ask him, "Where's Mom and Selina?" It's been a few days since the hospital visit, and the two of them have been MIA together a lot. I miss the hell out of Selina, but I know what she's doing is probably important and related to the women we rescued.

My dad shrugs. "Library I think," he tells me.

Carrying a tray of food and drinks for them, I walk into the library on the first floor of the compound. I'm surprised to see my mother and Selina hunched over a desk, poring over paperwork. My mom is on the phone, speaking with someone in hushed tones, so I motion with my head for Selina to come over to me when she looks up and sees me walking in.

"What's going on?" I ask as I set down the tray on a nearby table.

"I'm working with your mom on trying to reunite the girls in the hospital with their families."

"Oh, that's great, Lina," I tell her. She really took my advice to heart and is doing what she feels is right. "I told you that you'd be perfect for the job."

She smiles shyly and says, "You were right. I think this kind of work really suits me."

"So, the women are still in the hospital?" I ask.

She nods. "Your parents are paying for the medical bills. They're amazing like that."

I'm practically beaming with pride. My parents are incredible. Not many people would help others financially, especially people they've never met. But my parents don't bat an eye when they save these women from dire situations and then help them beyond what any ordinary person would do.

"Lauren is going to be moving back in with her grandmother as soon as she gets released by her doctor," Lina informs me with the biggest grin I've ever seen on her face.

"You did it," I tell her. She reunited the two of them, and now Lauren doesn't have to worry about her grandmother not wanting to be part of her life. "I'm so fucking proud of you, Lina," I tell her sincerely.

"Thank you," she says, blushing furiously at my praise.

"I'll let you girls get back to work but make sure you get something to eat. Okay?" I ask, motioning to the tray.

"Okay," she says before grabbing a sandwich and taking a bite. She closes her eyes and hums in approval. "I was starving," she says, her tongue snaking out to lick mayonnaise from her lip.

And, fuck, if that wasn't the sexiest thing I've ever seen in my life.

My cock instantly grows hard behind my zipper. Clearing my throat, I tell her, "Well, I better go."

"Maybe we can do a movie night again later?" she asks, surprising the hell out of me since the last time didn't exactly go so well.

"Uh, sure. That would be great," I tell her with a smile.

"Okay, great. Well, I better get back to work," she tells me.

"All right. See you later," I promise.

Fuck, I can't wait for movie night with Lina.

∽

Selina

"Draw me like one of your French girls, Jack," I tell Nico. We just finished watching *Titanic*, and it was amazing. I know it's considered to be an old movie to a lot of people, but I was seeing it with fresh eyes. And even though Nico admitted to having already watched it a few times before because his sister used to be obsessed with Leonardo DiCaprio, he still humored me by sitting through the almost three-and-a-half-hour-long movie with me without complaining even once.

His lips tilt up from my butchered movie quote as he flips to a fresh piece of paper in his wire-bound pad and props it up on a vintage drawing table in the corner of his bedroom. His thick fingers pick up a piece of charcoal, and his piercing gray eyes meet mine, unnerving me. "Just relax," he whispers.

I swallow hard and try to do just that on the leather armchair opposite of him. When I first proposed that he draw me like Jack did with Rose on Titanic, I thought it would be fun. But with the electricity circulating through the room that has my hair standing on edge and thick tension in the room that you could cut with a knife, now I'm not so sure this was a good idea.

This feels so much more...intimate. He's staring at me like he's truly seeing me, and I feel vulnerable. Even though I'm fully clothed, I feel completely naked under his intense gaze.

Sweat beads on my forehead, and I find myself squirming uncomfortably.

A dark chuckle sounds from behind the drawing table. "You

don't have to stay completely still, Lina. You can move...and breath," Nico reassures me with a gentle smile.

"I know," I say with a roll of my eyes. And just like that, it feels like most of the tension has fled the room just by him joking around. I try to force myself to relax. I'm thinking way too much into this moment. Nico is simply drawing me. No big deal, right?

My eyes focus on the movement of his long, thick fingers as they delicately blend shadows against the paper. My thighs clench together, and I realize I'm getting turned on by this.

"Have you done this before?" I ask him, curious. And I'm surprised by the bite of nervousness gnawing at my stomach in anticipation of his answer.

"No. I usually just draw and paint from memory," he admits.

For some reason, that makes me feel better...and less jealous. *Oh god, why would I even be jealous about that?* I think to myself. Maybe it's because a selfish part of me wants something intimate and special between just Nico and I and no one else.

My breathing becomes shallow as I watch him watching me with an intense, direct stare that has my heart beating in a strange pattern. *God, if we're not done soon, I'm going to develop some sort of heart murmur.*

A few minutes later, Nico, thankfully, tells me, "Finished."

I hop up and practically run over to him, anxious to see what he just drew. I stare at the charcoal drawing, my eyes narrowing at the beautiful girl. I can barely see me on the canvas unless I really focus hard on all the little details, like my freckles. "This is how you see me?" I ask.

"What do you mean? That *is* you, Lina."

I suck my bottom lip into my mouth, chewing on it with my teeth nervously. He can't be serious. The girl he just drew is beautiful, almost ethereal, and...*happy*. I'm none of those things. Or am I? *Am I happy?*

When I stare down at Nico's gray eyes, reflecting myself back in them, I think maybe I am happy with him...or at least I could be if I

KEEPING MY GIRL

let myself give in to what I'm feeling. Nico definitely doesn't make me feel unwanted or miserable. How fucked up is it that I can't even tell when I'm actually truly happy?

Nico must notice a change in my mood because he says, "You don't like the drawing?"

"No. I love it. I just...I don't see myself like you see me I guess," I mutter, feeling stupid that I can't even look at a drawing of myself without feeling a million horrible things.

"Lina," he starts. Then, he grabs my hand, gripping my index finger tightly in his grip. Together, we trace over my eyebrows, my eyes, the charcoal coating my fingertip. He takes me through the process, tracing over every one of his lines. "You're beautiful, Lina," he murmurs. "This is how I see you. And this is how the entire world sees you."

Turning to him, I straddle his lap, my legs falling to either side of his thighs. Swallowing hard, I muster up enough courage to speak. "I don't care how the entire world sees me. I only care about you," I confess.

He stares at me for a second, his eyes locked on mine. His charcoal-covered fingers grasp onto my face, and then he pulls me towards him. "Tell me I can kiss you, Lina. Please," he pleads with me.

He's asking for permission instead of just taking what he wants, and my heart soars with his words. He knows exactly what I need. And right now all I need is him. "Kiss me, Nico," I beg.

Our lips meet in a smoldering kiss. His thumb gently strokes over the small heart-shaped birthmark on my neck, and memories of our first kiss when we were teenagers come flooding back, hitting me with an unspeakable force.

A tiny spark kindles somewhere deep within me, making my pulse drift between my thighs. I'm panting wildly when we break the kiss and I look into his steel gray eyes. "It feels just like I remember," I whisper. Closing my eyes, I ask him, "Nico, can I tell you something?"

"Anything," he answers with a relaxed sigh.

Then, I open my eyes and meet his intense gaze. "You're the only person I've ever kissed. I refused to kiss anyone else. I wanted that to be a piece of me that no one else could ever have. I wanted you to own that part of me."

My tongue slowly edges over my bottom lip, and Nico watches the movement with rapt attention. I get a hint of the fire stoking in his eyes as my only warning before his hand grips the back of my head and he pulls my mouth to his once again. This time the kiss isn't so sweet and innocent. No, it's heated, all-consuming, soul-searing and threatening to ruin me for all other men on this earth. No one else will ever kiss me like this. And I don't want anyone else to ever try. I only want Nico.

His large hands cup my ass, grinding me down on his erection through his clothes. I gasp at the sensation, and he takes advantage, his tongue delving into my mouth hungrily. His tongue ravages mine as he devours me, swallowing the little moans that keep bubbling up from my throat.

His right hand slides from my backside to the apex of my thighs, his fingertips tracing the seam of my lips through my shorts and panties. "I want to taste you, Lina," he grinds out. "Can I taste you?" he asks, staring at me so desperately that I'm almost rendered speechless.

"Yes," I whisper before I can stop myself.

Gripping my thighs, he stands with me in his arms. I quickly wrap my legs around his waist as he carries me to his bed. My back hits the soft pile of sheets and comforters as he gently lays me down and stands at the edge, looking at me like I'm something delicious he wants to feast upon.

Oh god.

A shudder runs through me as he slowly pulls my shorts and panties off my hips and down my legs in one sweep. And then he gets on his knees, his head lining up perfectly with the apex of my thighs.

His charcoal-covered hands grip my thighs and bring me closer to his mouth, leaving dark finger-shaped marks behind on my skin. His tongue darts out and licks over his lips as his hungry eyes meet mine. "Is this okay?" he asks.

Again, he's making sure I'm all right, that he has my consent, and I can't even describe the feelings blooming inside of my chest at that moment. No one ever cared enough to ask for my permission before. And it's almost like I can't even breathe right now because I'm overwhelmed with the myriad of emotions flowing through my veins. All I can do is nod emphatically.

A slow, lazy grin spreads across his face as he gently spreads my legs wider to accommodate him. He hikes one of my legs up over his shoulder and buries his mouth against my tender flesh, licking me from entrance to clit, sending stars shooting behind my eyes as I moan.

His tongue flattens against my swollen, little nub, licking and tasting me until I'm crying out nonsensical words. I've never had anyone give me this type of pleasure before. It's never been about me in the past. It's always been about what pleasure my body could give someone else.

My hands reach out, grabbing onto the bedding and balling it into my clenched fists. My thighs quiver as I squirm and throb against his tongue. "Please!" I beg, my voice hoarse and full of lust.

"Mmm, fuck, Lina," his deep voice growls, reverberating against my flesh. "I love to hear you beg for me," he says before he flicks his tongue against my aching clit, setting my blood on fire, the warm glow of orgasm starting to spread within every nerve of my body.

As I'm getting closer to the edge, a bubble of panic begins to rise in my chest. My breathing picks up its pace until I'm struggling to get enough air in my lungs and it feels like I'm starting to drown.

"Hey," Nico says calmly. "Look at me. Focus on me, Lina. It's just you and me here. No one else."

"No one else," I say with a shudder. I stare into his eyes as he dips his head down to feast upon me again, the sight so erotic that the spark inside of me ignites into a full-blown inferno. I feel like I'm too close to the sun, burning up before I ever reach the surface.

"You taste so good, baby," he whispers between my thighs.

"Oh god," I murmur. I'm so close to the edge, I can practically feel myself beginning to fall. I shake my head, not knowing if I can do it, the bad thoughts beginning to creep in. "I...I don't know if I can," I mutter in frustration.

"Just let go, Lina. I'll be here to catch you. I promise," he says before flicking his tongue against my clit and licking me into obscurity.

My mouth opens on a silent scream as the unimaginable bliss hits me all at once. My hips shamelessly buck against his face as I reach the precipice and tumble right over the edge. The orgasm is so strong that I have to cling onto the blankets for dear life as I ride out wave after wave of violent, intense pleasure.

My cries fill the room as my entire body shudders. Nico keeps licking me, not relenting, drawing out every single ounce of pleasure from me that he can get.

Eventually, I begin to come down from the extreme high, my body going limp as I gasp for air and secretly wonder if a person can die from too much pleasure.

"That's my girl," Nico murmurs against my thigh before placing a kiss on my skin.

I expect him to fuck me then. I know he's probably hard and aching. But Nico surprises me when he climbs into bed beside me and draws the covers up over both of us.

He pulls me into his arms and holds me. Neither one of us speaks, and soon sleep comes over me, and I fall asleep in record time, feeling sated and safe in his arms.

CHAPTER 34

Selina

THE NEXT MORNING, I sneak out of Nico's bedroom and go down the hall to take a shower in my own room. I rinse the charcoal marks from Nico's fingers from my body, the water turning a dark gray as it swirls down the drain. I frown as I stare at the filthy water.

The bad thoughts that are always lingering in the back of my mind return at full force.

No wonder Nico didn't sleep with you. You're dirty. You're used up. You're a whore. He doesn't want you. Who would ever want you?

My fingernails claw at the sides of my head as I force myself into the stream of water, closing my eyes. I shampoo my hair, hating the bumps from old wounds and scars that my fingertips discover. Nico doesn't have a single blemish on him other than a few nicely healed scars. Mine are all ugly and jagged since most of them I had to try to sew or fix myself. I probably look like some kind of weird science experiment to him.

"Fuck," I cry out, choking on the water as the bad thoughts threaten to drown me.

I finish up my shower, and then step out, drying off quickly before wrapping a towel around my body. The moment I step into my bedroom, there is a knock on my door.

"Lina?" Nico calls from the hallway.

I step closer and force my voice to be steady when I tell him, "I don't feel very well this morning."

"Oh, all right," he answers, but I can tell by his tone that he's not entirely convinced of my excuse. "I can call Sarah if you —."

"No, I'll be fine," I say quickly, cutting him off. I don't want Sarah coming in here and realizing that nothing is actually wrong with me; that it's all in my fucked-up head. "I'll just...I'll see you later," I say.

I wait until I hear his footsteps disappear down the hall before I finally release the breath I was holding. I hate feeling like this. It was an amazing night, and now I feel absolutely terrible because I can't stop second-guessing everything.

Putting my palm to my forehead, I squeeze my eyes shut. *Why can't I just be normal?*

Sighing, I retreat back into the bathroom and start getting ready for the day. I blow dry my hair and get dressed in comfy clothes. My PT session with Dwayne starts in an hour, and I don't want to be late.

I make it downstairs and into the gym in record time, even beating Dwayne this time. He arrives about fifteen minutes later with two jumbo sized juices in his hand. He gives me one that has strawberries in it, *thank goodness,* and he takes the one that looks like green sludge. *Yuck.*

We start our session, but I'm honestly not feeling it. I can't stop thinking about last night and the consequences of what happened. What if I effectively ruined Nico and my friendship? Just the thought of him not talking to me anymore destroys me, eating me up inside.

"You seem distracted today," Dwayne says to me during one of my leg exercises.

"Uh, yeah, I just..." My voice trails off. I don't know if I should be even talking about this kind of stuff with Dwayne, but it's not like I have anyone else to talk to. I definitely can't talk to Nico. I'm already embarrassed and feeling guilty about everything that happened as it is.

"Spill the tea, Selina. I need something juicy to get me through my day," he says with a wink.

I can't help but smile. Dwayne has the ability to put me in a good mood no matter how irritable or upset I am before our sessions. "Um, did you ever...? Have you ever...?"

"Are we playing that game?" he asks, his eyes lighting up.

I arch a brow at him. "What game?"

"Never Have I Ever?" he questions. "I mean, I'm sure I could go steal some liquor from the kitchen if we really want to turn it up a notch."

I shake my head. "Liquor is the last thing I need right now," I tell him with a soft laugh. I've actually been enjoying being sober. For years, I used pills and alcohol to mask my real problems. And now that I'm in a better place mentally, I want to experience every minute of it, especially with Nico.

"Oh! Is this about...Romeo?" he whispers conspiratorially, using our secret nickname for Nico.

"Yes," I whisper back.

"Damn, maybe I *do* need a drink for this," he jokes. "What did Romeo do now?"

Dwayne is very aware of the situation between Nico and me. I didn't even have to tell him. He told me he could just *sense* the tension and attraction between us from day one. Whatever that means.

"Well, we were fooling around in his room last night."

Dwayne leans in, loving this story already, and I can't help but laugh at his rapt attention. "And?" he prompts.

"And he...went down on me."

"Hell yeah, girl," he says with an enthusiastic nod.

"But then afterwards...we just went to bed."

"Damn, Romeo didn't want anything in return?" he asks with furrowed brows.

"No," I shake my head sadly. "And I can't stop thinking about the reasoning behind it."

"Maybe he's waiting on you to make the next move for more," Dwayne suggests.

"Maybe," I drawl out before nodding my head in agreement. Dwayne is right. Nico is a gentleman like that. Never pushing, never asking for too much. What if he's just scared to push me too far? What if he's just scared period?

"Next time you get Romeo alone, let him know exactly what you want. That should clear up any confusion," Dwayne suggests.

I'm glad I spoke to someone about my feelings instead of just keeping them all to myself until they ultimately consume me. I actually feel a thousand times better than I did this morning. "Thanks for the advice."

"That's what I'm here for," he says with a big smile.

For the rest of our therapy session, I think about what Dwayne and I talked about. I think maybe I do need to just push Nico in the right direction. If I want something, I need to let him know what I want. And if he still rejects me after that, then I'll just have to deal with the consequences later.

CHAPTER 35

Selina

WE'RE WATCHING A movie in Nico's room. This has become an almost nightly routine with us, and I love it, but I want...*more*. The sexual tension has been building up between us, and I feel like I might finally snap tonight. It's been almost a week since he last touched me, licking me into oblivion, and I can still feel his tongue on me. The experience was otherworldly, like I was levitating, and I want to experience it again and again with him.

I've been waiting for Nico to make a move, but he's been stoic, not giving me any signs of wanting anything else beyond what we have right now. So, I decide that tonight is the night. I don't want to wait any longer. I've never initiated sex with a man before, however. I was always forced to do things I didn't want to do. And having never been in a real consensual relationship, I have no idea what to do. I've tried flirting but failed miserably; probably because I'm afraid my words will come out all weird and rough like a caveman — *me like you. Me want sex with you.*

I internally facepalm myself. Why is this so hard?

Because it's Nico.

Yes, that is precisely the reason why this is so difficult. Nico would never push me to do anything with him, knowing what I've been through. But that little voice in the back of my mind keeps wondering if he doesn't want me. My self-doubt creeps in easily, and I can't seem to get rid of her.

Nico would never want you. Nico is the perfect package, and you're nothing.

Shaking my head, I try to clear those evil thoughts from my head.

There's a sex scene in the movie, and Nico looks back at me nervously, like he's afraid of me seeing it...or maybe he's just afraid of it getting awkward between us. God, if I had one superpower, it would be the ability to read minds. I want to know what he's thinking, what he thinks of me.

Gathering all the courage I can muster, I get on my knees and crawl towards him at the foot of the bed.

"Not comfy?" he asks innocently as he glances towards me.

I shake my head.

He's lying on his stomach, his chin resting on his folded arms, his biceps bulging and testing the thread strength of his short-sleeved shirt.

Lying down beside him, I study his profile. His face is perfection — hard, strong lines like it was carved by stone but with soft features balancing it all out, like his long, dark eyelashes and striking, gray eyes that remind me of the sky on a cloudy day.

When Nico catches me staring, he asks, "You don't like the movie?"

"I don't want to watch the movie," I tell him, hinting at the fact that I want more. *So much more.*

He turns to his side, so that we're facing each other. "Well, then what do you want to do?"

"This," I whisper before I move closer and kiss him.

His lips are so soft and warm. They part on a groan, and I take the opportunity to taste him. My tongue tangles with his, and an intense feeling rushes through me straight to my core. Gently pushing him to his back, I straddle his hips and gasp when I feel his hard cock pushing up against where I need him the most. At least I know that I do turn him on. I was worried about that most of all.

But when I grind down on him, Nico suddenly pulls away. "Whoa," he gasps. "Lina, I don't think we... I don't know if..."

I stare at him as tears fill my eyes. That little bitch in the back of my mind was right. He doesn't want me. He'll *never* want me.

Climbing off the bed, I race out of his bedroom and straight to my room. I close the door behind me, quickly locking it before sinking to the floor.

I hear Nico's fist pounding on the wood a few seconds later. "Lina, let me in," he calls from the other side.

"No!" I yell back.

He tries the doorknob but has no success. "Damn it, Lina! We need to talk."

"I don't want to talk. Just leave me alone!" I don't care if I'm being dramatic. I was just turned down by the only man who ever gave a damn about me, so I'm allowed to sulk and cry and whatever the hell else I want to do.

The door vibrates against my back as Nico's fists meet the wood. "I will break down this fucking door!" Nico yells, and I can hear the anger mixed with worry in his voice.

He sounds like a mad man out there. And why does him acting like that turn me on even more? *Oh god, what is wrong with me?*

Standing, I flick off the lock and open the door. Nico pushes inside and stares at me with those gray eyes that I've dreamt about almost every night for the past decade.

"Whatever I did wrong, I'm sorry," he starts, apologizing and surprising me, as he closes the door behind him.

I thought he was going to come in here accusing me of trying to force him to do something he clearly doesn't want to do. "It's me who should be apologizing. I won't do it again," I say quickly.

"Do what again?"

"I won't try to kiss you...or touch you again," I promise.

"Lina, what are you...why wouldn't you try to do that again?"

"Because you obviously don't want me. You obviously think..." My words trail off. I can't even say my evil thoughts aloud. That will make them *too real*.

"I think what?" he asks, narrowing his eyes at me. He comes closer, gripping my arms firmly. "Tell me what I think, Lina," he demands, his voice dropping a few octaves.

"You don't want me. You think I'm...broken." I close my eyes, effectively blocking him out, because I don't want to see on his face that I'm right. But then I hear him...laughing? I slowly open my eyes, and sure enough, Nico is laughing at me. "You're an asshole!" I yell before I shrug out of his grip and stumble backwards, needing the distance between us before I do something I'll regret.

"Lina, you think I don't want you?" he asks with a cocked brow, the laughter totally erased and his expression deadly serious now.

"Yes," I confess in a whisper.

"There hasn't been a day in the past ten years when I haven't thought about you, Lina. And ever since you've gotten back, there hasn't been a minute or even a fucking second that has passed when you haven't been on my mind." He pins me to the wall with an intense look, his eyes darkening. "You think I don't want you?" he scoffs, as if the very notion is inconceivable. "I want you with every single fiber of my being. I want you more than I want to fucking *breathe* most days. I want to be with you more than I've ever wanted anything else in this entire world!" he shouts, exasperated.

His words render me speechless.

"You think because I don't fuck you that I don't want you?" he asks with a heavy sigh. "You're wrong, Lina. So fucking wrong." His searing stare causes my heart to skip a beat inside of my chest when he asks, "What can I do to prove it to you?"

The words are out of my mouth before I can even stop them. "Kiss me."

Nico moves towards me, eating up the space between us in just a few strides. Then, he captures my face in his large palms, pressing his lips against mine in a passionate kiss that has my knees growing weak.

When he pulls back, his eyes meet mine. "You're not broken, Lina. You're fucking beautiful and smart and funny and...perfect for me. I just didn't want to push you into doing something you weren't ready for." He captures my lower lip between his teeth and sucks. *Hard.* "Trust me, it's been so fucking difficult keeping my hands off of you," he whispers against my mouth. "I didn't want to push you away. I didn't want you to run. It would kill me to lose you again," he says vehemently, his eyes so mournful and lost in that moment.

"That will never happen. I'm here. I'm not going anywhere," I promise before I press my mouth against his. And when his lips part on a throaty groan, my tongue darts out and licks against his, tasting him. He's letting me take control, and I feel...powerful, for the first time ever.

I moan as his hands grip my backside, grinding me against his hard body, his erection pressing up against my stomach. Liquid heat begins to pool in my belly as his lips trail from my mouth down my neck. All my fears and bad thoughts disappear in that instant, and I know that I could easily get addicted to his touch.

Moving his lips back to meet mine, his hungry kiss consumes me, stealing every exhalation from my lungs. And suddenly, the kissing and touching isn't enough for me. It feels like my entire body is on fire, my skin burning like a torch is being held against it. I need more. So much more.

"I need you," I beg against his lips.

He hums in approval and starts backing me over towards the bed. Our clothes are unceremoniously removed in a hurry, piles of clothes fluttering to the floor like we're in a race to see who can get naked first. I'm nervous about him seeing me naked for the first time...but when I see his eyes feasting on my form, all doubts I had before suddenly float into the background.

I sit down on the edge of the bed, nervous but excited all at the same time. It feels like I've been waiting for this moment forever. Like all the roads we took with the bends and twists and turns all led us to here. And now that it's finally happening, it's hard to grasp the existence of it all.

"Fuck, you're gorgeous, Lina," Nico tells me before his tongue swipes over his full bottom lip. "I need to taste you again, baby."

Before I can even blink, he hooks his hands under my thighs and drags me down the bed towards him. The moment his mouth makes contact against my swollen little nub, I cry out, fisting the sheets in my hands. I watch him feast on me, the erotic sight turning me on like nothing else has ever done in my entire life.

His hands lock onto my thighs, holding me still, not letting me escape an ounce of the pleasure he's giving me. Each swirl over my clit sends me rocketing off to the moon, and he doesn't stop licking and sucking until I'm tumbling over the edge, calling out his name and panting like I've just run a marathon.

My body is trembling from the aftershocks as he continues to lazily sweep his tongue over my clit until I finally cry out, "Nico, please!" I have this building ache inside of me that's growing more painful by the minute. I need him inside of me.

"I'm here, baby," he tells me before crawling onto the bed above me. With his thick cock in his hand, he strokes it a few times, enticing me. I bite my lip, watching him, unable to look away. "Tell me what you want, Lina," he demands, staring into my eyes, as he rubs the crown of his cock over my wet slit.

He's asking for permission. Not just taking what he wants. And he has no idea how much that means to me. "Please, Nico. Please fuck me," I gasp out.

My words seem to please him. He closes his gray eyes for a moment before he opens them again, and I can see the raging fire brewing inside of him. He notches his cock at my entrance, and gently, so slowly it's almost torturous, he enters me.

I grimace, expecting pain. But I'm so wet from my orgasm that his thick cock slides in without even so much as a twinge of discomfort. "Wow," I pant out in disbelief. Even though I thought sex would always be painful for me, I still wanted to try it with Nico. Imagine my surprise that it's not and that it actually…feels good. My eyes roll in the back of my head as he begins to fuck me nice and slow. "Oh god!" I cry out.

He bends his head down, capturing my beaded nipple in his mouth before sucking and gently biting. The combined pleasure and pain has me seeing stars. It's never felt like this, and I can feel the tears gathering up in my eyes. All the fear and trepidation I had melts away with every kiss he places on my breasts.

"Is this okay?" Nico asks, his face etched with worry.

I realize I'm crying, but it's not because I'm in pain or uncomfortable. "I never knew it could feel like this," I confess in a rush.

His expression instantly relaxes, and his mouth comes down to capture mine in a soul-searing kiss. I dig my fingernails into the muscled flesh of his shoulders as his tongue delves into my mouth, ravaging me.

He fucks me nice and slow, making me take every inch of his cock, as his mouth guides down my throat to my breasts. He runs his thumb over the stiff peak of one breast as his mouth captures the other, licking and gently biting, lighting up every pleasure sensor I have in the process. His worshiping touch and the warm suction of his wet mouth as he latches onto my other breast turns me into a trembling mess.

My hands glide over the planes of his muscular back, touching every inch of his smooth skin as his hips piston, driving his hard length into me.

I didn't realize until that moment how badly my body had been starving, so desperate for his touch and pleasure. A delicious rush of sensation flows through me, and I feel so close to the edge. My fingernails score his back as I pull him impossibly closer, trying to hang on for dear life as my orgasm begins to rip through me.

"Come for me, Lina," he whispers against my lips.

I come apart at the seams at that very moment, crying out his name as I shatter under him. Nico rocks into me, drawing out the pleasure as his breathing grows louder, harsher. Then, he pulls out suddenly, his eyes locked onto mine in an unwavering stare as he reaches his own bliss. "Fuck, Lina," he groans deeply, gutturally, as thick ropes of his seed coat my stomach while he strokes his cock.

His biceps and thighs shake from the powerful orgasm, and I watch him in awe. He looks like some kind of powerful Greek god in that moment — hooded gray eyes, sexily mussed dark hair, and ripped muscles glistening with a light sheen of sweat from exertion.

The room grows quiet; our rapid, ragged breaths the only sounds filling up the space. I languidly lie in the bed as a warmth settles over my body, spreading from head to toe as I enjoy the post-coital bliss that I never had a chance to experience before.

"Are you okay?" he asks, his brows furrowed in concern.

Am I okay? I'm more than okay. I feel like a phoenix that's risen from the ashes to be reborn. Nico has done the impossible. He's pumped new life into someone who swore she was done living.

"Let's do that again," I purr.

A deep chuckle escapes him; but when I wrap my hand around the back of his neck and bring his lips down to meet mine, he realizes I'm not joking. He groans in approval as I reach down and stroke his hardening cock.

In a quick move, he flips me onto my stomach and enters me from behind. I cry out in surprise and then moan in pleasure.

We make love for the rest of the night. And when I wake up the next morning, I'm sore in all the right places and I have a permanent smile on my face.

CHAPTER 36

Nicholas

AFTER A LONG day of surfing, Lina and I sit on the beach, studying for her upcoming GED test. She has a few more days left before the big day, and I want to make sure she's prepared as much as possible for it.

We're still in our wetsuits, the sun beginning to set in the distance, as I read practice questions from my cell phone.

"Five," she answers, and I can't help but smile when I swipe to reveal the answer and she's right.

"That is correct," I tell her, doing my best Chris Farley impersonation from *Billy Madison*, a movie we just watched last night, while pulling my rash guard up over my head as seductively as I can.

Selina cracks up and slaps me playfully on my bare chest. "Be serious!" she says even though she's grinning from ear to ear.

I toss the shirt next to me and smile before running a hand through my damp, messy hair. I had to convince her to watch the comedy, but it was worth all the begging I had to do. Hearing Selina laugh through almost the entire movie made my night. No, more like my fucking *year*. I love seeing her happy. I want her happy, always, with me. *Only with me.*

"Okay, okay," I tell her before reading another question from the practice test.

"Uhm, Natural selection."

"That's right," I say with a grin. "You're gonna kill this test, baby."

"I hope so," she says, but I can hear the doubt in her voice.

"We can keep practicing," I offer.

"Maybe later. Let's just enjoy the sunset together," she says softly before moving closer to me in the sand.

I wrap my arm around her, holding her tightly to my chest. I kiss the top of her head, breathing in her scent. She smells like strawberries and the ocean, and it's a wonderful combination.

Neither of us says a word as the sun sets, disappearing beyond the horizon. Only when it gets dark to the point that we can't see much around us do I finally break the spell we're under and tell her, "We better go home."

Standing up, I reach my hand down and pull her up and into my arms. Grazing my fingertips along her cheek, I study her beautiful face in the moonlight before placing a tender kiss against her lips. Ever since we've crossed the line from friends to lovers, I haven't been able to keep my hands off of her. Not that I think she minds. Half the time, Lina is the first one making the move, which I couldn't be happier about.

I was so afraid of pushing her away, of losing her that I almost fucked up and lost her by keeping my distance. I'm so fucking happy that we found each other somewhere in the middle and that we're in a good place now, though.

"Movie tonight?" I ask her. Movie nights have become a regular thing between us.

"I had something different in mind," she says, and I can hear her breath catching in her throat as my fingers trail down her slender neck.

"What do you have in mind?" I ask, staring down at her as her eyes slowly flutter shut.

"A shower. Together," she says before placing a kiss upon my lips.

I hum in approval. "I like that idea."

"And then..." Her voice trails off when she places another kiss on my mouth.

"And then?" I urge, desperate to know what comes next.

"And then you'll see," she promises with a sexy grin.

"Oh fuck, I can't wait until *and then*," I tell her.

Selina giggles and kisses me chastely before taking off in a sprint towards the pack of cars sitting in the parking lot. "First one to the car gets to pick the next movie we watch!" she throws behind her shoulder.

I grab my shirt from the sand and chase after her, loving the feeling of adrenaline when I finally catch up to her and pin her up against the car.

"I win," she says breathlessly.

"Good," I whisper. I don't even care that she gets to pick the next movie. I would watch paint dry on a wall if it meant I could cuddle with her in my room all night long. I capture her mouth with mine, shoving my tongue into her mouth and devouring her as she moans and grinds against me. Her legs wrap around my waist, and I pin her against the car while I kiss her senseless. She releases the softest whimpers against my lips, and the sound drives me crazy. Fuck, I can't wait to get her home so that I can ravish her in my bed.

Someone clears their throat loudly, and I suddenly remember that we are not alone. I glance over to see Tommaso, one of the guards, staring at us with a grin on his face. He shakes his head at me.

"Sorry about that, Tommaso!" I call over to him. These guys are probably ready to call it a day, and I don't blame them. They've been sitting for hours in cramped SUVs, watching us run around on the beach and surf. "We'll be heading home now," I tell him before opening the door for Selina and shutting it once she's inside.

Before I climb into the driver's seat, I hear Tommaso on his phone saying, "The lovebirds are finally on their way home," and I can't help but smile.

CHAPTER 37

Nicholas

I'M PACING THE kitchen floor, waiting patiently for Selina to return home. She went for her GED testing early this morning. I sent two carloads of bodyguards with her, not taking any chances. I stare down at the last text from one of the guards.

On our way back.

That was twenty minutes ago. The black SUVs should be pulling up the driveway any minute now, and I can't wait to see her. She's been studying so hard for that damn test, and I know she will be super bummed if she doesn't pass. I have no doubt in my mind that she passed with flying colors, however. My girl worked her ass off. And if the universe isn't a totally cruel bitch, then she'll make sure Selina passed.

Light reflecting off the SUV's windshields catches my eye, and I look out the window, waiting patiently in the kitchen. I watch as Selina steps out of the back, the sun hitting her blonde hair, making it appear as if she has a halo around her angelic form. It takes all of my willpower not to run out the door and scoop her up in my arms.

She's become a constant in my world, and I can't imagine my life without her now. Just the thought of losing her again keeps me up at night and has me waking up in a cold sweat and panting like I just ran a marathon.

I'll do whatever it takes to keep her safe, and I know without a doubt that I would kill anyone who tried to come between us in any way.

When Selina enters the room, my patience finally snaps. I walk over to her and envelop her in my arms, inhaling the familiar strawberry scent of her hair. She lets me hold her for a few minutes before pulling away. She glances up at the huge *congratulations* banner I hung earlier and frowns. "What if I hadn't passed?" she asks.

"So you did pass?" I ask, pulling her back into my arms and squeezing her tight. "I knew my girl would kick that test's ass!" Releasing her, I walk over to a bottle of champagne and pop the cork before pouring us two glasses. "Congratulations, Lina," I tell her before handing her one of the flutes.

She takes the glass from me and sips the champagne. "Thank you," she says, absolutely beaming.

I glance at the clock. It's only ten in the morning. We could have a full day of celebration at this point. "What do you want to do today? Anything. Just name it."

Her eyes light up when she says, "Let's go for a drive."

I smile. She's been having fun driving the different cars in the garage. Her favorite, though, is my dark blue McLaren 720S. She loves how fast it goes, and I love to watch her drive it. It's fucking sexy as hell. "All right. That sounds like fun."

"Let me go change first, though," she tells me before finishing off her champagne and setting the glass down.

I watch her walk away, her cute ass swaying under her tight jeans. My cock instantly lengthens in my pants, and I bite back a groan. Scrubbing my hand down my face, I wonder how long I can go today without being inside of her. I think our record at this point is just a few hours. God, I'm such a goner for that girl.

∼

Selina

I thought I needed drugs to get that ultimate high to sustain life. But, in reality, all I needed was Nico. He's my newest addiction — a drug so sweet and perfect that I'll never be able to rid him of my system. He's running through my veins, pumping adrenaline into my once cold, dead heart, making me feel alive again. Every day with him is an adventure, and I absolutely love that.

And when we make love, the feelings I get are so addictive that I just want more of them. All the time. I'm insatiable. And I'm thankful that he is too. What once was a small spark between us has completely ignited into a full-blown forest fire. I just can't get enough.

"Slow down, Lina," Nico warns as I take a turn too fast.

I manage to get the car back under control. I've been driving more and more, getting the hang of it, and today I want to be fast and reckless. I glance in the rearview mirror, and the SUV that had been tailing us is no longer in sight. Gripping the steering wheel, I pull onto a side road. We're out in the country, in the middle of nowhere, not even a house in sight except for maybe at the end of this dirt road.

Nico leans forward in the passenger's seat and looks in the mirror. "I think we lost the bodyguards," he says with a frown.

"Good," I tell him before I unbuckle my seatbelt and scramble out of my seat and onto his lap.

I catch him off guard, and I can see the moment he realizes my intentions. His pupils dilate as he focuses his gray eyes on mine. "I fucking love it when you're bad," he hisses through clenched teeth as

I grind down on his thickening cock. "We don't have much time," he warns.

"We don't need much time." For some reason, driving...and maybe just freedom, in general, gives me such a rush. My panties have been soaking wet the entire drive. And every time I would glance over to Nico, I would get the image in my head of riding his cock in the car, and it turned me on even more.

Wasting no time, I unzip his pants. He helps me with the next part, pulling his pants and boxers down to his knees until his thick, hard cock is free, bouncing up towards his stomach.

I wore a skirt for this very reason, so all I have to do is push my panties to the side before I'm sinking down on his delicious length.

"Wait," Nico breathes, but then he groans as I seat myself, my slickness coating him the whole way down. "Oh fuck, you're ready for me, aren't you, sweetheart?" he moans.

I ride up and down on his length, kissing his neck, whispering in his ear, "I'm always ready for you."

"Kiss me," he demands. "Kiss me like you're mine."

My mouth claims his in a soul-stealing kiss. "I'm yours," I breathe against his lips. "I'm only yours."

His gray eyes darken as his hand grips the back of my neck and pulls my mouth back to his. He kisses me like our plane is on fire and going down. He pulls me so close that there isn't any space left between us as his cock drives in and out of me in a relentless rhythm, my hips slamming down to meet each of his thrusts. "Oh fuck, Lina, you feel so good, so tight," he growls deeply.

I don't know if it's the excitement of having sex out in public and anyone could see us or the fact that the bodyguards will be coming soon and catching us, but I reach orgasm in record time. It washes over me with violent crescendos, and I suddenly break our kiss, my moans filling the interior of the car, as my thighs shake from the intensity.

Nico grips my ass, taking over and driving his cock up into me over and over again until he too falls apart, his cock pulsing deep inside of me, spilling his release.

He holds me then, our hearts racing together, our breathing ragged. "Fuck, that was hot," he whispers against my neck.

"Yeah," I manage to say.

I see headlights shining in the rear window, and I watch as the black SUV pulls into the lane behind us. "Shit. They found us."

"Thank fuck these windows are tinted. I don't want anyone seeing you but me," Nico growls.

I can't help but smile at his possessiveness. I love that he wants me and only me and that I want exactly the same thing. We have a mutual obsession with each other. I don't know if it's healthy or not, but I could care less. I love it regardless.

His softening cock slips out of me easily, and then I fix my panties and skirt before climbing back over into the driver's seat. Nico's phone rings a second later, and he's quick to answer it.

"Yeah, sorry about that, Tommaso. We didn't realize we lost you, so we pulled over so you guys could catch up." He looks over at me with a salacious grin on his face, and I cover my mouth to keep a giggle from slipping past my lips. "We'll be heading back to the compound now," Nico informs him.

I start the car and turn around in the grass beyond the dirt lane. I take my time now, not wanting to piss off the bodyguards again. Nico's father has been putting more bodyguards on all of us when we venture out of the house. I'm definitely not complaining about the extra protection. Anything that keeps me safe and able to stay with Nico is fine with me.

I'm driving down the highway towards the compound when I feel Nico's hand on my bare thigh. His pinky is dangerously close to my panties, and my breathing begins to pick up speed. I don't know what it is about him, but everything he does turns me on now. It's like I was so numb to everything for such a long time, and now it's like a switch has been flipped. He makes me *feel*...everything. He's brought new life into me, and I couldn't be happier. It's like I'm a completely new person, making up for lost time with a man I truly care about. *I feel free.*

"Is my cum leaking out of you and soaking your panties?" he asks, his voice rough with lust.

His question sends a shiver through me. "Yes," I answer.

"Naughty girl," he says before his fingers move under my skirt to the apex of my thighs. He runs his finger along the wet seam of my panties, pressing his fingertip against my clit, and I bite my lip to keep from moaning out loud.

I glance down to look at what he's doing, but Nico *tsks* at me. "Keep your eyes on the road, Lina," he warns.

My eyes go back to the highway as I anxiously try to concentrate on driving and what he's doing to me at the same time. Nico pulls my panties to the side, and I feel his finger dip inside of me, gathering his seed before he brings it up to my clit. All of this feels dirty and wrong...but so damn hot.

He strokes my clit with his cum softly, and I grip the steering wheel tightly, my knuckles turning white from the pressure. "This is very dangerous, Mr. Vitale," I breathe.

"I'm beginning to think you like dangerous, Miss McCall."

He's right. I love the thrill. I never knew I would be someone like that, but here we are. I love almost getting caught when I'm with Nico. The danger gets me off.

"Please, more," I sigh. His light touches just aren't enough. I need more. So much more.

He possessively cups my pussy then, his thick fingers entering me, fucking me as his thumb presses against my clit. I groan out loud, almost losing control of the car. A car beside me blasts their horn, scaring the hell out of me. "Oh fuck!" I cry out, feeling both scared and thrilled beyond measure.

"Is this the *more* you spoke of?" he whispers against my throat before I feel his lips sucking on my skin.

"Yes!" I gasp. I'm so frustrated with having to keep the car on the road that my brain feels like it's being torn in two between responsibility and pleasure. "I need...I need to pull over," I whine.

"No, no, no," Nico chastises me. "Keep driving, Lina." He drives his fingers further into me, causing me to moan loudly. "You like the danger of it, don't you? You're gripping my fingers so tight, pulling me so damn deep inside your greedy, wet cunt," he growls.

His filthy words are not helping the situation. And just when I think I'm going to scream in frustration, I feel my orgasm hit me like a blinding force of light. I grip the steering wheel tightly, forcing my eyes to stay on the road as my entire body shudders. Tendrils of warmth and pleasure unfurl within me as I cry out in anguish, "Oh god! Oh my god!" I shamelessly grind against his hand, and Nico doesn't stop until I'm literally slumped against the steering wheel, completely spent and fighting to keep the car on the road.

"That's my girl. You did so good, baby," Nico praises me, his fingers slowing until he finally removes them. He gently fixes my panties and skirt before sitting back in his seat.

I'm panting as I struggle to maintain my grip on the steering wheel, my legs still shaking from two intense orgasms almost back-to-back.

"Next exit," Nico tells me nonchalantly, as if he didn't just give me two of the best orgasms in my entire life, as if we didn't almost wreck and die on the highway...several times.

I put on the turn signal, my body going through the motions as I desperately try to come down from my high and concentrate. Thank goodness we're not far from the compound, and I feel a hell of a lot better when we're pulling up to the gate. The guard at the front checks our car in, and I drive through.

When I'm parked, I finally breathe out a sigh of relief. Nico and I climb out of the car, and I glare at him over the hood of the car.

"What?" he asks, feigning innocence, and I can't help but smile.

Tommaso, one of the bodyguards, steps out of the SUV that was tailing us and asks, "Were you having car trouble?" Concern laces his features as he says, "You were doing sixty and then ninety and then forty-five on the highway, and I saw you swerve a few times."

Nico flashes me a cocky grin before turning to the guard. "Nah, Lina is just learning how to drive. I've been trying to teach her, but she's a terrible student," he deadpans. "She'll get better with more practice, I'm sure."

"Oh, okay," Tommaso says with a nod of understanding before giving me a small, uneasy smile and then turning away to continue with his shift.

I walk over to Nico and smack him in the stomach with the back of my hand. "Asshole," I mutter under my breath.

"You love me," he retorts with a chuckle before walking towards the house.

My steps falter behind him. I know Nico was just joking around, but his words have a profound impact on me. I never thought I'd ever be capable of loving someone; never wanted to love anyone or allow myself to be that vulnerable in a relationship. But I know everything is different when it comes to Nico. And I think the impossible is happening — I am starting to fall in love with him.

CHAPTER 38

Nicholas

"YOU'RE NOT CONCENTRATING...once again," Renato tells me before swinging out towards my face with his fist.

I barely manage to pull away before his fist can connect with my cheek, feeling the *whoosh* of air by my ear as he follows through with the hit. Thank fuck we're just using fists today and not knives or half of my ear would be laying on the floor right now.

"Do you want to end up back in Sarah's office?" he mocks me.

We've been training for about an hour in the gym, but I'm not feeling it. This morning was amazing with Selina. I took her driving, and it turned into so much more than a simple driving lesson. The fact that she planned the whole excursion and wanted to fuck me so badly that she drove like a madman to lose our tail has me fucking hot and bothered all over again.

"Time out," I tell Renato before going to sit down. I feel like a damn teenager, thinking about girls in the middle of the day and sporting a boner while in public. Fuck, she makes me feel so many damn things. She's all I can think about. And the sex with her is amazing. To say I'm addicted to the way I feel when I'm around her... or inside of her...would be the understatement of the fucking century.

I love the fact that she gets off on danger. The risk of getting caught turns me on too. I think it's funny she thought I'd actually let us wreck on the highway today, though. At any given second, I would have taken the wheel, but she was strong and focused, taking everything I was giving her and not letting us wreck. I wouldn't let anything happen to her, though. Not a single hair on her head will be harmed while she's with me. That I can certainly vow.

"Thinking about Selina?" Renato asks as he sits on the bench next to me, the wood creaking under his weight.

I nod and flash him a grin. "How'd you know?"

"Because she's all you think about, man. Plus, you've got this goofy fucking grin on your face." He snickers when I give him the finger. "Man, I'm just glad to see you happy for once."

"I wasn't happy before?" I question even though I know I wasn't.

"No. You were a miserable fucker for years after Selina disappeared. I'm glad you found her. And I'm glad she has you now."

"Thanks, man," I tell him. Renato isn't one for sappy moments, and I know he'll try to change the mood in three...two...one...

"I can only imagine that goofy grin you've been wearing the past few days is because you guys are finally fucking," he suggests.

And there it is. "So what if we are?"

"Hell yeah," he says with an emphatic nod. "Attaboy." And then he mutters under his breath, "At least someone is getting some pussy around here."

My brows crease at his words. I just figured he'd been fucking my sister for years, but maybe I was wrong. I've caught them making out in dark corners of the compound before, but maybe she's saving herself for marriage or something. Who knows when it comes to Aria. We were really close when we were kids, but now I feel like she's distancing herself from everyone. I know she feels like a prisoner here, like a princess locked in a gilded cage kind of spiel, but I also know it's for her own damn good. Look what happened to Selina. And maybe we shouldn't be holding Selina's past against Aria, but we all do it. We have to keep Aria safe and *here*.

The thought of anyone taking my sister or, God forbid, Selina again has my blood boiling. My parents made it their mission in life to take down people like Constantine Carbone, and I want to continue that mission now and long after they're dead and gone. If I could save a million girls like Selina, I would. And I will.

"You done resting, princess?" Renato asks.

"Yeah, let's go," I tell him with a glare.

"Oh shit. He's back!" he says with a clap of his hands. "This should be fun."

"Very," I say before standing. With my repressed anger and frustration over my terrible inner thoughts, I'm ready to tear someone's head off. Looks like Renato will be the one going to Sarah's office later after all.

CHAPTER 39

Nicholas

AFTER I'M DONE with my work for the day, I sneak down to the gym where I know Selina's getting her physical therapy session.

The therapist has her lying down on a bench while he stretches out her legs and thighs. The way his hands are touching her has me instantly seething. And if Dwayne didn't have a boyfriend and would be more likely to hit on me than Selina, I would be cutting those hands right the fuck off.

As I grow closer to the two of them, Dwayne looks up and smiles. He cocks his head to the side, probably taking note of the tension in my shoulders and the frown that's present on my face. "We're almost done here, Nico," he tells me with a wink, perhaps knowing what's got me all riled up.

"How's my girl doing?" I ask, laying it on thick even though Dwayne is not a threat. There's just something about Selina that makes my inner caveman act out whenever I'm around her. I want her more than anything in this world, and I feel protective of her, obsessively so. I'm sure it's my own psychological trauma of having her taken away from me all those years ago and the constant fear I have of losing her again, but some of it is just primal instinct to take care of her and protect her at all costs. I've never felt that way over someone else before. Just her.

"Honestly, your surfing excursions have done wonders for her. I was just telling Selina that I don't think we need to continue therapy. This is our last session."

"Oh, thank fuck," I groan out loud and then snap my jaw shut when I realize what I just said.

Selina's brows dip before she smiles and gives me a knowing look. Then, she turns her attention to Dwayne. "Thank you. For everything."

"No problem. I'll talk to you soon, Selina." He stands and walks out of the gym, leaving the two of us alone. It's late in the evening, so I doubt if anyone else will be doing any sessions here tonight.

I go over to the pull-up bar and grip it in my hands before pulling myself up to my chin and dropping back down repeatedly.

Selina watches me for a few reps before she stands and walks over to me. "So, you're jealous...over Dwayne?" she asks incredulously. "You know he has a boyfriend, right?"

"Doesn't matter," I tell her simply.

"I think it might," she says with a laugh.

I drop off the bar and face her. "You really have no idea how beautiful you are, do you?"

With a concerned look on her face, Selina walks over to me and places the back of her hand against my forehead. "Are you sure you're feeling okay?" she jokes with a sly grin.

I grab her hand and place a kiss on her palm. "I feel just fine." I won't press the subject. I know Selina has a hard time believing just how beautiful she is. In my eyes, she's the epitome of perfection. She may not see it, but I'll always be here to make her feel special and beautiful just like she deserves.

Frowning, she jumps up and does a few reps on the pull-up bar. My cock twitches in my pants as I watch her pull herself up and drop down over and over. She's gained so much strength since she arrived, and I couldn't be prouder. Pretty soon she'll be able to kick *my* ass, and the thought of her trying makes my dick rock fucking hard.

When her eyes meet mine, she gets a telling look on her face. She probably thinks everything she does turns me on.

And she'd be absolutely right.

"You know, Dwayne has the most amazing hands," she says as she pulls herself up on the bar again, making it look easy. "I miss his hands already," she drawls. "Maybe I should schedule some...*private* sessions with him."

"Lina," I warn, stepping up behind her and watching her firm ass bobbing up and down in front of my face. "Don't poke the beast."

"But what if I want the beast to *poke* me?" she throws over her shoulder, flashing me a look that has all my blood rushing straight to my cock.

Grunting, I jump and grab the bar on either side of her hand, locking my legs around hers and doing pull-ups with her plump ass pushing against my erection. "See what you do to me?" I growl into her neck before biting gently, followed by a lick to soothe the pain.

She moans, grinding back against me, and I'm a fucking goner. Dropping down, I wrap my hands around her waist and help her down, sliding her down the length of my body, so that she can feel how hard I am for her. With my mouth at her ear, I whisper, "I think you forgot that this room is soundproof. No one will be able to hear you scream."

A shudder runs through her, and she turns in my arms to look at me with a lust-filled gaze. "Promise?"

I groan. "My naughty girl," I tell her before my mouth crashes down on hers. Backing her up to the wall, I turn her around and drop to my knees. My large hands grab her curvy ass, squeezing and kneading her, my fingertips occasionally brushing against the apex of her thighs. Every soft brush elicits a moan from her beautiful mouth.

"Tell me what you want, Lina. I want to hear the words coming out of your beautiful mouth."

"Make me come," she moans against the wall.

Her words go straight through me down to my heavy cock. "Fuck," I hiss before I rip down her leggings. I bury my face between her thighs, licking her pussy before dragging my tongue up her slit to her little asshole and then back again. Her entire body trembles beneath my hands as I pin her to the wall, eating her like a starving, dying man. And I am starving for her. Always. Her pussy is a delicacy and makes my mouth water whenever I think about it. She tastes sweet, like a forbidden nectar that I'll never get enough of. My tongue is buried so deep between her legs that I'll no doubt be tasting her sweetness for weeks.

She's mumbling nonsensical things to the wall when I push a finger...and then two inside her soaking wet cunt. It's weeping for me, and I couldn't be happier. I curl my fingers inside of her until I reach the sweet spot that has her crying out. My thumb presses against her little clit while I finger fuck her pussy. But that isn't enough for my greedy girl, and I know just what she needs.

I flatten my tongue against the rim of her puckered hole, licking her until her legs begin to shake.

"Oh god! Oh my god, Nico!" she cries out, practically screaming.

I can't help but smile before I lick her again, flicking my tongue over her tight, little hole, until she finally reaches the precipice of her orgasm. She tumbles over the edge, moaning and crying as I keep her pinned against the wall, holding her weight up in my arms as her pussy floods my fingers and my tongue.

I don't stop until she's nothing but a trembling mess and her moans begin to die down.

I stand, capturing her in my arms, not wanting to ever let her go. But when I hear her sniffling, I fear I went too far. Terrified, I grab her chin and force her gaze to meet mine.

She looks up at me with tears in those distinctive blue and green eyes and then tells me with a sexy grin, "Your turn."

∼

Selina

Nico made me cry. But not in a bad way. It was in a very, *very* good way. The orgasm he gave me was so damn strong that I lost control of my emotions. It feels like I was waiting a million years for that kind of release.

It also proved that I can just let go. I don't have to reaffirm every few seconds that he's here with me. I just *feel* it now. I feel his constant presence deep down in my very soul.

I watch in awe as Nico puts his fingers inside his mouth, tasting me. His eyes close slowly as he moans in appreciation. And when he pulls his fingers free, he tells me in a husky sigh, "You taste so damn good. So fucking sweet."

My clit throbs from his filthy words. I didn't know words could turn on a person so much, but Nico has a way with them. He can make me go from the Sahara to the Pacific Ocean with just a few choice words.

He gave me a powerful orgasm that I'm still feeling the aftershocks from, and I desperately want to return the favor. Falling to my knees, I grab the waistband of Nico's sweatpants. I look up at him, and he has a concerned look on his face. I'm sure he's wondering if this is okay, if we should even be doing this, if I even want to do this. And the answer to all of those questions is yes, and I plan on showing him with my mouth just how okay all of this is.

I'm tired of living in the past. I'm tired of being afraid. I want to have a normal relationship with a man that I trust with my whole heart, body and soul. And I know Nico would never push too far or make me do something I didn't want to do.

Tugging down his sweats, I watch in awe as his hard cock bobs up towards my face. He's so long and hard, it makes my mouth water. My hand begins to tremble as I wrap my fingers around his cock, but I force it to steady along with the bad thoughts trying to enter my head. I focus on the moment. I focus on Nico and how much I want to make him feel good.

Gripping his length, I lick around the crown softly and gently. This elicits the sexiest growl I've ever heard from deep inside his chest, and it sets my blood on fire. Feeling empowered, I move my hand up and down his shaft. Then, I flatten my tongue and lick up a bead of pre-cum, moaning at the salty taste of him.

"Fuck, Lina," he groans.

"Feed me your cock, Nico," I whisper as I stare up at him.

He hisses between clenched teeth before gripping the base of his cock and gently pushing the head past my lips, filling my mouth. Moving my head, I lick and suck at his velvety steel length, drawing him as deep as I can into my mouth and then back out over and over again.

I place my hands on his thighs, controlling the depth as I suck him. He doesn't once try to thrust it down my throat. He remains completely still, and I don't know if he's even aware he's letting me take control, but it makes me feel powerful and urges me on even more to make him come.

I pull back completely, his cock releasing from my mouth with a *pop* before I suck him back in, taking almost the entire length of him. That motion alone causes his thighs to tremble under my hands, and I grin around his cock, loving every minute of pleasure I'm giving him.

I keep repeating the action until he growls out, "Enough."

With brute strength, he lifts me up in his arms, cradles my ass and impales me on his cock before I can even blink. I struggle to breathe as he fills me up to the brim, his cock hitting my cervix, mixing delicious pain with a lot of pleasure.

He gently lays me down on a weight bench, the same one where he watched Dwayne working out my muscles after our therapy session, and I wonder if he's doing this on purpose. Claiming me on this same bench like a jealous barbarian. The thought crosses my mind, but then all thinking goes right out the window as he lifts my hips and drives his cock into me, hitting that special part inside of me that only he can.

"Oh god!" I cry out. I can feel a million emotions building up inside of me again as he hits that spot over and over again. "Nico!" I scream right before I tumble over the edge, becoming a blubbering mess once more and shattering around him.

"Fuck yes. Cry for my cock, Lina," he hisses out before he groans out his own release, his hips pistoning erratically before finally stopping. "Oh fuck, Lina. I'll never get enough of you," he sighs contentedly as he holds my legs tightly in his arms.

As we both attempt to catch our breath, Nico stays inside of me for a few minutes, placing gentle kisses on my calves and ankles before eventually pulling out of me.

He helps me up from the bench and then leads me to the shower room. Once we're under the hot spray, we can't keep our hands off of each other. And as we make love under the cascade of water, I realize I never want to live in a world without Nico by my side. I want him to be my forever.

CHAPTER 40

Selina

A SOFT KNOCK comes at my door late on a Saturday night. I open it, thinking Nico is going to be on the other side, but I'm stunned to see his sister standing there. Aria is dressed up like she's getting ready to go to a party in a short, gold, sequin mini dress, matching high heels and a full face of makeup.

"Bored?" Aria asks me with a Cheshire cat grin.

"Very," I confess. Nico was with his father the entire day, and we barely got to see each other. I'm sure they were doing important business, so I can't complain. Nico was so tired when he got home that he just wanted to go to bed and promised he'd make it up to me tomorrow. And I've just been sitting here thinking about all the ways he'll probably be making it up to me...

"Want to go out?" Aria asks, snapping me back to the present. "My friend is DJing at a club tonight, and I'm dying to see her do her thing."

Hesitating, I glance down the hall to Nico's closed bedroom door. "Uh…"

"Don't worry. My brother doesn't have to know shit. It will be just us girls."

A nervous smile forms on my lips. I really want Aria to like me, and this might be my ticket into getting to know her better. She's just like her brother — a closed book until you really put the time and effort in. "Okay, sure," I tell her with a nod.

She glances down at my pajamas and asks, "Got anything to wear?"

I look down at my attire, suddenly embarrassed. "No?" I say, and it sounds like a question more than an answer.

"Don't worry. I have plenty in my closet. Come with me." She holds out her hand, and I take it, the smile never dropping from my lips as she leads me through the compound and to her room.

Aria is shorter than me, so finding something that actually fits is quite a daunting task. We spend about twenty minutes raiding her closet until we finally find a dress that doesn't show my ass cheeks.

"I love that dress on you," Aria tells me when I step out of her bathroom.

I glance down at the flowy silver dress and smile.

"I have a pair of kitten heels that might fit you," she suggests.

I slip into the pair. "They're a little tight, but I think they'll work for tonight."

"Perfect."

We make our way downstairs and into the garage where there's a car waiting. I'm expecting to see a few carloads of bodyguards, like how it normally is when Nico and I venture out, but I'm surprised to see only a driver in the front seat and no guards in the back.

"We don't need more guards?" I ask Aria, trying to keep the tremor of fear out of my voice.

She simply smiles and waves my concerns away in the wind. "We'll be fine. There are going to be tons of people there. Nothing is going to happen."

KEEPING MY GIRL

Anxiety gnaws in the back of my mind on the way to the club, and I can't stop sawing my bottom lip between my teeth in nervousness. I know Nico wouldn't like this. If he finds out about us going out, he's going to be pissed. And angry Nico is never a good thing.

When the driver pulls up to the large industrial-looking building, he tells us, "I'll be parked a few blocks away. Just text when you're ready to leave."

"Thank you, Marco," Aria calls when she jumps out of the back of the car, turning and waiting for me to join her.

Steeling my nerves, I climb out and stand beside her, looking around. God, I wish I had a cell phone so that I could at least text Nico to let him know what we're doing and where we're going, but then I remember the control room. Aldo probably knows that we left and already told him. I mean, I hope so anyway. I don't know exactly how that all works when one of the family members leaves the compound. I don't know how much of a leash Aria is on, but at the moment I'm hoping it's extremely short.

Aria grabs my hand and pulls me towards the entrance. There is a long line of people wrapped clear around the block, but Aria goes to the guard at the front and says her name. The big, burly guy with a bald head checks his list and then steps aside for us to go through the front door.

Inside, it's loud and bright with numerous neon-colored lights moving in various patterns across a huge dance floor. The club is packed to the brim with people drinking, dancing, and talking.

We go to the bar first, ordering and downing a few shots of tequila while we sit on uncomfortable stools, waiting for our sexes on the beach to be made all while simultaneously warding off a few cocky guys who approach us, looking to score.

After Aria tells yet another guy to get lost, she turns to me and says, "You need to relax, Selina."

I don't think I've ever been able to relax in my entire life now that I think of it. Nodding, I try to force my body to stop being so wound tightly. It, unfortunately, doesn't work. After being on high alert for so many years, afraid of what will come next, my body has been conditioned into a state of constant awareness and anxiety.

Our drinks arrive a few minutes later just as an upbeat song begins to play over the speakers. Aria jumps up and grabs my hand. "Let's dance!" she shouts over the music.

With the liquor coursing through my veins and making me feel bold, I follow her onto the dancefloor. Just her presence alone makes the crowd part like the Red Sea. She's beautiful, strong, and confident, and I wish I could be like her for even just a minute. She commands the room, all eyes on her, and I just dance beside her in wonderment.

She moves her body to the music, her long, chocolate brown hair swaying to the movement. And when she asks me to join in, I put my arms up in the air and move in sync along with her.

"Hell yeah!" Aria calls out with a big grin.

With the alcohol giving me liquid courage, I dance my heart out, never having felt more alive...and *normal*. I give in to the music, close my eyes and let it take over my body and soul. It feels so liberating, just being able to drink and dance like a regular twenty-something. So many things people just take for granted. After having been locked away in a cage for most of my life, I'll never take anything for granted again. And I'll remember this night for the rest of my life as the first of what I hope are many good times to come.

I open my eyes to turn around to thank Aria for taking me out tonight, but my vision somehow locks on a dark figure on the second floor. Most of him is hidden by the shadows, but his hands and how they grip the handrails in front of him have me paralyzed. *Those hands.* I would recognize those hands anywhere.

Suddenly, my drink slips out of my hand and splatters onto the dance floor.

"Whoa!" Aria calls out, bumping into me and stealing my attention away from the man. "Okay, you're cut off!" she jokes. But when she sees my face, she sobers quickly. "What? Selina, what's wrong?"

I look away from her and back to where I saw the man, but he's no longer there. "Constantine is here!" I say in a panic. My eyes frantically dart around the second floor, desperate to catch another glimpse to be certain, but I can't find him again.

"Are you sure it was him?" she demands, grabbing my arm and shaking me.

"Yes! No!" I shake my head, wishing now that I was stone-cold sober. "I'm not a hundred-percent sure, but I think it was him."

"Shit!" Aria mutters under her breath as she pulls her cell phone from her clutch. "I'm going to call Renato just in case. He'll know what to do."

She takes my hand and leads me to the corner of the club. We're in the shadows, hidden from the neon lights, and I can't stop searching for *him*.

"Renato, it's me," Aria says into the phone. "Listen, don't freak out, but we're at the club."

"Damn it, Aria! Which club?" I can hear him yelling from the other end of the call.

"Liquid Lounge," she responds. Renato must have some choice words with her, because she pulls the phone away from her ear and rolls her eyes. "I don't need your shit right now, Renato. I need your help." She swallows hard before saying, "Selina thinks she just saw Constantine Carbone here."

I watch Aria's face morph from merely concerned into pure panic. Now she knows exactly how I'm feeling.

"He said we need to get out of here. I'll text the driver to come pick us up. He's only a few blocks away. Then we can —."

She never gets to finish that sentence. A loud, deafening boom sounds, and the music suddenly cuts off.

Pop, pop, pop, pop!

I pull Aria down to her knees, sheltering her as the gunfire goes off. The crowd of people erupts into panic, many screaming as they start running for the exits. I push Aria under a table so that we don't get trampled to death as the shooting continues to explode through the entire club. Dead bodies begin to fall around us until the place looks like something out of a war movie.

"Aria! Aria!" I can hear Renato's frantic screams from the cell phone, which is now lying on the floor next to our feet.

People are crying, screaming and trying frantically to escape, and anyone that moves is just being mowed down by the gunmen. I hold my hands over my ears, trying to silence the horrific sounds as panic bubbles up inside of my chest.

The gunfire suddenly comes to a stop. Aria looks at me with a wide, unfocused gaze. "We need to get out of here," she pleads, her voice trembling. I think she's going into shock.

"Stay low," I tell her quickly.

We climb out from under the table, and Aria snatches up her phone at the last second, holding it in a vice grip in her hand.

The nearest exit is by the restrooms, and so I pull Aria along towards them.

"I wouldn't do that if I were you!" a deep, familiar voice calls out to me.

My body locks up like a statue, and my feet suddenly freeze to the floor. I can't even force myself to move, so I yell to Aria, "Go! Get out of here!" She needs to save herself. If Constantine is here, he's here for me, not her. She needs to get as far away from me as possible if she has any hope of escaping and getting help.

"I'm not leaving you!" she cries, tears streaming down her pretty face as she pulls on my arm.

"Get out before it's too late!" I hiss at her, pushing her away from me. It's me he wants. It's always been me. I refuse to let her get into this mess with me. She doesn't deserve to witness the horrors I have. If I have to sacrifice myself to save her, I will. I *always* will.

Sobbing, she finally turns and runs out the door at the end of the hall. And a sense of relief passes through me knowing that she won't be caught up in this mess.

I turn and look upon the devil himself. Constantine is in his normal attire — a dark and expensive tailored suit that costs more than most people's monthly rent. His short, salt and pepper hair looks immaculately styled; not a single hair out of place.

"Did you miss me?" Constantine asks with a wry smile. He looks the same as the last time I saw him. Still as handsome as ever and pristine. Still with that ever-present cruel smirk gracing his lips. Still *evil*.

Aria's screams tear through the hallway, and I watch in horror as one of Constantine's goons manhandles her back into the club and forces her to stand beside me.

"I'll go with you," I tell Constantine quickly. "Just let her go."

He lets out a deep, hearty laugh. "Oh, you think you make the rules now, my little pet?" he asks.

I cringe at his nickname for me. I never thought I would hear those words come out of his mouth again. I had nightmares about it, but I didn't think I would have to live it all over again.

I was safe.

I was actually safe.

And I left my sanctuary.

What the hell was I thinking?

I want to be mad at Aria, but she didn't force me to go. I wanted to go. I just wanted to be normal. Was that so much to ask for?

Yes, the little nagging voice in the back of my head tells me. *Look what happened the moment you let your guard down.*

For years, I've never let my guard down. Not even once. I never could when I was living in constant fear and distress.

Constantine walks over to us. His hand reaches out to touch me, but I grimace and move away from him. "It seems my little pet has lost her manners," he says through gritted teeth. "Don't worry, I'll teach you your manners again. I'll beat the fucking defiance out of you until you can no longer walk." He hauls his hand back and slams his fist into the side of my head.

The side of my face explodes with pain. Grunting, I fall to my hands and knees. I can't even remember the last time I felt this much pain. I've grown weak in my time apart from him. It used to take a hell of a lot more than just a punch to make me crumble.

"Leave her alone!" Aria starts screaming, and I wince.

Looking up, I watch Constantine walk over to her. His fingertips graze along her cheek and her jaw, before he wraps his hand around her neck and lifts her face to get a better look. "And you must be Aria Vitale. My god, you look just like your mother," he says in awe, and I can see the lust in his eyes. "Oh, I'm going to have fun with you. All the fun I was denied with her thanks to your no-good father."

Anger boils up inside of me, overflowing to the point where I can't contain it anymore. All the years of abuse. All the years of fear. Everything has built up to this.

Screaming, I pull myself up to a standing position and lunge for Constantine, determined to scratch his eyeballs out. My nails manage to score his cheek before I'm suddenly hauled backwards by one of his men. The man holds my arms down in a vice grip, and I fight him like a wild animal until I wear myself out and go limp in his hold.

Constantine pulls a white handkerchief out of his suit pocket and wipes at his face, staring down at the blood when he pulls it away. A hearty chuckle escapes his chest before his dark eyes lock onto me. "Save your strength, little pet. You're going to need it for what I have planned for you," he threatens. Then, he looks to his men. "Hurry up and frisk them, and then let's get the hell out of here."

"Where are you taking us?" Aria screams.

I know she still has the phone hidden somewhere. Hopefully Renato is still listening, but I doubt if Constantine will give our next location out that easily.

"We're going on a little boat ride," he says with an evil grin before leaving the club, walking over dead bodies as he goes.

Police sirens can be heard in the distance while four men roughly search Aria and me, tearing at our clothes and putting their fingers and hands in places they shouldn't be.

"Don't you dare touch me!" Aria screeches. "Don't! Stop!" Despite her best efforts to fight the men off, they manage to manhandle her until they find what they're looking for.

"Cell phone," one of the men calls out as he pulls it out of Aria's bra. He takes the device, drops it to the floor and smashes it against the concrete with the heel of his heavy boot.

A sob escapes Aria then, and I know exactly what she's thinking. They'll never be able to find us now. We'll be taken, and there's not a damn thing anyone can do to change that.

CHAPTER 41

Nicholas

IT'S EITHER LATE or early as fuck when loud banging on my bedroom door wakes me out of a dead sleep. My first instinct is that something happened to Lina, so I jump out of bed and rush to the door. When I open it, I expect to see her, fresh from a nightmare or some other problem she needs me to help her with. But instead, Renato is standing there. His eyes are wide with fear, and he looks like he's barely holding it together as he tells me, "They're gone. He took them."

My brain is working on overdrive, trying to decipher what exactly he's telling me. My hands grip his shoulders, and I shake him, forcing him to focus on me. "What? Who are you talking about, Renato? Who's gone?" I demand in a rush, my questions running into each other.

"Aria and Selina are gone. Constantine has them," he grits out.

I stare at him in disbelief, my hands slowly dropping from his shoulders. "No," I tell him, shaking my head adamantly. This must be some type of living fucking nightmare that I can't wake up from. "No, you're wrong." Hurrying down the hallway, I stop at Lina's room. I burst through the door, expecting to see her sleeping, but her bed is empty, not even showing signs that it's even been slept in tonight. "No," I gasp around the large lump forming in my throat. "How did this even happen?" I would have known if there was an attack on the house. I would have been alerted by sirens and alarms.

"Aria thought it would be a good idea for them to sneak out in the middle of the night and go to a club."

My hands curl into fists at my sides. "What the fuck?" I scream. Before I can even second-guess my actions, I drive my hand through the nearest wall. My knuckles scream in agony as chunks of drywall and paint chips fall to the floor when I withdraw my hand from the fist-sized hole.

"I can't believe Aria did something so stupid," Renato says, shaking his head. "We have to get them back. Who knows what the fuck is happening to them right now? They could be..." He doesn't finish that sentence, and I don't even want him to.

"Have you told anyone else yet?" I ask in a rush, cradling my cracked and bleeding knuckles.

"No. I went straight to you when they smashed Aria's cell phone."

I wince. We don't even have a way of tracking them now. "We need to wake up my father and Aldo. Aldo will be able to track them through cameras in the city. The sooner we find out where they're going, the better."

"Constantine did say one thing before the call ended. He said, 'we're going on a little boat ride.'"

Fuck.

If Constantine disappears on a yacht somewhere out in the middle of the ocean with the girls, there's no telling when we'll ever see them again...if ever.

"Let's go," I say urgently, running down the hall with Renato quick on my heels.

I pound on my parents' bedroom door. My dad answers it a few seconds later. His eyes are full of sleep, but his body is on high alert, muscles taut under his white tank. "What's wrong, Nico?" he asks, closing the bedroom door behind him.

I know he doesn't like to worry my mom unless he absolutely has to, and I'm all right with keeping her in the dark on this. I know she'll do nothing but panic and worry. "Aria and Selina are gone," I tell him. Then, with a grimace, I add, "Constantine Carbone took them."

"How the fuck did this happen?" he asks. I explain everything that Renato told me, and my father's eyes widen and then narrow. "Does Aldo know?" he asks urgently.

"Yes, I already called him. He's working on it, trying to figure out where they're going."

"Let's get to the control room. Tell me everything on the way," my dad says in a rush.

We meet Renato in the backyard, and the three of us hurry to the control room in tense silence. There's nothing to say; nothing to make this situation any better. My sister and girlfriend are gone, and they were taken by the worst person on the fucking planet. Who knows what horrific acts he's committing on them right now.

I squeeze my eyes shut and stumble against the wall going down the stairs.

"You all right, man?" I hear Renato ask.

I nod slowly and then force my eyes open. I need to get my shit under control. Selina and Aria need me to be clear-headed. I can't think about what *could* happen. I just need to find them and bring them home before anything *does* happen.

"I'm fine. Let's go," I tell him, urging him to keep going.

The room is buzzing with adrenaline, and the smell of coffee hits me like a brick wall as I look around at our IT guys diligently working on several computers. Aldo's fingers are moving feverishly over a keyboard, and the three of us move behind him to stare at his monitors. He's putting in some kind of code, and there's camera footage jumping around from one angle to another on one of the wide screens.

"Aria only took one guard with them, and he was told to wait in the car a few blocks away," Aldo informs us. "He had no idea what even happened until the cops showed up." Then he adds, "I'm hacking into the city's live traffic cameras. I'm trying to track them from the club to see which direction they were going."

My father scrubs a hand down his face. "I can't believe Aria would do this. How did she not realize the danger they were in?"

"She couldn't have known Constantine would show up like that," I tell my father. Aria isn't reckless. She's just very naïve at times...which isn't totally her fault. My parents sheltered her too much; not that I can really blame them after what happened with Selina, however. *Fuck.* I could go around in circles a million times trying to make sense of it all, but now isn't the time for pointing fingers.

"How did he find them?" my father asks the million-dollar question that is on everyone's mind.

Renato shrugs. "Coincidence?"

I shake my head. "No. More like convenience."

"Are you sure Dr. Catalano checked her for tracking devices?" Aldo asks me, and I can't say the thought hasn't crossed my mind in the past thirty minutes.

"The doctor said she couldn't find any," I answer, but now I'm second-guessing Dr. Catalano's opinion. If she just did a quick search on Selina's body, she wouldn't have found anything. I'm sure Constantine wouldn't have made a tracker easy to find.

"We should have been more thorough, ran a scan on her," my father says through clenched teeth.

"It would explain how he found her," Aldo suggests. "That's the most plausible reason at this point."

"Fuck," I mutter under my breath. I think back to the time when Selina told me about Constantine mysteriously finding her and murdering the family that was helping her. No wonder she was always trying to leave here. She knew deep down he would find her again even if she didn't know the logical reasoning behind it. And I dismissed her fears like a fucking idiot. I made her feel safe when she truly wasn't at any point. And look what happened. I failed her. I failed them both.

My father clasps a hand over my shoulder. "You didn't fail anyone," he says, and I realize I must have spoken the last part of my thoughts out loud. "We're going to find them. We're going to bring them back home where they belong," he tells me.

I give him a nod. Even though his words make me feel minutely better, my stomach is still doing nervous flips. This is Carbone we're talking about. He took Selina from me once before and was able to disappear for a fucking decade before I was able to find her again. I don't think I could live without her, knowing she was out there in the world with him, being his plaything to torture and maim.

My hands clench into fists at my sides. No, I can't think like that. There is no other option at this point but to find them. I won't let her disappear again. She's my girl. I won't stop until I find her. And once I do, Constantine will pay for what he's done to her with his life.

CHAPTER 42

Selina

WE'RE NEAR THE water. I can feel the humidity in the air, and I can practically taste the salt in the air mixed with the coppery tang of my blood. It's such a familiar, unwanted memory. Nausea wracks my stomach, twisting and turning painfully until I almost throw up. I manage to keep it down, swallowing hard and focusing on my breathing.

Aria groans from beside me, and a sense of relief floods through me. She had been screaming and kicking, so one of the guards knocked her unconscious outside of the club before they shoved us in the back of a black windowless van. I tried my best to wake her on the way here, but she never came to. Perhaps it's better that way. The less she has to experience, the better.

We were taken to a large warehouse that houses boats and yachts. Four men strung us up on a rafter and left us alone. It's been at least an hour since we arrived, and my arms and hands are numb from lack of circulation.

"Wh-what...where are we?" Aria asks, slowly coming to. She tries to move her arms, and then the panic sets in when she realizes our predicament. She struggles, her breathing picking up speed as she starts to wheeze and panic on the verge of hyperventilating.

"Aria, it's okay," I try to reassure her, but I know my words are useless right now. We're screwed — completely vulnerable with no end to our torture in sight. It can only get worse from here. That has been my attitude my whole life, and nothing is going to change that now. But I have to be strong. For Aria.

"It's not okay," she whines, tears streaming down her delicate cheeks. "We have to get out of here, Selina!" she pleads as if I hold the key to our freedom somehow.

But even if we weren't strung up like pieces of meat in this warehouse, there would be no easy escape for us. Constantine's men are everywhere. And anywhere they are not stationed, I'm sure there are motion-activated cameras detecting every little movement and alerting his guards within a matter of seconds.

Constantine pays his men a lot of money to comply with his orders, no matter how depraved they might be. There is no leaving here on our own volition. At least not alive anyway.

Heavy footsteps echo in the warehouse, growing closer, and I quickly shush Aria. She's still whimpering, but at least she has enough sense to not talk or struggle.

The biggest, most dangerous predators do not like their prey docile and compliant. They want their prey to fight for their lives. And that's exactly how Constantine is. He enjoys delivering pain and causing fear. We have to make ourselves appear weak and vulnerable even if we're not.

I close my eyes, and I know that it's Constantine coming closer just by the sound of his footfalls against the concrete floor. It's sad that I know him so well. I could pick him blindly out of a crowd just by his smell...and taste.

My body begins to tremble on its own accord. Perhaps it's the coldness seeping into my bones. Or maybe it's just the fear of the unknown creeping into my soul. I don't know what Constantine is going to do to me for betraying him. And even though Nico is the one who killed Gino and kidnapped me, it will still be a betrayal on my part from Constantine. I will pay for Nico's actions and sins that night. But as long as I take the brunt of Constantine's anger and no one else, I'm willing to do just that. I'm willing to sacrifice myself for any of the Vitales, especially Nico.

"Hello, my little pet," his deep timbre sounds from a few inches away as he stops walking.

I slowly open my eyes and face my tormentor. "How did you find me?" I ask bravely.

He seems taken aback when I speak out of turn, especially considering I didn't address him properly. "I told you I would always find you, my sweet Selina." He moves closer, walks behind me. Carefully, almost tenderly, he lifts my hair from my neck and brushes it aside. Feeling along my scalp, he stops when he reaches a bump. I've felt that bump a million times before. A raised scar from one of my many head wounds, or so I always suspected. I was always recovering from something or other, so it was hard to keep track of all my scars.

"A tracker," he explains, debunking my theory, and my blood runs cold.

All this time he knew exactly where I was. But he knew he was no match for the Vitale family, so he came at me when I was the most vulnerable — when Aria decided to sneak out of the safety of the house and go to a club. He was there all along, waiting with bated breath until he could get to me safely and easily. And I stupidly handed myself over to him on a silver platter.

He releases my hair and walks until he's standing before me once again. "I never lose what's mine," he tells me, his voice deceptively calm. "It just took a little while longer to get to you, but I knew I would have a chance eventually. You know how patient I can be."

I swallow hard at his words. Yes, so very patient. Waiting hours, days, weeks, months, years to break me down. Grooming me to be his *little pet.*

Constantine moves closer until I can feel his breath on my lips when he requests, "I want vengeance on the man who killed my son. You were there long enough to know the schedules of the guards, the layout of the Vitale compound. I want to know the access points. I want to know when they're at their most vulnerable. You're going to give me every single thing I want."

I'm glad that Constantine doesn't know exactly who killed Gino, but I'll never give him what he wants. I'd rather die than speak Nico's name and give him up like a traitor.

Suddenly, his hand snatches out and grabs a fistful of my hair, bending my neck at an awkward angle and making me cry out in pain.

"Don't touch her, you bastard!" Aria screams from beside me.

Oh god, I just want her to be quiet. Constantine releases me with a chuckle. And then he turns his attention to Nico's sister. "And what should I do with my *new* little pet?" he asks out loud.

"I'll never be your pet, you fucking psychopath!" Aria shouts.

I can almost see the wheels inside Constantine's head turning. I can almost smell the arousal coming from him. I know everything Aria is doing right now — the screaming, the fighting — is doing nothing but turning him on.

He walks over to her and reaches out to touch her. She's quick to kick out at him, nearly missing his balls and catching his thigh instead with her unsteady foot. "Don't you dare touch me!" she screams.

"Oh, I'm going to do so much more than touch you, my little *principessa*," he says through gritted teeth. "I'm going to hurt you. I'm going to bend you until you fucking break," he threatens, sending another tremor through me. With a snap of his fingers, two guards come forward. "Let's show my new little pet some manners. Cut her down."

The tallest guard brandishes a knife. In a few quick movements, he saws through the rope, and Aria's body falls to the concrete floor in a crumpled heap. She yelps in pain, and my teeth clench together and tears fill my eyes as I imagine the kind of pain she's in right now from that hard fall.

"No! Please!" I scream. "I'll do anything you want, Constantine! Kill me for your son. Take my life. Just let her go!"

Constantine doesn't even spare me a glance as he instructs his guards, "Hold her down. I'm going to take what I want from the little bitch before you two get your turn."

One guard throws Aria to the cold, unforgiving concrete and pins her arms down. She struggles with all of her might until the guard who cut her loose holds a blade to her face. Then, she suddenly stills as an anguished sob escapes her lips.

"Don't make him carve into that perfection," Constantine warns. He goes to his knees, prying her legs apart.

I scream and twist against the ropes, my arms and hands crying out in agony. "No, Constantine! Please don't do this!" I cry out. "I'll do anything you want. Anything!" I scream out, begging, pleading.

I can hear his belt buckle and the zipper of his pants going down, and I squeeze my eyes shut. I can't stop this from happening. And I also can't watch this horrific act, the same exact thing that happened to me so many times over the ten years. *I can't.*

My breathing becomes labored as I struggle through a panic attack. My heart feels like it's hammering its way out of my chest. I haven't had to deal with the harsh reality of Constantine's sick ways in a long time. I always had the pills to help me get through the worst of it. But right now it's just me. *It's just me.*

I'm expecting to hear Aria's cries as Constantine violates her, but instead I hear her scream out, "No, no, no! Please! Please! I'm a virgin!"

My eyes snap open on the last word. I hope I only heard them in my head, but when my stare meets Aria's wide, innocent eyes, I know she actually said it.

Constantine immediately stops. He slowly tucks himself back

into his pants and stands up. I can see the look of confusion on Aria's face and then the relief as to what is happening. She thinks she's safe. But little does she know she just sealed her fate.

"No," I whisper right before Constantine announces, "Take her to the doctor and get him to examine her. If what she said is true, put her on the next boat to the island."

The island. The place I've heard Constantine bragging about numerous times before. I struggle in my restraints, desperately trying to get to her, to save her from that awful fate.

The men wrestle Aria into a standing position. "Where are you taking me?" she screams.

"Why, you're going to auction, my dear," Constantine explains with a sneer. "Your virginity is about to make me a lot of money. Some retribution for my son's death, if you will."

Tears stream down Aria's cheeks, and she fights the men as they lead her away.

"Aria!" I cry. "Aria!" I wish I could go with her, protect her somehow. "Please, Constantine," I beg him as he walks over to me. "Don't do this to her. Take your anger out on me, but don't hurt her. I'm begging you."

"Oh, don't worry, pet. I will be taking my anger out on you. But nothing is going to stop me from selling that little Vitale bitch to the highest bidder. Let's just call it compensation for everything her family has stolen from me over the years...including you." An evil smile spreads across his face that makes me shiver. "A big *fuck you* to the Vitales!" he announces with his middle fingers up in the air. Then, he turns to walk away, throwing over his shoulder, "When you're ready to give me the information I require, then I'll cut you down and we can finally go home where you belong, my little pet."

The light is turned off before I hear a door close. I'm left in the dark silence where the only sounds I can hear are my screams.

CHAPTER 43

Nicholas

THE ENTIRE CONTROL room is on edge, everyone buzzing with barely controlled rage, the tension so thick in the room that you could literally cut it with a knife. Constantine has Aria and Selina, and there's not a goddamn thing any of us can do about it.

"They could be in another state...or hell, another country by now!" I yell, exasperated, running my hand through my hair and pulling at the ends in frustration.

It's been hours, and Aldo isn't any closer to finding out where Constantine has taken the girls. We lost the trail on them somewhere downtown, and he hasn't been able to pull enough camera footage to find out where they went. And all of our men out there searching the streets, abandoned buildings and warehouses have come up empty.

My father's expression is solemn when he announces to the room, "I'm going to call my contact person with the FBI. We need their resources and manpower."

"The FBI?" I scoff. "If they help us, then Constantine will never get what he truly deserves." Which is a long, gruesome, and torturous death. Only the best for that bastard, in my opinion. I want to see him die and rot with my very own eyes.

"And if they don't help us, we could lose them forever," my father says vehemently. "We need all resources on this. We've helped them out many times in the past. The least they can do is help us now when we need it the most. I have all the right connections to take care of this and walk away clean with no questions asked."

I reluctantly nod in agreement. If my father is anything, he is a very smart man when it comes to matters such as this one. "Do what needs to be done," I tell him.

He gives Aldo a nod, and I watch as Aldo begins typing on his computer, probably setting up the secure line we'll need to contact the FBI.

I pace the concrete floor as my father gets on the phone, my hands curling into fists, my biceps trembling as anger begins to boil inside of me. I've never felt so goddamn helpless before in my entire life. Maybe back when Selina was first taken from me, but I was a dumb kid. I'm an adult now. With resources. There has to be a way to get them back safely. I don't want to involve law enforcement, but every second, every minute, every hour that ticks by lessens our chances of finding them.

My father's murmurs in the corner of the room cease, and I stop pacing to turn to look at him. "We move in one hour," he announces to the room.

One hour. Fuck. That's longer than what I wanted to hear; but considering everything that needs to be put into place before we can get to Aria and Lina, it could have been way worse.

One hour. I check my watch, set the timer and watch the seconds tick down.

I'm coming for you, Selina.

CHAPTER 44

Selina

ALL I WANT is to be at home in Nico's arms. I don't know how I didn't realize it before this moment. He's my home. He's my...everything. And I love him. I love him with all of my being, soul and body.

And if I ever escape from here, if I ever make it out of here alive, I want to tell him all of that. Because if I die before he knows how much I care for him, how much he means to me, I won't be able to rest in peace. I will haunt this earth forever, mourning my mistakes and missed opportunities.

"Are you awake, my little pet?" Constantine's voice instantly breaks me out of my reverie, forcing me to come to terms with my present and horrible situation.

I look him dead in the eyes. I want him to feel my hatred, the hate I have carried around for him for years. It's been lingering deep inside of my chest, just waiting for the right opportunity to show itself.

A high-pitched feral scream breaks free from my lungs, and I relish in the surprised look he gets on his face. It's nice to be the one scaring him instead of the other way around.

Constantine quickly schools his features and takes a step towards me. When my scream dies in my throat, he tells me, "My, my, little pet. If I wanted to hear you scream, I would just fuck that tight, little asshole of yours." A devilish smirk forms on his lips, and I want to bite it off of his face.

He comes closer to me, and I strain in my bonds, snapping my teeth together like a wild dog, wanting to actually bite him if he comes any closer.

His hand snatches out to grab my throat before I can even blink, before I can even react. His chokehold on me grows stronger with every passing second, and I struggle to breathe as he crushes my windpipe.

"It's a shame I'll have to retrain you. I don't know what the Vitales did, but they gave you some sort of backbone while you were gone." His hot breath fans over my face as he promises, "I'll remedy that soon enough. I'll break every bone in your fucking body if I have to until you obey."

I struggle against him, but my efforts are proven futile. My vision starts to blacken around the edges, and I fear that this is the end for me. It's hard for me to remember the number of times I thought I would die at the hands of Constantine. There are just too many to count.

"I could end your life at any given second," he snarls into my ear. "Don't you fucking forget that!"

He releases me then, and my entire body sags towards the ground, my shoulders screaming in pain from the strain. I cough and sputter as I suck in lungfuls of precious air.

"You're mine!" he says before he lashes out, punching me in the stomach.

I gasp from the pain, all the air suddenly leaving my lungs in a rush as a silent cry leaves my lips.

"You've always been mine," he tells me, spittle flying from his mouth and onto my face. "And you'll *always* be mine."

He turns and walks away from me, running his fingers through his hair, messing up perfection. Now I know he's really upset. If Constantine is anything, it's a perfectionist.

And knowing that he's on edge, I decide to defy him even further. Instead of being the docile, little mouse that I always used to try to be, I decide to let him know exactly how I feel. Looking up at him through blurry vision, I tell him loud and clear, "I don't belong to you. I never did. And I *never* will."

Maybe it's my last act of defiance. But if he's going to kill me, I want him to know that he'll never own me. My heart belongs to Nicholas Vitale. And I will love him until my last dying breath.

"What the fuck did you just say to me?" Constantine asks, turning quickly on his heel and heading straight towards me.

He raises his fist in the air, and I close my eyes, trying to ready myself for the blow, but it never comes.

"Put your fucking hands in the air!" I hear someone cry out.

My eyes flutter open, and I see a man dressed in all black holding up a rifle with the words SWAT written across his chest in big, white letters.

I watch in utter disbelief as Constantine puts his hands in the air and follows the man's next instruction, which is to get on his knees.

Thinking I must be dreaming or maybe I'm already dead, I don't allow myself to feel relieved until I see Nico coming into the room behind more SWAT members.

A sob bursts free, and my entire body sags in relief when he comes running towards me.

"Help me get her down!" Nico yells as he comes for me, lifting me up in his arms to take some of the tension off of my shoulders. "It's okay. You're safe," he says as I tuck my face against his chest.

I vaguely feel my numb hands vibrating as someone cuts through the ropes, and then I'm free, falling into Nico's arms.

"I've got you, Lina. I'm here. I've got you," Nico whispers to me.

I want to sink into his arms and stay there forever, but I can do that later. Even though it kills me to say the words, I know I have to tell him. Hopefully it's not too late. "They took Aria. She's gone! They took her to that island!" I gasp, trying to hold myself together but failing miserably.

His face drops at my words, but he simply holds me tighter. "We'll find her," he assures me. "We'll make him talk." Nico's carries me towards the exit, his gaze hardening into a murderous glare as his eyes rest upon Constantine.

There's a strong sense of urgency inside of me when I cry out, "Wait!" I want to watch my captor, my tormentor get his justice. No, it's so much more than want. I *need* to see this.

Nico reluctantly stops in his tracks and turns me to face the bastard that stole my childhood away from me.

Constantine is down on his knees, his arms behind his back as they secure handcuffs around his wrists. He looks up at me, and I smile at him as widely and brightly as I can. I want him to know how happy this is making me. I want him to know he can't hurt me anymore. I want him to know that, by making me suffer, he sealed his fate behind bars. Nothing will get him out now. No technicality in the world can help him. The SWAT team obviously observed the abuse towards me, and my testimony alone will lock him away. And as long as I'm alive, I will testify against him every single fucking time he tries to get parole or overturn his case. I will let the world know what a terrible man he is. I will show the world my scars to prove it if I have to. I will do anything just to keep him from hurting one more person.

And it's not until I watch them loading Constantine into the back of a black van that I feel like I can finally breathe again. Nico takes me to a waiting SUV, and we climb into the backseat where I allow myself to touch, to feel Nico. My needy hands grip his t-shirt, bringing him impossibly closer to me. I can never get close enough to him. I want to bury myself inside of him and never leave.

Nico holds me the whole way home.

Home.

I never really had one before. My mother jumped from trailer park to trailer park, couch surfed or stayed in motels until she could get her fix, dragging me along for every second of her drug-filled antics.

When the car stops outside the Vitale compound, I lift my head and peer into Nico's eyes. "You're my home," I tell him.

Wherever he is, I will be too. And I will be happy.

∽

Nicholas

Selina is recovering nicely in her room, sleeping peacefully thanks to a sedative. It was almost impossible to calm her down after we got home. She wanted to go find my sister. And while I feel the same way, we must let the authorities handle it. We got them involved, and now we have to, unfortunately, play by their rules.

If we had known beforehand that Aria was missing, we would've approached the situation entirely differently. And I would have taken pleasure in torturing Constantine until he talked. Then I would have killed him with my bare fucking hands, strangling the life out of him until I saw his evil soul leave his lifeless body.

My muscles ripple with anger, and I land my fist on the punching bag before me. I've been working out for hours, trying to calm myself down to no avail. I'm too angry, too sad, too...everything. The emotions I'm feeling are overwhelming me, and I feel like I'm drowning in them.

Lying there in wait until they gave us the go ahead to burst through the door to get to Selina was torture in and of itself. They almost put me in handcuffs because I refused to back down. I went in with the SWAT team, unprotected, at my own risk, not giving a single fuck. And I'd do it all over again.

Seeing Selina hanging there...fuck, it's going to be an awful and unwanted memory ingrained in my mind forever. Every time I close my eyes, I see her. Helpless. Her tear-streaked face crumbling with disbelief and then relief the moment her eyes landed on me.

I punch the bag again, my muscles straining and vibrating against the force of the blow. If only it were Constantine's face I was hitting and not this stupid bag.

Renato enters the room, and he looks like he's barely holding it together. When his eyes lock onto mine, there's a silent understanding that passes between us. He lost the girl he loves. I know the hell he's going through right now, and I feel for him immensely.

Hopefully they find Aria before it's too late. Selina mentioned Constantine wanting to sell her, auctioning off her virginity at the island that we never were able to find and probably never will.

Just thinking about it has my blood boiling.

What should have been a simple, fun night out for Aria and Lina turned into something horrific and cruel. Aria is gone. And Selina... well, she barely survived. Who knows what that bastard would have done to her had we not come to save her.

Renato runs his hands through his hair as I land a few more punches on the bag. "I was just down in the control room. They still haven't found her," he says, updating me on my sister, as his fingers tug at his hair in frustration. "She could be halfway around the world by now."

"Don't say that." I take a step back and close my eyes. The old feelings and emotions I had when Selina went missing all come rushing back full force. When someone in your life goes missing, your mind goes on a journey of all the possible situations and outcomes; none of them good. You imagine the worst-case scenarios over and over again until you're almost crazy with grief. "They're going to find Aria," I assure him. "We have the entire police force and the FBI looking for her right now."

He shakes his head sadly. "I don't know what I'll do if I lose her, man." Then he adds, "I love her."

I give him a nod. His words don't come as a shock to me at all even though he's never voiced his feelings before now. "I know you do." I don't know if Aria reciprocated those feelings or not, but I know Renato has been in love with her since the day he met her. They spent a lot of time together, but I think it was more out of convenience for Aria since my mom and dad pretty much kept her under lock and key over the years. Although now I can see why they were so strict with her and why they were always trying to rein me in as well.

There are a lot of bad people in this world, and all they need is one opportunity, one single moment to prove how awful they truly are.

"We'll find her," I grind out as my fist lands on the bag multiple times. "And I'm going to make sure that bastard Constantine pays for what he did."

CHAPTER 45

Selina

I WAKE UP with a start. The last thing I remember was the nurses trying to calm me down before they stuck a needle in my arm, sedating me. Everything is fuzzy after that.

I'm in my bed, so Nico must have tucked me in. But where is he now?

Movement from my right catches my attention, and I see a dark figure sitting in the chair I usually read in by the window.

"Nico?" I whisper.

"Yeah," he says. He sits forward, his elbows on his knees, the moonlight streaming through the window highlighting his handsome features. In one hand is a rocks glass with a dark amber liquid, the ice clinking against the side of the glass with his movement.

"Any news about Aria?" I ask even though I'm afraid of the answer.

"Not yet," he says, his voice heavy with emotion.

"It's my fault," I tell him. "If I wouldn't have left the house..."

"It's not your fault. We had no idea about the tracker."

The tracker. I told Nico about it after I was rescued. My hand instinctively moves to the back of my skull. There's a bandage over the place where the tracker once was. They must have removed it while I was sedated. "I didn't know about it," I mutter quickly. "If I had known —."

"No one is blaming you for anything, Lina," he assures me.

I take some solace in that fact, but guilt and shame are still scratching away furiously at my insides. Everything is my fault even if no one sees it as such. Aria is gone because of me. She's out there, all alone, scared, not knowing if she'll ever come back home again.

And I know *exactly* how she feels.

I lived through all the up and down emotions that trick your mind into thinking you're on some kind of crazy, evil roller coaster. And just when you think things can't get any worse, they do.

Shuddering, I throw the blankets off and go to stand. My legs are unsteady, and I almost fall. I catch myself on the bed. "Damn, that sedative is strong," I curse.

"You were inconsolable," he reminds me. "And plus, they wanted to get that tracker out of you." He sets down his glass and comes over to me. "Please get back in bed."

He moves to grab my arm, but I shrug it off. "I can't just sit here while Aria is out there. God only knows what he's doing to her! I need to help. I need to do something!"

I don't realize I'm near hysterics until Nico suddenly grabs me and pulls me close, crushing me to his chest. The first of many sobs let go, and my fingers wrap around his shirt as I slowly release some of my repressed guilt.

"It's my fault. It's my fault. It's my fault," I chant against his chest as my tears soak the material of his shirt.

"No, it's not," Nico whispers into my ear as his hand gently caresses my back up and down. "There's only one person to blame."

He's right. Deep down I know he's right. And even if I have to live with this survivor's guilt, or whatever the hell you want to call it, Constantine is the one who needs to be punished. He is the one behind all of this. If it wasn't for him, none of this would have happened.

"There has to be something I can do," I plead with him.

"I could take you down to the control room. Aldo might have some questions to ask you about locations of places you've been with Constantine. Maybe he can figure out where he might have taken my sister."

I nod. "I can do that. Yes, anything he needs. Anything to help."

"As soon as you're feeling better," he adds on the little caveat.

"No," I tell him with a firm shake of my head. "Now. It has to be now." I won't wait another minute or even another second without trying to help them find Aria. It's the least I can do. "I have lots of information I could help Aldo with. The sooner, the better," I plead with Nico.

He stares at me with those gray eyes that I love so much and then gives me a nod. "All right. Let's go then," he tells me before hooking his arms under my legs and lifting me. "But I'm carrying you the whole way down there. And if you show any signs of stress or weakness down there…"

"I won't," I assure him. I'm completely focused on finding Aria right now. I can recuperate and dwell on everything later. She is my main focus, my main priority. And I won't be able to fully relax until she's found.

∼

After hours of talking to Aldo about different places, cities and countries Constantine frequented or regularly visited, I'm mentally exhausted, and we're no closer to finding Aria. Aldo promised to take all of the information I gave him and run it until it either gives us a hit or a dead-end. I'm praying and hoping for the former.

When Nicholas escorts me back to my room, I'm too wired to sleep.

"Let's take a shower," I suggest. I need to get Constantine's scent off of my body. I swear I can still smell him and feel his touch. I shudder in response to my inner thoughts. And, without another word, I walk into the bathroom and begin stripping out of my clothes.

Nico follows suit, slowly removing his clothes while I test the water in the shower. Once I feel like it's hot enough, I step in. A few seconds later, Nico joins me. I'm careful not to wet my hair, because I don't want to mess up the bandage on my head where they removed the tracker. I hold my head out of the stream while I get my body wet.

Nico grabs a bottle of his body wash and squirts some into his hand. And then I feel his gentle touch on my back. I'm so overwhelmed by tonight's events, Aria's disappearance and Nico's gentleness with me that I begin to cry. And it seems like once the dam breaks, the flood gates open, and soon I'm sobbing.

Nico turns me around and captures me in his arms. I hold on to him for dear life. "I didn't think I'd ever see you again," I murmur against his chest.

"I wouldn't have let him take you again, Lina. I would have spent the rest of my days on earth searching for you until I found you. I would have scoured heaven and hell for you. There is no way I would have just let you go. You're my girl," he tells me heatedly.

My hands skim up his shoulders to his face, and I place my hands over his scruffy cheeks and force him to meet my eyes. "I love you, Nico."

He stares at me, a myriad of emotions crossing over his features.

"Say something," I say nervously with a soft laugh.

He blows out a breath and stares into my eyes as he confesses, "I love you, too. I've always loved you, Lina, even from the first time I laid eyes on you. Probably before I even knew what love was. I have loved you for every second, every minute, every hour for the past ten goddamn years." He cups my cheek with his palm and gently runs his thumb over my lower lip, his eyes tracing the movement. "I guess I was just waiting for you to catch up."

Nico's words overwhelm me to the point that I'm incapable of speech. Gripping his neck, I pull his face down to me until our lips meet in a passionate kiss.

My hands roam over his broad chest and then lower until my fingers are running through the soft hairs of his happy trail that lead down to the deep V of his pelvic muscles. But before I can get too far, Nico's hands grip mine, stopping me. His eyes darken as his jaw tightens. "We can't, Lina. You're hurt," he says.

"Please, Nico. I need you," I beg. I can worry about my bumps and bruises...and everything else later. Right now, I need to feel him inside of me. I need him to feel how much I want him, need him... and love him. I need the connection that only him and I share.

Nico reluctantly releases my hands, and I continue my journey. His abs tense as my hands lightly brush over them, and I hear him blow out a staggered breath. Reaching down, I touch his hardening cock, rubbing him from root to tip, earning me a delicious, deep moan. Nico's gray eyes flare with desire.

I watch him grow thick and hard as I stroke him. And when a small bead of pre-cum leaks out of the tip, I swipe the drop with my finger and then stick it in my mouth, tasting him and moaning in approval.

"Fuck," Nico growls, and I can see the exact moment when his control finally snaps. Backing me against the tiled wall, his erection digs into my thigh as his tongue laves over my breasts, slowly sucking on each stiff peak.

My hands dive into his damp hair, holding him to me, needing more. So much more. His teeth scrape over my nipples, biting down gently before soothing the pain with his tongue. Liquid pleasure floods through my veins until it feels like every nerve in my body has awakened just for him. I think I could come just like this, with his wicked mouth on my breasts, but Nico has other plans.

His hand slowly ventures down to my wet core; and the moment he touches my clit, it feels like fireworks exploding behind my eyes. My body trembles as he sinks a thick finger inside of me, pumping in and out while he works my clit with his thumb. His worshipping touch leaves me breathless and needy.

"Please, please, please," I beg in a whisper, needing the pleasure only he can give me.

"Come for me, Lina," he demands.

And I do.

I tumble over the edge so quickly that it takes my breath away. My mouth opens on a silent scream, and Nico takes full advantage, thrusting his tongue into my mouth, tasting and devouring me while I shatter around his hand.

He doesn't even give me a moment to recover before I feel his cock notched at my entrance, and then he's filling me up in one slick stroke.

I cry out, and he gives me a few seconds to adjust before he begins to slowly rock into me, taking his time as the warm water rains down around us and the steam encases our connected bodies.

Gripping my left leg, he lifts it up before driving his cock back into me. The new angle causes him to hit the spot inside of me that makes me sees stars. "Oh god, Nico!" I moan.

Nico pins me against the wall as he takes what he wants. What he needs. I can feel the tremor in his muscles as he's trying to hold it together. Tears fill my eyes as his lock onto mine and I see the raw, undiluted emotion there. We almost lost each other again. And the actuality of the situation seems to hit us both at the same time.

"I love you," he whispers urgently.

"I love you, too," I whisper back.

He moves faster and deeper, giving me every inch of his length. He drives into me, capturing my lips with his. The kiss is raw, heated and full of emotion. Even though he just told me he loves me, he's making me understand his true feelings without words. He's letting me know just how important I am to him in the way he holds me so tightly against him, as if he's afraid that I'll be taken from him again.

But even if I would somehow disappear, I would find my way back to him. He's my entire world now, my friend, my lover, my...*everything*.

I whimper against his mouth as my orgasm detonates within me, completely destroying me in the process. Nico lifts his hips, driving his cock in and out and milking every ounce of pleasure he can get out of me until he joins me in bliss. His warm breath skims across my lips in a low moan as he buries himself inside me one final time.

"I'm never letting you go," he utters before sealing his vow with a kiss.

CHAPTER 46

Nicholas

ARIA HAS BEEN missing for weeks. The FBI hasn't even seen a trace of her, and our family has grown desperate for answers. Every interrogation the authorities do with Constantine turns up nothing. He's not talking, not giving up one fucking inch to help us. Not that any of us thought he would.

I'm still angry with the fact that we got the police and FBI involved instead of taking matters into our own hands. Had we known that Aria was missing, we would have never asked for their help. We thought we were doing the right thing, to get Constantine Carbone locked away forever and for justice to be served for all of his victims. We wanted them to have the chance to testify against the bastard, to somehow right all the wrongs.

But if I could go back in time, I would have tortured him until he gave up Aria's location. He's essentially under protection now, locked up in prison. I can't lay a finger on him, and that fucking infuriates me.

"Whoa!" Renato calls out as I narrowly miss his face with my fist. "Sorry, man."

He throws down the punch mitts that were on his hands and says, "Maybe we should take a break."

I nod in agreement and walk over to a bench on the other side of the gym and take a seat. I grab my bottle and squeeze some water into my mouth. We've been training for hours, and my muscles are trembling from the exertion. Sometimes working out is the only way I can get my frustration out. And I definitely don't want to accidentally snap on Selina. She's been through more than enough shit in one lifetime. She doesn't need me taking my internal shit out on her.

My cell phone rings, and I retrieve it out of my black gym bag. "Unknown number," I announce with a frown. "Hello?"

"Nico. It's me." I hear Aria's eerily calm voice on the other end of the line.

My heartbeat instantly doubles in speed. "Aria? Where are you?" I demand. Thinking quickly, I open an app that Aldo installed on my phone for just this kind of situation. It will trace the phone number while simultaneously sending out an alert to Aldo's computer so that he can try to garner as much information as he can.

At the mention of her name, Renato comes rushing over. His eyes are wide and glued to me.

"I'm safe," she says, but I don't believe it. She sounds...strange. Something is very wrong.

"What happened? How can I find you?"

"I'm okay," she says vaguely, not giving me much, and I know deep down she's hoping that I'm tracking the call and able to find her. "How are mom and dad doing?" she asks.

"No one is going to be okay until you're home," I tell her adamantly. "Please, give me any information you can, but only do it if you're going to be safe," I carefully instruct her.

"Remember how I always wanted to go to Mexico?" she asks. "It's really beautiful here."

She's in...Mexico. What the fuck? I take a mental note of every single fucking word she's telling me...and not telling me, for that matter.

"Are you okay?" I ask.

"No," she says, her voice breaking on a sob, and it feels like my heart is sinking like a stone down into my stomach.

I get a text from Aldo, and I pull the phone away from my ear to glance at it.

It reads: **Tracing the call now. Try to keep her on the phone.**

So the app is working. Good.

When I put the phone back to my ear, I ask her, "Describe where you are. Are you in a house or an apartment?" I need her to give me something, *anything*.

"It's big, secluded. Lots of men with weapons," she whispers.

"What else can you tell me, Aria?" I prompt.

"I..." Her voice fades away as I hear something in the background. Fast, heavy footsteps. Then I hear someone talking in a deep voice, demanding the phone, and a sliver of fear runs up my spine.

"I was sold to a man," Aria blurts out, the true panic in her voice evident now. "Please, help me, Nico!" she cries into the phone. "His name is Mateo, and he's —." Her voice cuts off abruptly before she can give me any other information.

"We're going to find you, Aria. We're not going to stop looking for you! Do you understand me?" I practically scream into the phone.

She doesn't answer. I hear a rustling noise, and it sounds like she's struggling with someone. And then the line goes dead.

"Fuck!" I yell, gripping the phone so tightly in my hand that I hear an audible *crack*.

"Is she okay? Where is she? Did they hurt her?" Renato fires off the questions frantically.

Quickly, I type a short text to my father while I tell my friend, "She was sold to a man and is being held captive in Mexico."

"Mexico?" Renato repeats while running a hand through his hair. "Holy shit."

My father instantly responds, telling me to meet him in the computer room. "We need to go see Aldo. Maybe he was able to trace the call somehow or can find out more information on this guy."

Renato nods before running out of the room. I grab my stuff and chase after him. I just hope Aldo can help us somehow.

～

I watch Aldo's fingers move across the keyboard in a blur as he types in all the information I was able to give him. Behind him, my father paces impatiently.

"I wonder how she was able to get to a phone," Renato wonders aloud.

"My baby girl is smart," my father answers in a gruff. "I just hope she's not suffering for her bravery." He grimaces and stops pacing, gripping the edge of a desk in a white-knuckle grip. "We need to find her as soon as possible."

Aldo's fingers finally stop moving, and he moves his right hand to the mouse, clicking on a few things. "I think I have a hit."

We all gather around the huge monitor screens as a grainy picture of a man appears. He looks to be in his late twenties, early thirties with black hair and dark eyes.

"This is Mateo Navarro," Aldo announces.

"This is the bastard who bought my daughter?" my father asks, fuming.

"I'm not a hundred percent sure just yet, but I would say this is the man. He's almost a ghost on the internet. He's really good at hiding his tracks."

"That doesn't bode well for us," I mutter.

Aldo's expression sours. "I'll get as much information on him as I can, try to figure out what we're dealing with."

My father scrubs a hand down his face. "Looks like we're not going to get Aria back anytime soon if this guy is a goddamn ghost."

"I'll work night and day on this, sir," Aldo promises. "I won't stop until we know everything we can on this asshole."

Dad gives him a nod. "Keep working. I'm going to go tell my wife that Aria called. It might lift her spirits a little. I want everyone to keep her in the dark about everything else, however. She's been suffering enough. She doesn't need to know that the odds are stacked against us right now."

We all agree to that. My mom has been worried sick about my sister. The last thing I want to do is break her heart even more.

EPILOGUE

Nicholas

EVEN THOUGH OUR lives have been pretty much turned upside down with my sister's disappearance, it's Selina's birthday today, and I'm determined to make it a great day for her. I can internalize everything, worry about it all later and manage to keep a smile on my face. I can do that much at least for my girl. She deserves nothing but the best today.

It's been a week since Aria called me. We haven't heard anything else from her, but Aldo has been gathering as much information as he can on the man who bought her. Soon, we'll be traveling to where my sister is being held captive and rescuing her. But for today, it's all about Selina and celebrating another year of her being on this earth with all of us.

I've been preparing her party for over a week now, keeping my mom, who has been sick with concern over Aria, busy and distracted.

Mom picked out all the decorations and the food. I kind of just stood aside and let her take control of everything.

Keeping my mother occupied wasn't an easy task, but it definitely worked. I saw her smile today while we were putting the decorations up, and I haven't seen that smile since before Aria went missing. And the fact that she's not still in her bed, crying and is actually up and awake, running around, decorating and making a fuss over every little thing is a wonderful sight to see.

Selina has no idea I was even planning anything. I played it off that I had no idea of her upcoming birthday. And I can't wait to see her face when she walks into the kitchen, which looks like a party shop exploded inside of it.

My mom decided on the colors rose gold and brown. There are helium balloons floating near the ceiling, streamers, a happy birthday banner with Selina's name on it hanging in the back of the room, complete with a huge balloon arch with the number twenty-four under it. A huge three-tier birthday cake sits front and center on the island, surrounded by lots of Selina's favorite foods and snacks; and, of course, there's a giant container of mint chocolate chip ice cream in the freezer.

"Think she'll like it?" my mom asks, fussing with the candles on the cake. She wants to make sure everything is perfect.

"Mom, Lina is going to love it," I assure her. I strain to keep the smile on my face. I can see the tiredness in her eyes, and I know she hasn't slept much since Aria went missing. I can't even count the number of times I came downstairs in the middle of the night and saw my mother sitting in the kitchen, crying to herself.

My dad sits at the island, swirling a glass of whiskey in his hand, his tattoos peeking out from the cuffs of his black suit jacket. "What's not to love? I think it looks great, honey," he tells her.

Mom walks over to him and places a kiss on his cheek. "Thank you, Luca." Then, she turns to me and says, "Now we just need the birthday girl."

"On it," I tell her before grabbing my cell phone. I send a quick text to Selina's new iPhone, asking her to help me in the kitchen with something.

Her response is: **What did you burn this time?**

I can't help but grin. She knows I'm a disaster in the kitchen, having helped me put out numerous fires and throw away a lot of ruined dinners. I swear I could burn water at this point.

"She's coming," I tell everyone.

Benito walks in a moment later. "Am I late?"

"No, you're just in time," I tell him.

He makes a beeline for the cake, intending on swiping his finger through the thick icing, but my mom quickly slaps his hand away. "Don't you dare touch that cake, Benny," she scolds him.

"Sorry, Verona," he says sheepishly before going to take a seat at the island beside my father. He harumphs in disapproval and then pops a chip into his mouth, surreptitiously watching my mother out of the corner of his eye to make sure he doesn't get in trouble for sneaking a potato chip.

I shake my head and chuckle. Only my mom could slap a huge beast like Benito and get away with it.

A few minutes later, the door opens and Selina walks into the room as we all yell, "Surprise!"

The look on her face is priceless. She's completely shocked. And then…her face crumbles as tears instantly fill her pretty eyes. She looks around the room and whispers, "This is all…for me?"

"Of course, beautiful," I tell her before scooping her into my arms in a huge hug. "Happy birthday," I whisper into her ear.

"I've never had a birthday party before," she confesses in the crook of my neck while wrapping her arms around my waist and squeezing me tightly.

"Just another one of your firsts that I get to claim," I tell her before pulling back and pressing a kiss to her lips. "Now, go blow out the candles and make a wish."

My mom has just finished lighting them by the time I let Selina go, and she walks over to the island. Little flames dance in her beautiful blue and green eyes as she stares at the cake with the biggest grin on her face I have ever seen. "Wow," she whispers in awe. "That cake is almost as big as Benito," she quips.

Everyone laughs, and Benito just shrugs and nods his head in agreement. My mom went all out on the cake, and now I'm glad that she did. It was all worth the look on Selina's face.

"You better blow them out before the house burns down," I joke.

Selina laughs and then closes her eyes before blowing all the candles out in one breath. Everyone in the room claps.

"I'll cut the cake," my mom announces.

"I'll help," my dad offers.

As the two of them work as a team on the cake and Benito puts his huge muscles to the test scooping the ice cream, I pull Selina aside and ask her, "So, what did you wish for?"

"I wished for Aria to come home," she says in a whisper.

Of course Selina wouldn't wish for anything for herself. She's fucking amazing like that. "That's a great wish," I tell her before placing a kiss on her forehead.

Pulling out my phone, I text Renato to join us for ice cream and cake, but he refuses. He's down in the control room with Aldo, combing through notes, documents, and internet leads. My friend hasn't been the same since my sister went missing. He's just been...lost.

If Aria could only see what all of us are going through right now, I'm sure she would come home in a heartbeat if she could. I just hope she's okay, wherever she is.

"Birthday girl is first," my mom announces, handing Selina a plate full of food.

"Thank you," Lina tells her with a huge smile on her face. I'll never get tired of seeing that smile. She's been so happy since she's been home. I can only hope to see that same happiness on Aria's face soon.

"Nico, you're next," Mom says before handing me a plate.

"Thanks," I tell her.

We all sit around the kitchen, eating, talking, laughing and enjoying each other's company. There's nothing like a birthday party to bring family together. And that's exactly what we are. One, big, happy family.

∼

Selina

After the birthday party, Nico informs me that he has yet another surprise. I don't know if I can handle any more surprises for one day, but he assures me that I'll love it, so I go along with his plan.

When the car comes to a stop, Nico says, "Okay, you can open your eyes."

And so I do. Confused, I stare around the familiar parking lot and eye the beach and ocean in the distance. My face instantly lights up when I turn to him and ask, "We're going surfing?"

He chuckles. "That's not exactly what I had planned." He gets out of the car and comes over to open my door. "Come on, I'll show you."

He grabs a bag out of the backseat and then we walk hand in hand down to the beach. The smell of salt water and the sound of the ocean waves crashing against nearby rocks soothes my soul. The beach isn't crowded at this time in the evening, and it's almost like we have the whole place to ourselves except for a family building sandcastles near the water and a few fishermen by the pier.

Nico pulls a blanket out of the bag and shakes it out before laying it down on top of the sand. Then, he kneels down on it and motions for me to sit. I sit down on the blanket, cocking my head to the side as

I watch him pull numerous things out of the bag. I still have no idea what he's up to.

I watch as he places down a few juice boxes. The label looks so familiar, and a memory niggles at the back of my mind. Next is a bag of Doritos. Oh god, I haven't had them in forever. Then a container of...chocolate and marshmallow cookies.

His words from that day come rushing back to me. *"I'll pack us those juice boxes that you love, a bag of Doritos, and some of those chocolate and marshmallow cookies that you keep sneaking out of the jar in the kitchen."*

And then he pulls out a container and unsnaps the lid. All the air leaves my lungs in a rush. "You made me PB and J with the crusts cut off," I whisper, my voice breaking. It's the picnic date we never got to go on because my mother took me away. "You remembered," I tell him, my voice full of emotion.

"I remember everything about you, Lina," he says softly.

I crawl over to him and place my lips against his in a heated kiss. "You're amazing. Do you know that?" I ask him when I pull away.

"I know, but it's still nice to hear," he jokes.

I can't help but laugh.

We eat our picnic lunch in peace, enjoying the sounds of the ocean, kids playing in the sand and watching the sun begin to set on the horizon. After we finish eating, Nico hands me a small box.

"What's this?" I question, staring at the box with a raised brow.

"It's your birthday present," he says with his lips tilting up in a smile.

My brows furrow. "But you already gave me, like, a gazillion presents today." He's done more than enough to make my day special. In fact, he's gone above and beyond.

"Yeah, well, this is the most important one," he informs me.

I open the box slowly and carefully and am stunned to see a ring in the middle. It's not a big flashy diamond, and I couldn't be happier. Nico knows I wouldn't want something like that. No, instead, this is a handcrafted ring with little words stamped all over the thick, white gold band.

"I wanted to give you something that would mean something to you. To us," he explains.

I carefully take the ring from the box and look at the words etched into the band. Tears burn the back of my eyes as I read over the tiny quotes. *"We'll always have Paris,"* I recite. *"If you're a bird, I'm a bird."* I can't help but smile. *The Notebook* is definitely one of my favorite movies now. We've been watching so many sappy love movies lately, and I wondered why Nico never minded. Now I know why. He was waiting to see which quotes meant the most to me so that he could do...this.

"I would rather share one lifetime with you than face all the ages of this world alone."

Who knew I would be such a big *Lord of the Rings* fan? I know Nico was happy about that one.

"I'll never let go." My face grows very serious as I meet his gaze and adamantly tell him, "I would have made room on that door for you."

Nico chuckles. "So, do you like it?"

I shake my head. "No, I don't like it. I love it. It's absolutely perfect, Nico." I tackle him backwards onto the blanket, placing numerous kisses on his face before saying, "It's perfectly us."

Nico takes the ring and slips it down over my left ring finger. "Lina, will you marry me?" he questions with a grin.

"Yes, I will marry you," I answer without even hesitating.

I place a kiss on his lips before settling down beside him on the blanket as the last rays of sunshine cast over us, warming my skin.

"So, do you want a big wedding?" Nico asks as he holds my hand, staring at the ring on my finger.

I shake my head. "Just you and me. And your family." Then I quickly add, "But we'll do it after Aria comes back home." The wedding wouldn't be complete without her here with us, and she *will* be here for it. I can sense it deep down inside of my bones.

"That sounds perfect," Nico says, humming in approval while kissing the top of my head. "I love you, Lina," he whispers into my hair.

"And I love you, Nico," I whisper back. "Forever."

"Forever," he agrees.

THE END

ABOUT THE AUTHOR

Thank you for reading! If you enjoyed reading *Keeping My Girl*, please consider telling your friends and posting a short review on Amazon. Word of mouth is an author's best friend and much appreciated. Shouts from rooftops are great too.
You can find all of my books exclusively on Amazon and free for Kindle Unlimited subscribers: http://amazon.com/author/angelasnyder
And please sign up for my newsletter to be notified of all of my new releases, giveaways, sneak peeks, freebies and more: http://eepurl.com/cNFoo5

ALSO FROM THE AUTHOR

Keeping My Captive, Aria Vitale's book, is available to pre-order on Amazon!

Keeping My Captive

(Book 3 of the Keeping What's Mine Series)

When I first saw Aria at the auction, it was like some twist of cruel fate bringing us together. There's just something about her that I could not resist. I had to make her mine.

But now that she's under my power, I quickly realize I've gotten more than I bargained for.

Aria isn't just a pretty doll to play with. No, she's so much more than that.

And no matter how many times I try to bend her, she just won't fully break.

When I find out the truth about Aria's family and where she came from, I know my feelings for her will bring an all-out war against me and my empire.

But I'll do anything to protect and keep my little captive. She's mine now, and I'm never giving her up.

Find *Keeping My Captive* on Amazon here: http://mybook.to/KeepingMyCaptive

Printed in Great Britain
by Amazon